Nathaniel

Holly Moral

Contents

Nathaniel

At first glance, nobody would be able to tell that Nathaniel Jean had a problem. Or second glance, or third, or fourth. Nobody would imagine him losing entire nights of sleep to conflicted thoughts and tear-stained cheeks. Nobody would know that he was flawed.

After all, he had everything. He was a captain of his school's soccer team and one of the top players in the state. He had a big house, a loving family, and money to spend. He had friends, he had fun, he had faith.

He never meant for it to happen, he really didn't. He never wanted to look at another man in the way he should have been looking at another woman. The idea had disgusted him for most of his life—living in a heavily catholic town with heavily catholic parents, homophobia was the only response he knew. That didn't change when he first realized that he didn't like girls.

No, Nathaniel Jean was still homophobic. He hated the idea of a man sleeping with another man. He was raised on the idea that gays went to hell, and he believed it. He despised gays.

Therefore, he despised himself.

Nathaniel Jean hated himself more than he'd ever hated any friend that had betrayed him, any enemy that angered him. How could he love himself when his very existence was, in his mind, wrong?

It wasn't a lesson he could learn on his own. He needed help, even if he didn't know it.

Nathaniel Jean was more fortunate than most, because help did arrive for him. Help by the name of Lucas Morgan, they boy he'd always known but never known. The boy with big dreams and bigger talent. The boy who was out and proud, with loving parents and a hateful brother. The boy who was way too wise to be only seventeen years old.

The boy that changed Nathaniel's life over the course of their thirty-six week long senior year.

Prologue

Growing up, I'd always idolized my cousin Kenneth. He was five years older than me, which, to a boy as young as I was, instantly made him crazy cool. It only added to my awe that he seemed to be good at absolutely everything. Sports, school, music, video games—you name it. He was perfect in my eyes. My idol.

It started when I was five, the first time I met him that I was old enough to actually remember. He showed me all of his Pokémon cards—he had so many—and even gave me a few. That was when I decided that he was awesome.

I never saw him too often. His visits were biannual, since his family lived all the way in Manhattan. That was another thing I loved about Kenny—as a kid growing up in Nowhere, Nebraska, his stories of the Big Apple amazed me. The busy streets, the museums and theaters, the subways and skyscrapers, the diverse people; I'd never experienced anything even close in my catholic, suburban town. Kenny always promised he would take me someday, and I believed him. Years later, my dreams still lived in the Big Apple.

I'd always wanted a brother growing up. The only sibling I had was my little sister, and she bored me with her Barbies and My Little Pony. So, despite our scarce interaction, I saw Kenny as a big brother figure. He was smart and athletic and charismatic, which meant a lot to a shy, scrawny kid who'd barely dodged being held back in the first grade.

It was no shock that my favorite parts of each year were when Aunty Lacy and Uncle Brock came to visit. For four weeks a year—three in the summer and one in the winter—I got to spend time with Kenny. I would hang onto him like a leech whenever he was around, but he never seemed to mind. Maybe that was weird, since most preteen boys wouldn't want to hang out with their clingy little cousin, but he seemed to enjoy spending time with me, playing video games or kicking around a soccer ball or doing whatever we were doing.

That all changed when I turned ten. Kenny was fifteen at the time, and his family had joined us for their yearly summer visit as usual. Our parents called my cousin and I to join them for dinner; we'd been playing soccer in our backyard. I didn't want to go inside yet—Kenny had just laughed and told me that I was getting better at soccer than him. After that, I wanted to keep playing, to show off and earn more praise. Our parents insisted, though, so we reluctantly went inside, not expecting the hell that was about to break loose.

Dinner started off fine. At one point or another, my mom started prying the way aunts do, asking Kenny how school was and what clubs he was in, how his friends were and if he had a girlfriend. Casually, as if it were nothing, Kenny said that he didn't want a girlfriend. That he didn't like girls that way, but he had a sort of, unconfirmed, boyfriend. I thought that was cool. Weird, yeah, but since it was Kenny, and everything Kenny did was awesome, I instantly approved. My parents didn't.

The rest happened so quickly, I couldn't keep up. All I could recall were shocked expressions, then my parents yelling, his parents yelling back, yelling, yelling, yelling. A few words stood out—disgusting, homophobic, small-minded, sinful, faggot. Some of them, I'd never heard.

Within thirty minutes, Aunt Lacy and Uncle Brock had stormed out, taking an overwhelmed, crying Kenny with them.

I was ten years old, I had no idea what was happening. When I asked my parents, they simply said that Kenny was sick and that they didn't want him to get me sick as well. That night, my dad suggested we pray as a family. I remember the way he asked God to "heal that family" and "cure Kenny" and "protect Nathaniel from their sinful ways". As he tucked me into bed, he kissed my forehead and told me to be wary of people like Kenny. That they would try to corrupt me. I argued that Kenny was nice. He said he had thought so, too.

That Sunday, at church, the pastor preached about homosexuality, a word I was relatively unaware of. I understood its meaning soon enough, though, and I wondered if the sermon was a request by my father and mother. The news about Kenny spread quickly, and suddenly kids I didn't know were approaching me at school, asking me what it was like to have a "faggot" cousin. Adults would hold my hands and pray for me and hug me whenever they saw me, as if there had been a death in our family. I suppose, in a way, there was, because Kenny was dead to us now.

It wasn't easy to shake my love for him. He was my favorite cousin, my brother, my idol. But my parents worked hard. They took down pictures of him. They cut off all communication with that part of the family. And every chance they received, they emphasized the danger of homosexuality and the "evil" inside of Kenny for practicing it and his parents for support-ing it. The entire town seemed to be determined to make me believe that

Kenny, what he was, and how his family supported him, were wrong. I did. Of course I did.

After all, my parents and my town were all that I knew. Both had raised me and shaped me into the child I was. Their words were gold. It took time, but eventually, I didn't idolize Kenny anymore. I saw him as what everyone around me wanted me too: a disgusting sinner. They made it clear that being anything other than straight was wrong, and I trusted them. The model image I'd had of Kenny had been completely, totally, ruthlessly destroyed.

Then, in seventh grade, I met a boy. Or maybe 'met' was the wrong word. I'd been introduced to him sometime before, because everybody knew everybody in our town and he'd been living there as long as I had—which was, to clarify, since birth. Yet it wasn't until I was twelve years old that I began to know him.

I actually met his twin brother, Shawn Morgan, first. We were on our middle school's soccer team together. I didn't know Shawn—or anybody on the team—very well, because I was still shy and nervous and had a hard time bonding with other boys, especially popular ones like them who had no interest in a quiet kid like me.

Our end-of-the-season party was at Shawn's house that year. When all of the pizza was finished and the boys had all clustered into their friend groups, I found myself, unsurprisingly, alone on the back porch. That was when Lucas Morgan approached me.

He was scrawny like me, but that was where our similarities ended. Where my hair was blonde, his was black. Where my eyes were blue, his were green. Where I was shy and isolated, he was charismatic and popular like his brother. Yet, unlike his brother, Lucas actually took an interest it talking to me. Suddenly, the party didn't seem so bad.

It only made sense that we became friends. Lucas was nice and funny and quirky and had a shiny charizard. We would talk at school in classes that I hadn't even realized we had together. I liked him.

Too much.

We were only a few weeks into our friendship when I started noticing that my heart would beat faster and my palms would get sweaty when he smiled at me. I realized how pretty his light green eyes were, how pretty his face was in general. I was crushing on him.

That was when I cut him off. In a panic, I blocked his number and avoided him and completely deleted him from my life, just like I'd deleted Kenny. I couldn't delete the impact he'd left on me, though.

Because, as I continued to grow to thirteen, fourteen, fifteen, I realized that Lucas wasn't the only boy I noticed. It didn't help that boys, including myself, were all starting to exercise more, growing less lanky and more muscular. Girls were getting better too—curvier and prettier—but I hardly noticed. I tried to notice, but no matter how much I forced myself to appreciate a young lady's beauty, I couldn't make myself want it. Even as I became more attractive and outgoing and gorgeous girls started flirting with me and competing for my attention, I could only pretend to flirt back. I didn't want to pretend.

I understood what was happening by the time I was sixteen. I was the one thing my parents would never want me to be, the one thing I'd never want to be. I was totally, unquestionably gay. That wasn't, in any way, okay with m e.

It started off with denial. I told myself that I couldn't be gay. It wasn't possible. I was normal, and any weird feelings I had were a phase.

The second stage was anger, because I was gay. When I glanced at the other soccer players changing in the locker rooms, it wasn't because something strange had caught my eye. It was unfair. It was so fucking unfair! What did I ever do? Sure, I wasn't the best guy around—popularity changes people. But I surely wasn't the worst, was I? Why did I have to be cursed? Why was I such a faggot?

The final stage—which had enveloped me during my junior year and refused to dissipate since—was despair. Despair because I would never be the man my parents wanted me to be. Despair because I would go to hell. Despair because I was a monster. Despair because I would never be able to love, or like, or even tolerate myself.

After all, I'd been raised homophobic. My family was, my school was, my town was. I hated gay people, I truly did. I hated my cousin Kenneth. I hated Lucas Morgan, who was outed in sophomore year. Oh, I really hated Lucas Morgan. But the hatred I had for him, or Kenny, or any enemy I'd come to know, didn't compare to the despise I held for myself.

You'd think that the strain of carrying this burden, the burden of being something so horrible, would lessen with time. That I'd become more used to it, that it wouldn't still plague my thoughts every night after nearly two years of realization.

That was about as far from the truth as one could get. The longer I had to keep this dirty secret, the longer I had to watch Lucas Morgan get picked on in the hallways knowing I deserved the same myself, the less sleep I seemed to get.

Especially since the one thing that had kept me sane for the entirety of my sophomore year was the rule I'd set for myself to never act on my sexuality, emotionally or physically. Just because I was gay didn't mean I had to show it, or even think it. Maybe if I cut boys out of my life, I could get them out of my heart, just like I'd done to Kenny and Lucas. Kenny was no longer my cousin, and Lucas was no longer my crush, so why couldn't boys no longer be the objects of my interest?

At least, that was the plan. But of course, nothing can ever be that simple. It might've actually worked, you know, if Lucas fucking Morgan hadn't decide to weasel his way back into my mind at the end of Junior year. If I'd never gone to see the school's production of Wicked with a date. Because maybe then I wouldn't have been reduced to a puddle of awe as I watched Lucas Morgan perform. Maybe then I wouldn't have caught a certain bitch called 'feelings'.

It didn't help that there was a new player on the school soccer team this year—senior year. You guessed it: Lucas Morgan.

1 : Nathaniel Jean's Little Big Problem

Video on the side has nothing to do with the chapter or the book in general but it's great so you should watch it, it's called "The bro duet" and it's super gay but #nohomo

"Fuck."

I blinked, unimpressed, at Trevor Cazamm as he suddenly halted in the middle of the hallway, holding out his arm and forcing me to stop as well. "What'd you forget?" I asked dryly; we've done this drill before.

"My cleats."

I snorted loudly and resumed walking, not surprised in the slightest that Trevor would manage to forget something so pivotal. He scrambled to catch up with me, going into some long story about how he must have left them in his living room, at which point I promptly tuned him out.

Trevor is my best friend, I guess. I mean, he's the closest friend I've got out of all the assholes in my shitty little town. Would I die for him? Hah, I wouldn't give up ten bucks for him, and I was sure he felt the same about me. We were friends because we were available—we were both popular, we'd played on the same club and school soccer teams for years, and he was the most tolerable out of the rest of the soccer players. That wasn't to say that Trevor wasn't entirely superficial like the rest of them, but he was a slight improvement.

Then again, all of the "superficial" soccer players were also supposed to be my friends. They considered me a friend, sure, and they were certainly convenient to know, given that they were pretty much the reigning elite class of Listrough High School. Our football team sucked more ass than a gay porn star, and so the students and faculty turned to us soccer players for someone to glorify.

There was Damien Diggory, our goalie. Tall, handsome, and as dumb as a rock. He was undoubtably popular, and so intimidating in stature and demeanor that no idiot would dare even look at him the wrong way. Guys like Damien were good to have around, because they offered security.

Next was Cameron Schetwaldski, the best midfielder his age in Nebraska. Cameron was absolutely full of himself and an overall pain in the ass, but he was funny and quick-witted. People liked him for that, and it was nice to have someone around who could always ease the tension.

Tyler Fiero—our left and best defender—was another notable character. He was just a character in general, really. A serious prankster, loud, stupid, and obnoxiously quick to start a fight for someone his size—that is, five foot six and one hundred twenty-five pounds. Hanging around a person as memorable as him had its perks; he was such a distraction that my mistakes often went unnoticed.

Trevor Cazamm was our next best midfielder, and probably the smartest guy on the soccer team. Which is sort of like being the fastest snail. He was nice, yeah. Funny. Popular. A god guy to have around for light support every now and then. A bad guy to have around to truly lean on in times of weakness, because he'd step out of the way and let you fall without a second thought.

Possibly my least favorite member of my little "friend" group was Shawn Morgan. He was a great forward, but a pretty shitty person overall. Not that I'd ever voice that, because he was possibly the one person at our preppy private school that had more power than I did. Unlike me, Shawn had always been popular. He'd had girls fawning over him since his sandbox days, and loved to abuse the power he seemed to hold over women. Almost as much as he loved to abuse his brother.

When word got around that Lucas Morgan was gay—to this day, I still didn't know how anybody found out—Shawn was the first to show his distaste, and he didn't do it alone. He had enough supporters as it was, being the so-called "king" of our school. It didn't help that our entire town was very catholic and very conservative. That said, Shawn had more than enough people to back him up if he wanted to bully his brother, and nowhere near enough opposers. Homophobia was a part of our brand here in Nowhere, Nebraska.

Shawn never hit Lucas—at least I don't think he did—but he sure gave him hell at school. My "friends" were always more than happy to join in the verbal harassment.

Not that I was any better than them in that aspect. I didn't exactly partake in their bullying, but I didn't attempt to stop it, either. I was stuck firmly in the bystander category, with zero intention of leaving. Why would I? I hated Lucas Morgan, after all. Let my "friends" pick on him—it was none of my business.

I wasn't better than them in any aspect, really, except for maybe my skill as a forward. I wasn't smarter than them, I wasn't much nicer. I was hot headed, I was arrogant, I was a player, I was fake, and I was definitely intimidating. I was what I needed to be: untouchable.

Damien Diggory, Cameron Schetwaldski, Tyler Fiero, Trevor Cazamm, and Shawn Morgan were only a small selection of the players from the soccer team, but they were easily the most popular, and so they were what I considered my immediate friend group. I couldn't honestly say that I genuinely cared for any of them, but it wasn't as if the lying phased me. After all, lying was all I did. It was how I survived.

"Dude, you still there?"

I put on a bored expression and glanced down at Trevor with a shrug. "Yeah, why?"

"You were, like, seriously spacing out," Trevor told me.

Again, I shrugged. "Sorry," I said half-heartedly. "What were you saying?"

"I was saying..." I tuned Trevor out again as we headed to the boys' locker room. As if I cared.

Trevor was lucky. It was only the first day of tryouts—it was the first day of school, period—and we both knew from having tried out for the last three years that we never so much as looked at our cleats on the first day of tryouts. Today was the day that coach would drill us into the ground. As long as we had our running shoes, we were fine. Unless Trevor managed to forget those, too.

"Fuck!"

Trevor was stood in front of his gym locker, naked from the waist up, staring at his open Adidas bag and letting out a stream of very creative curses. "Dried up ass balls" was my favorite.

"Forgot your sneakers?" I guessed.

"I must have left them by—"

To prevent him from going into another long tangent that I really did not care to hear, I reached into my own Adidas bag and threw my back-up running shoes at him. Now, let's make this clear—they were not back-ups that I'd packed with the fear of forgetting my own shoes. No, I'd been bringing them especially for Trevor after this exact routine happened in freshman and sophomore year. They were old sneakers, pretty worn out and probably not suitable for providing proper support during long runs anymore, but that wasn't my problem.

"Thanks, dude," Trevor said with a heavy sight of relief. "You saved my ass."

"What's new?" I teased. Trevor rolled his eyes and reached out to roughly shove my shoulder.

"You're such an asshole."

"What the hell?!"

Trevor and I both shared a confused glance at the angry exclamation that had come from the center of the locker room—the wide area between the two middle locker rows, the only space wide enough for large groups to congregate. The voice was obviously Shawn's, but he usually didn't get worked up until we were at least on the field.

"What the hell do you think you're doing here? Get your ass home!"

"Dude, calm down," a second voice, one that was familiar but not recognizable, said. A loud murmur was floating through the room now, and, overcome by curiosity, I crept out from behind our row of lockers to see what was happening. It didn't take long to figure out what the the commotion was about. "I'm here to try out, just like you."

Stood leaning casually on the table that stood against the western wall of the room, facing Shawn Morgan with a Nike duffel bag slung over his shoulder, was none other than his brother—his gay brother—Lucas Morgan.

Shawn looked absolutely mortified. "You?" He hissed. "Trying out? Have you lost your mind? Get out!"

"Yeah!" Tyler Fiero joined in all too enthusiastically. "I don't want your eyes all over me while I change, perv."

I caught several of the other players consciously covering their bare chests with their arms and shirts.

"Well you don't have to worry about that," Lucas Morgan said, and I caught the hint of a challenge in his eyes. "You aren't really my type. Usually I go for guys with brain cells."

All around me, boys snarled and hissed in protest, sounding almost like animals. "Watch it, fag," I heard someone snap.

Yet nobody stepped forward, or made any move to act in any physical manner. They never did.

I'd always found that sort of strange, because, although Lucas Morgan was tall and fit—I was pretty sure he worked out more than several of the other boys in this locker room—we always outnumbered him. He was strong, but the majority of us were probably stronger. If just two were to step forward and challenge him, I was sure he'd stand little chance. Yet nobody ever laid a hand on Lucas. They threw words—harsh words—but kept their sticks and stones to themselves.

"We don't want you here," Damien Diggory growled. Several boys nodded and spoke in agreement, but I couldn't help but think that his words sounded a bit cliche and stupid. Then again, most of the things that Damien said did.

Still, I couldn't help but also agree. I certainly didn't want Lucas Morgan in here, or at tryouts, or—God forbid—on the team.

Lucas, however, simply shrugged. As usual, he wasn't phased. "Sucks, man. Wish I could help, except I really don't."

Clearly having heard enough, Shawn stepped forward, getting right in his brother's face. "Listen here," he spat. "You better watch your fucking tongue, faggot, because there's one of you and forty-five of us. You do the math, since you're such a smartass, and figure out the probability of you comin' out of that fight in one piece. Stay if you want, I don't give a shit. It'll be great to watch your pansy ass fall on its face when you realize you can't play for shit. But quit acting all tough, fairy, because we could flatten you in two seconds if we wanted."

Lucas blinked, looking boredly down at his brother, and said, "You done?"

Shawn's fists clenched at his sides, and I wondered if this would become the first time anyone saw him lay a hand on his brother.

"Dude," I sighed, not in the mood to watch a fight to break out and end up with one less forward on the team because the idiot got himself suspended. "Let it go. You're just wasting your time, he's not worth it."

I felt two glares focused on me then. One, Shawn's, went away after a moment as he grumbled in reluctant agreement and turned on his heels with a huff to find his locker. The other players followed his lead, turning grudgingly back to their clothes. I noticed that they all avoided the locker row where Lucas stood, as if he would try to molest them as they changed. Then again, maybe he would.

I still felt eyes on me, and I uncomfortably glanced at Lucas Morgan. He was still glaring at me, although he didn't seem quite angry. The gaze he fixed me with was more analytical and thoughtful, almost as if he knew something that I didn't.

He stared at me unwaveringly, and I felt the hairs on the back of my neck stand up as his light green eyes searched me. The feeling that I was being studied made me feel more than a little uneasy, so I said, "What are you staring at, creep?"

Lucas smiled, catching me entirely by surprise. It wasn't a nice smile, but it wasn't a mean one, either. "Nothing," he said, and started looking through his duffel bag. Our short interaction had clearly come to an end.

Not for the first time, Lucas Morgan took us all by surprise.

Tryouts that day consisted more or less of nonstop jogs, sprints, and workouts for three hours. We'd all expected Lucas to fall behind, to struggle at the back of the group with all of the newcomers. He didn't. Hell, he kept up better than some of the seasoned players.

I could tell that this bothered Shawn. I'd never seen a truly murderous look until I caught a glimpse of his face when Lucas passed him during a one-on-one sprint.

Guys like me, Shawn, Cameron, and the other best players never really gave our all during tryouts. Our positions on the team were pretty much secured, and our "mediocre" was usually better than the other contenders' top effort. Why waste our energy?

Yet, in that moment, Shawn put on a burst of speed that I only ever saw in games. It was clear in his expression that he was absolutely determined to leave his brother in the dust, and for a moment it seemed like he would.

However, it turned out that Lucas hadn't quite been giving his all, either. He too sped up, and was only a fraction of a second behind Shawn when he finished the sprint. Judging by Shawn's expression, the win itself wasn't enough. He'd wanted to embarrass his brother, and, as usual, had failed.

By the time we were all back in the locker room, changing and preparing to go home, everybody seemed a bit sour. None of the boys trying out, not even the lousiest freshmen, liked the idea of the gay guy outrunning them. Yet I doubted that was the biggest concern. They were all scared that Lucas Morgan would be able to play as well as he could run. Then he would make the team. That was a nightmare to them. To me, too. Because Lucas Morgan was my little problem.

I thought this over as I washed the sweat and dirt from my skin. "Little Problem" was not an adequate description of Lucas Morgan, not even close. He was a big problem, a massive one. My only one, in a way. At least, he was the source of all of my problems.

If it wasn't blatantly obvious by now, Lucas Morgan was completely, totally, unchangeably gay. What might be less obvious was that I was, too. Now, I wasn't naive enough to blame Lucas for my sexuality, to say that he "turned me gay". I could say, however, that he made being what I was infinitely harder, and he didn't even have to try.

After I'd gotten over my crush on Lucas in the seventh grade, I'd assumed that I was done with him. Even when he was outed sophomore year, I remained unaffected. I was doing the only thing I could to cope with the nagging hatred alway clawing at me from the inside out—I buried myself in my school and sports and social life and church until I had no time to focus on feelings. I couldn't like boys if there was no room in my mind for romance, and if I didn't like boys, maybe I would be on my way to becoming the man I was supposed to be.

But no, Lucas couldn't let me have that. On a date with some girl who wanted to see the school's production of Wicked, Lucas managed to push aside my distractions enough to make room for feelings. Feelings that I didn't want.

It was breathtaking, watching him perform. I never stood a chance.

And so I found myself back at square one. All of the work I'd done to force myself not to like boys, to like girls instead, was in vain, and it was all Lucas' fault. Finally, just as I'd begun to be able to sleep properly again, I found myself enduring more restless nights. God, I hated him. Really, really hated him. And liked him. At the same time. A lot.

I ran my hands down my face, frustrated with the whole situation, and that was when I noticed how wrinkly my fingers had become. I'd been in the shower, thinking, for way too long.

With a towel wrapped around my waist, I went back to my gym locker and hastily grabbed all of my things. It wasn't until I was fully dressed and headed out that I realized I wasn't alone. A lone figure was sat in the row across from mine, slumped over with his head in his hands. I knew right away that it was Lucas.

On one hand, he looked somewhat distressed, and it would be the nice thing to do to ask him if he was okay. On the other hand, I had no desire to talk to him at all whatsoever, and it's not as if I was known for being particularly nice. No, I continued on my way. Or, well, I tried to. I hadn't taken two steps when Lucas looked up from his hands and said, "Subtlety isn't really your thing, you know?"

I scoffed and rolled my eyes. "Yeah, okay." As I took another step to leave, his voice called out.

"Why are you still here?"

I should have kept going. I had no reason to talk to him, and there was nothing stoping me from leaving. Yet his voice planted my feet to the ground, and I realized then that he had a lot more power over me than I'd originally thought.

"Long shower," I answered shortly. Then, for some reason, "You?"

Lucas stood, grabbing his duffel bag and backpack. "I'm leaving now. Just didn't feel like walking quite yet."

Despite myself, I raised my eyebrows in surprise. "Don't you have a car?"

He laughed humorlessly and nodded. "Technically, yes. Shawn and I share a car. But it's hard enough to get him not to leave without me in the morning—there's no way he'd wait for me now. Not with how pissed he i s."

This was where I offered him a ride, right?

Let's see. Do I offer to spend an extra fifteen minutes in an enclosed space with the boy I was trying to get out of my head, or heartlessly leave him to walk home in the heavy late-summer heat?

I shrugged and resumed walking, leaving Lucas Morgan standing there, staring after me with that analytical look of his.

I didn't sleep well that night, but that was no shock. I hadn't had a decent night since I went to see that damned musical. Not that it really mattered—the next school day was more than mundane, what with teachers still getting organized and learning names and explaining rules. I didn't need much energy to get through it.

Tryouts would turn out to be a different story. We ran for most of it, even harder than we had yesterday, and settled down for a scrimmage at the end. I think what tired us out even more than the tough work was watching Lucas play, because we all knew by the end of the second day of tryouts that he would be making the team. Turns out, he did play as well as he ran, and none of us were happy about that. Especially Shawn. He wouldn't talk to anybody as we walked back to the locker room, and he stormed out as soon as he'd grabbed his bags—without even changing—no doubt leaving his brother to walk home again.

The next two days of school—and the final two of tryouts—went by pretty quickly. I refused to so much as glance in Lucas Morgan's direction, but my friends had other ideas. I could tell just how frustrated they were by his talent at soccer by the way they upped their hallway antics. The insults and jeering that he usually dealt with whenever we passed turned into shouting and even some minor shoving. Yet Lucas remained stoic, and that only seemed to aggravate them more.

Surprise surprise, Lucas made the team. The twenty other boys—straight boys—that did not make it were clearly enraged, but what could they do? They would look like idiots if they tried to poke fun at the guy who'd clearly outdone them. I say this as a fact because a few of them—mostly wannabe rockstar freshmen—did try, and consequentially did look like idiots the moment Lucas opened his smart mouth.

The most frustrated, by far, was Shawn. He, too, ended up looking like an idiot, as he'd been so sure on the first day that Lucas would make a fool of himself. Instead, Lucas would probably end up on our starting lineup.

The locker room cleared out quickly on that fourth day, without the usual celebration by the people who'd made it, without the congratulating and high-fiving and smiling. Nobody was in a good mood, not even the freshmen and sophomores who'd made the team for the first time. That goes to show how strong homophobia really was at this school.

I actually wish I'd made my departure as early as the others did. Instead, I ended up getting caught by the rain. My car was all the way in the school parking lot, and I didn't fancy the idea of walking through the sudden downpour to reach it. Instead, I ended up stuck in the smelly room, sitting on the bench in the middle of my locker row, waiting for the rain to at least mellow a little.

I looked up in mild surprise as Lucas Morgan—of course he was still here too, just my luck—sat down next to me on the bench. Had he gone insane? "Dude, move," I snapped.

Lucas turned to me with a raised eyebrow, and I felt anger spark in my nerves at the arrogant expression on his annoyingly attractive face. "Why?" Was all he said.

"The hell do you mean, 'why'?" I said incredulously. "How about because I said so?"

Lucas laughed, which only helped to further my anger. "You know, you don't scare me, Nate. Not than any of you soccer fuckboys do, but especially not you. You're too nice to be scary."

I scoffed at that; this guy didn't know me at all. "I'm not nice," I told him honestly.

He shook his head in a way that was infuriatingly confident. "Yeah you are."

"You don't know me."

Lucas shrugged. "I don't have to. It's pretty obvious in the way you act—you never jump in when your friends are picking on me, sometimes you even tell them to stop—"

"I tell them to stop because they're being stupid, not because I'm defending you," I protested.

"And you just don't give off the mean-boy vibe," Lucas continued as if I hadn't spoken. "You try to, but you don't. Plus, guys like Damien and Shawn and Tyler, they've always been jerks. But I knew you once, and you weren't—"

"You didn't know me!" I snapped. No way was Lucas about to bring up seventh grade, when he fucked with my life. "And you still don't. So how about you quit trying to be so wise, huh? You're dumber than I thought if you believe you know a single damn thing about me."

I stormed off then, not caring about the rain, just needing to distance myself from Lucas as quickly as possible. I didn't get out, however, before I heard him say, "I know more than you think."

That sentence sent a shiver down my spine that I blamed on the rain. I brushed the comment off, refusing to admit to myself that he got to me.

Yet he did get to me. That night I lay awake, thinking about how much I hated how clever he was and how I'd be spending the next few months playing soccer with him and how annoyingly right he always seemed to be and how much I wanted him. Thinking about how much I absolutely despised him, almost as much as I despised myself, yet couldn't keep his face out of my head. Thinking about the fact that I was everything my parents loathed, everything my entire town loathed, everything I loathed. Thinking about the fact that there really was no cure to my disease, that I would be impure forever. Thinking about the fact that I deserved every bit of harassment that Lucas got, yet I hid in the shadows as he was persecuted for a sin that I, too, was guilty of.

2: Nathaniel Jean's Soft Spot

A /N: I just wanna add a quick disclaimer and make it known that this story doesn't reflect my religious beliefs or opinions at all. The setting of this story is a very Catholic town, so it only makes sense that Catholicism plays a part in the characters' lives. However, nothing said in this story is meant to disrespect the Catholic religion or push it on anybody who doesn't identify with that belief system. Any jokes made about the way Catholics in the community behave are directed towards the people, not the religion itself, and I am in no way trying to brand all Catholics as acting these ways. These people just happen to be Catholic and assholes. This particular story is simply describing this particular town in which these particular people act this particular way.

All religious beliefs (or lack thereof) should be respected and considered valid, so for the love of god please don't do the annoying thing that I see in so many Wattpad stories where you get into arguments in the comments with other readers over your opinions. It's just a story, guys.

Alright that's it lmao enjoy

With the next week came the first practices—Monday through Friday, from three to six—and the true start of the soccer season. As much as I loved soccer, this part of the year was usually hell, because I also had club practice from seven to nine on Mondays and Wednesdays. In other words, my life was about to become exhausting.

One good thing came from the rigorous schedule, though. I realized after that first week that with school practice, club practice, and homework, I was so tired by the end of the day that I fell into a long sleep each night. I hardly had time to wallow in my self pity.

And I needed the distraction. Ever since the start of senior year, it was as if Lucas Morgan was everywhere.

We had no classes together—thank god—yet we seemed to pass each other at least once between each period. I tried to avert my gaze whenever he was within ten feet, but the effort was in vain. Not because I couldn't resist looking at him when he was nearby—I wasn't that weak. No, it turned out that my friends would be the banes of my existence. For whatever petty reason, they found it absolutely necessary to stop Lucas in the middle of the hallway and harass him for a solid thirty seconds every single time they saw him until he got bored and walked around them.

Then, at around two forty-five each afternoon, I'd see Lucas again in the locker room. After that, I'd be subject to the view of him stretching and running and dribbling nonstop for the next three hours. None of the boys even bothered him during practice anymore, after the coach yelled at Tyler for mistreating a teammate.

At six o'clock sharp, we'd be back in the locker rooms, and I'd have to try my absolute hardest not to look as he changed, or to feel guilty as I saw Shawn leave without him. I'd been tempted more than once to offer Lucas a ride, and the thought that I was starting to go soft for the boy only made me angrier.

So yes, the distraction was very much appreciated. I would realize, though, at the beginning of the third week of school, that I couldn't stay distracted forever.

That Monday, all of the boys rushed out of the locker rooms as soon as they'd grabbed their items, hoping to beat the rain that was obviously coming; the sky had been growing darker and darker all day, and the air was disgustingly humid. Everybody except for me, because I was a stubborn idiot who refused to step foot in my car without showering first.

Naturally, as luck would have it in my oh-so-cliche life, I found myself joined with unwanted company when I emerged from the shower.

"Good job on the field today."

I tried not to feel overwhelmingly annoyed that Lucas was talking to me, but I couldn't stop my eye from twitching at his compliment. He knew that I didn't want to speak to him, now or ever, so why was he even trying? Maybe he knew that his mere existence bothered me, and got a kick out of pushing my buttons.

Of course, I didn't respond. Instead, I pulled my hoodie over my head and grabbed my bags, perfectly prepared to ignore him and walk out in the now-pouring rain.

"Aw, thanks pal! You did good too!" Lucas' voice, sarcastic as ever, rang shrilly in my ears. Okay, he was definitely trying to get me mad.

"The hell is wrong with you?" I snapped, whipping around with a glare and hoping to intimidate Lucas enough to get him off my case. I'm not sure why I even bothered—nothing intimidated Lucas.

As suspected, the boy was not bothered. "Nothing, really," he shrugged, then laughed dryly. "Well, I guess your friends would disagree, huh? Dude, it's fucking obvious what's wrong with him!" Lucas' voice was mocking again, but this time I knew that he was imitating someone else. His voice had dropped to sound lower and somehow dumber, just like Damien Diggory's. If I didn't hate him so much, I'd be impressed by the impersonation. "He's gay, bro! I bet he, like, likes dick and shit! Haha!"

I blinked, unamused by his little drama display, and said, "Your point?"

Again, Lucas shrugged. "I don't know, I guess I just don't get the whole homophobia vibe from you. You don't really care that I'm gay."

Oh boy, was he wrong. He was so wrong, yet he sounded so right, as if he knew everything. It was infuriating, his know-it-all attitude. I had several choice words floating through my head for him, begging to be shouted, but instead I rolled my eyes and said, "Go suck a dick, Morgan."

Lucas laughed. "I'd love to!"

For several reasons that I don't care to admit, my cheeks burned red at the sexual statement. I should have just walked away then, showed him that I didn't care what he said, but he'd gotten to me again. And he knew it. He knew that I didn't handle anger well, that I was easily provoked, and he was using it to his advantage. "You're fucking sick, you know that?" I snarled.

Lucas glanced down at himself, then up at me with a raised eyebrow. "Really? Because I feel great."

I took a deep breath through my nose in an attempt to not do anything stupid, like hit him or kiss him or anything in between. "Dude, what do you want from me?" I sighed, trying my best to keep my voice level.

"A ride home would be nice."

My brain didn't process his words for a few seconds. Then, shocked by his straightforward request, I merely stared blankly at him for several moments. Finally, when I realized that he'd actually said that, I scoffed. "You're kidding, right?"

Lucas crossed his arms over his chest. "Why would I be kidding? It's raining cats and dogs out there, and I sure as hell don't wanna walk forty-five minutes through that."

I shook my head in disbelief. "Forget it," I said shortly, and turned on my heels to leave.

"Please?"

Fuck. He was not allowed to pull the 'please' card on me.

I didn't have to say yes. I sure as hell didn't want to. It would give me certain satisfaction to know that Lucas Morgan, my unbeknownst enemy, had to walk home through the rain while I was available to give him a ride. Refusal would be so easy, too. All I had to do was say 'no'. Maybe even throw in some curse words, just for good measure.

I turned back around and stared straight into his green eyes. The expression in them had changed drastically since my last words—the snarky glint was gone, replaced by something almost like hope. God, it would be so nice to reject him now. To see that hopeful look fall from his face.

"Fine, you can have a ride, but if so so much as look at me I'm leaving you on the side of the road."

Dammit.

Where had that even come from? Judging by his expression, Lucas was just as surprised at my generosity as I was.

I wanted to backtrack, to say 'never mind' and leave Lucas here. But then I'd look pathetic. I'd dug myself a lovely hole, and there was no climbing out now.

"Uh, what?" He asked, bewildered.

"You heard me," I grunted reluctantly, mentally cursing myself over and over. "Now hurry up or you're walking."

I didn't wait for his response. I turned and stalked out of the locker room, the sounds of Lucas scrambling to gather his things following me out. By the time I was halfway down the pavement, he had caught up with me.

Lucas wisely said nothing as we hurried through the parking lot to my Mercedes. By the time I sat behind the wheel, we were both soaked to the bone.

The drive was quiet and extremely awkward, so I turned on the radio. A Migos song began playing and Lucas, infuriating as ever, snorted. I glanced at him, one eyebrow raised, and said, "Is there a problem?"

He shook his head and glanced down at his lap, but I could see him biting his lip, holding in a snicker. That bastard.

Ten minutes later, I pulled up to his white-picket-fence house. "Get out," I told him.

Lucas turned to look at me and did the most aggravating thing he possibly could have. He smiled. Not a mocking, sarcastic grin, but a sincere, toothy smile. When he smiled, he showed off a single dimple in his right cheek that I used to love when we were friends. I still loved it.

"Thank you," he said.

"Get out," I repeated, and he laughed.

"Getting out," he narrated as he climbed out of the car and shut the door behind him. I wasted no time in pulling out of his driveway and driving away from him, probably much faster than was safe during such heavy rain.

It was supposed to be a one-time thing. A mistake I made in a moment of weakness.

Yet three days later, the sky decided to spill its guts on us again. Apparently Lucas was feeling bold, and I was feeling stupid.

I really needed to stop making the mistake of staying after practice to shower. I couldn't help it, I hated the feeling of walking around covered in dirt and sweat, and I didn't want to get my car dirty. Then again, I hated Lucas Morgan, too, yet I kept practically walking into encounters with him.

"Hey," Lucas greeted as I passed the bench where he sat, clad only in a towel from the waist down.

I didn't return his greeting. Instead, I rudely said, "Look away, pervert."

I heard Lucas snicker behind me as I changed into my regular clothes. When I finished dressing he asked, "Can I open my eyes now?"

I turned around and saw him still sitting on his bench, this time with his hands covering his eyes. Before I could respond, he dropped his hands and looked up at me. "Oh good," he said, grinning. "I was scared I'd go blind when I saw your pale-ass stomach. Thanks for the warning—really helped a brother out."

I gritted my teeth and clenched my fists. He was asking for trouble. When he'd gotten into the habit of riling me up, I didn't know, but I didn't like it one bit. "Who the hell do you think you are?" I asked, narrowing my eyes in a glare. "Learn to watch what comes out of that mouth of yours."

Despite my subtle threat, Lucas didn't seem worried. Instead, he grinned. "How sweet," he said, his words coated in sugar.

I flipped him off and grabbed my duffel bag and backpack. "You can be as sarcastic as you want, you're the one hauling your own ass home."

Lucas shrugged. "Nothing I'm not used to."

As much as I tried to fight it, guilt nibbled away at the lining of my stomach. "Well maybe if you weren't such a cocky little shit, you'd have a ride," I said matter-of-factly. Lucas laughed, as if the idea was funny.

"We both know that's not true," he said with a roll of his eyes that I knew wasn't directed at me. "If I was straight, I could be as much of an ass as I wanted and Shawn would still give me a ride."

Mentally, I agreed with him. I wouldn't give him the satisfaction of letting him know that, though. "I wasn't talking about Shawn."

Finally, I got a reaction out of him. His eyebrows shot up and surprise registered momentarily down him face, before he pushed it out of sight. "You're saying you'd give me a ride, then?"

"Would have," I corrected. It wasn't true, of course; I'd had no intention of offering. A little white lie never hurt anyone, though. "But you've gone and pissed me off, so you can forget that."

Lucas pursed his lips and stared up at me quizzically. "I don't believe you," he said. "There's no way you'd have offered me a ride."

I shrugged, enjoying the hesitation I saw flicker across his expression. "Guess we'll never know, huh?"

A glimmer in Lucas' green eyes told me that I hadn't won just yet. "You could always prove it," he said; he stood up then, grabbing all of his things and taking a step towards me.

"Oh yeah?" I challenged. I wished that I could look down on him and intimidate him, but we were nearly the same height. I had maybe an inch on him, at most. "How?"

"You could give me a ride anyways," he said triumphantly. I muttered several curses—I really should've seen that coming.

I tried to reject him smoothly, saying, "How about no?" Lucas' smirk never wavered, though, and as I walked out of the locker room, he was right in step with me.

"You're stubborn, you know that?" I snapped as he followed me out to my car.

"Yup," Lucas said.

"And annoying," I added.

"Yup."

"And this doesn't change anything."

"Nope." Lucas was smiling. His grin had always been a little lopsided. The left side of his mouth turned up just a little higher than his right, so it always seemed like he was smirking.

"I still hate you."

"Of course."

The drive to Lucas' house was just as tense as it had been Monday, but I tried not to dwell too long on the fact that the object of both my affection and my loathing was sitting inches away from me. I didn't turn on the radio because I wasn't about to sit and listen to him snigger about my music taste, so the silence was even more awkward.

Lucas must have felt it too, because as I drove I caught him fidgeting with just about everything—his phone, his hands, the drawstrings of his hoodie—out of the corner of my eye.

"You know—"

I quickly cut him off by saying, "One more word and I'm leaving you here." We were at a red light, still a solid six or seven minutes from his house. That would not be a fun walk.

I chanced a glance at Lucas to see him pouting slightly. He was so irritatingly cute, he gave me a headache.

"Permission to speak?" He requested sarcastically.

"Nope," I said.

"Anyways," he continued as if I hadn't spoken, "As I was saying, it's weird. How you guys work, I mean. How this whole town works, really." He paused as if waiting for a response, but I provided none with the hope that my lack of interest would convince him to shut up. Of course, it didn't, and he continued. "You all preach goodness. You live and breathe the Bible, but you do it sort of . . . selectively. You believe in kindness, yet you're horrible to anyone that's different from you. That's weird, right? You know what else is weird? The Bible says, 'Therefore what God has joined together, let no one separate.' Yet half of the families in this town are divorced. Nobody gives them any problems, nobody tells them they're wrong, but the entire town hates me just for being who I am.

"Example number two. Catholics feel very strongly about premarital sex and abortion, right? Yet Katy Holman, at sixteen years old, found out she was pregnant in January and got an abortion that same month. She stopped getting shit for it by February. I came out—against my will—in Sophmore year, and I still haven't stopped getting shit for it two years later.

Even Katy Holman has the nerve to call me a sinner. I just think it's so strange, how that works. It's a constant cycle of hypocrisy."

I said nothing. I kept my eyes on the road and carried on as if I hadn't even heard him speak. Lucas huffed softly, but he didn't sound annoyed. Just tired. He made no move to talk again, and I made no move to kick him out of the car until I'd pulled into his driveway.

"Get out," I grumbled, turning to Lucas with a glare. His hand reached for the door, but stopped midway. He dropped it back to his lap and looked at me for a long, unsettling moment. "Don't make me say it again."

Lucas smiled. "You know, as much as you pretend to hate me, I don't think you really do," he said complacently. "I mean you sat through my rant and didn't kick me out, that's gotta mean something. I think I'm growing on you, Nathaniel Jean. Maybe you've got a soft spot for me."

"I swear to god if you don't get the fuck out of my car—"

"Alright, alright," Lucas raised his hands in submission. "I'm out. Thanks for the ride, see you at school."

For the second time, I sped away from Lucas' house as if the furies were chasing me. When I arrived at my own home, I saw another car in the garage. My parents had left for Colorado on a business trip a week before school started; they were finally back.

Nobody greeted me when I entered the house. My mother was in the kitchen, judging by the smell, and my father was lounging on the sofa watching the news. Neither of them so much as moved when they heard me enter.

"Hi dad," I said in an awkward, half-hearted greeting.

My father didn't glance up from the TV, but he said, "Hello, son. How's soccer?"

That was it. No 'how's school?' or 'how has your day been?' or 'how are you feeling?' He didn't care about any of those things. He only asked about soccer. Not that that was anything new.

"The usual. Coach is already drilling us for States and we haven't even had our first game," I told him. My father hummed.

"As he should," he said. "Anyone new we've gotta worry about?"

I shrugged, even though he couldn't see me with his eyes glued to the TV. "Not really. There're a couple of sophomores and freshmen that made it. They're pretty good, but not that good. None of them are even on the starting lineup." Our school didn't have a junior varsity team, so varsity tended to have players from every grade. That meant that each year there was an oncoming threat of talented young players, but nobody stood out this year. "You know that family that just moved in, the Andersons? They have a boy one year below me who plays midfield really well, and we have a new defender that's pretty good. Other than that, everything is pretty much the same."

"Who's this new defender?" Dad asked. "Is he gonna take Fiero's spot?"

I really did not want to tell my dad who he was. Of course, he would find out eventually, but I'd rather not be around when it happened. "No, he plays center."

"And his name?" Dad pressed. I groaned internally.

"Lucas."

"Lucas . . . ?"

Here goes nothing. "Lucas Morgan."

Instantly, my father's eyes were on me. Funny how I had to mention someone else to get his attention. "What?" He snapped. "You're joking."

Reluctantly, I shook my head. His eyes widened. Here it comes.

"They let that fag on the team?" He exclaimed. My mother entered the living room, her hands dusted with flour, at his outburst. "Has your coach gone mad? How could he even let that queer try out?"

I shrugged. I did not want to have this conversation, now or ever. "He plays well," I said simply. "None of us like it, but we've gotta deal with it."

"What's going on?" My mother asked, glancing between my dad and I. That was it. No greeting, no 'honey I missed you!'

Dad sneered. "That Lucas boy is on the team."

My mother gasped, which really didn't seem necessary to me. "Lucas Morgan?"

I decided to take my leave then, before they started discussing the horrors of a gay boy living in their town, let alone playing on my soccer team. I didn't want to hear them talk about how despicable Lucas was—I'd heard it all before.

I slipped out of the living room, unnoticed by my parents, and disappeared down the hall until I reached the stairs. The moment I set foot on the second floor of our house, I ran into my younger sister. Jenna was texting on her phone, not watching where she stepped, and would have fallen on her butt had I not caught her.

She yelped in surprise and nearly dropped her phone. When she realized what she'd ran into, she rolled her eyes. "Jeez, you're like a brick wall, Nate," she huffed.

I shrugged, albeit a little smugly.

"I work out," I said. "You should try it sometime."

Jenna slapped my arm playfully and smirked. "We both know I can outrun you, hotshot."

Jenna was only fourteen years old, but she was probably right. She'd run track all three years of middle school and always came out on top. Now, she was running cross country for the school, but everybody knew that track and field was her passion. She was a sprinter. She could outrun most of the boys on the high school's track team when she was in seventh grade, so I didn't doubt that she could leave me in the dust now.

Still, being the stubborn brother I was, I said, "In your dreams, shortie."

Jenna rolled her eyes again, but changed the subject. "How come you're home so late? I know my practice ends before yours, but still, you take forever."

"Caught in the rain," I said smoothly. It wasn't exactly a lie, it was just short of the whole truth. "That's all."

Jenna seemed to accept the answer, because she said, "I'm not sure why I asked, since I don't actually care, but whatever," and stepped past me, probably headed to her room. I followed suit and headed to my own room, already knowing that I wouldn't be coming out again for the remainder of the night. If I tried to eat dinner, it wouldn't stay put. I felt sick.

Lucas had a way of saying things, manipulating his words until I wouldn't be able to forget them. I wondered if he knew, or if verbal influence just came naturally to him. Or maybe I was just easily influenced. Whatever the case, I couldn't refrain from considering everything he'd said. I used homework as a distraction for a few hours, but when I was done and had no choice but to lay down in bed and hope for sleep, my mind resumed its chaos.

My first thought: Lucas used to be popular. He was attractive and charismatic and nice, it made sense. He'd had a lot of friends, none as close to him as his brother. They were a dynamic pair. Shawn always seemed to be on top, but Lucas wasn't far behind. Shawn was the sporty one, Lucas was the creative one, and their differences made them work.

It was like a switch flipped in sophomore year. As soon as word got out that Lucas was gay, he became an outcast. His 'friends' all left him, and his brother was the first to go.

When he was first outed, the pastor had preached about homosexuality week after week, until eventually Lucas and his parents stopped going to church. Shawn, of course, still went every Sunday; it almost seemed like an act of rebellion, to show that he wanted nothing to do with his brother. Lucas was shunned by nearly the entire school; even teachers and administrators alienated him. I remembered seeing him walking once, then watching as a mother grabbed her son's hand and crossed to the other side of the street. Everybody in this town treated Lucas Morgan like the antichrist.

Yet Katy Holman, who'd committed what people here considered a sin, was only scolded, maybe temporarily punished. Her friends were still her friends, nobody gave her trouble at school, and she was loved throughout the town. What made Lucas different from her?

I wasn't sure how long I spent pondering the answer. Time made no difference, anyways, because I came out empty nonetheless. When I finally gave up on formulating an explanation, a new question bloomed.

How did he do it? He wasn't completely happy, I could tell, but he wasn't in despair, either. I wasn't sure how I knew, but I was positive. Lucas Morgan was, if nothing else, satisfied with himself. He wasn't shy to speak of his sexuality, and he did it with pride.

That made me angry.

Lucas and I were the same. We had the same nasty problem. But we were total opposites. Where I hated who I was, Lucas didn't, not in the slightest. I thought that everybody in our small town was right for believing what they did, but Lucas seemed convinced that they were wrong. He wasn't supposed to be happy. He was supposed to be like me, torn apart from the inside out with guilt. He was supposed to think that gay wasn't okay, he was supposed to fear the consequences of his being. Yet he didn't. He was so goddamn content with himself.

I wasn't sure why this infuriated me so much. Maybe I was angry because I wanted him to see himself the way I did. Maybe I was jealous.

Jealous of the guy who was estranged by his entire community. That's rich.

The next day, it was raining again. I stayed after to practice to shower as usual despite the darkening sky, so I wasn't surprised when Lucas approached me, or when he asked for a ride home. I didn't even bother to argue. Thankfully, he didn't say a word the entire way.

The sky was cloudy all day on Monday, but it didn't seem to be in any rush to release. As I prepared to leave the dressing room, I saw Lucas staring at me expectantly. It wasn't raining yet, but it could start any moment.

"Just hurry up," I huffed. Lucas didn't need to be told twice.

The sky was clear on Tuesday. Yet as I left the locker room, Lucas was at my side.

"It isn't raining," I deadpanned. Lucas didn't so much as slow his stride.

"But it's hot," he pointed out. "I could get heat stroke."

I rolled my eyes but didn't bother to argue. I still hated Lucas, but I liked having someone else in the car with me. "Don't start thinking this is an every day thing," I warned. Lucas raised a single eyebrow.

"Isn't it?"

Apparently it was.

3: Nathaniel Jean's Worst Moments

The last week had been harder than most, and my lack of sleep was starting to take a toll on me. Two to four hours a night wasn't enough, yet I couldn't seem to get any more.

As usual, Lucas Morgan was to blame. He hadn't uttered a sentence during the car rides I'd given him all of last week, but his words from the week before still clung to my memory and refused to let go. Each night, as I tried to sleep, they made their attack on my mind.

I didn't know what to think anymore. This small town in the middle of Nowhere, Nebraska has always been my home. The people here had shaped my thoughts and beliefs as I grew. It was here I learned that men were to love women and vise versa, no exceptions. But if Lucas could be so proud with himself, there had to be others who were, too. Kenny was.

Now it was a question of who was right, and who was wrong. Up until that Thursday, I wouldn't have hesitated to say that my town was right. That Lucas and Kenny and anybody who believed that what they—we—were was okay, was wrong. Now, I wasn't sure.

I wanted to be sure. I'd spent my life being sure. Yet I couldn't help but wonder what my life would be like if I didn't see my sexuality as a sin. Would I be happy? Would I be confident, like Lucas?

Internal conflict was no stranger to me. The matter seemed so black and white, yet there was no easy answer. Back and forth, my brain fought throughout the nights. And it was starting to show.

Half-dressed for school on Monday morning, I stopped as I passed the floor-length mirror propped against my bedroom wall. Dark shadows framed my eyes. My pupils seemed dilated. I looked duller somehow, as if sleep deprivation was sapping the life from my skin.

I spent another minute staring at my reflection in the bronze-rimmed mirror, something I didn't do often. I could've looked worse. In whole, my appearance hadn't changed drastically. My body was still toned and sun kissed from all my time playing soccer. My hair was still dirty blonde. My eyes were still blue. I was still spotted here and there by large freckles—beauty marks, maybe. One was still on my left cheek, another still against my hairline, a third still right below my ear. Several still dotted my torso and back. I was still me.

I knew I was attractive. People didn't hesitate to tell me so. It was a fact—on the outside, I looked good. If only everybody knew that what was inside was much uglier.

My body was just a mask, and I hated that. My entire life was, really. Everybody assumed that Nathaniel Jean was perfect. When people looked at me, they saw the good-looking star athlete with a lot of money and a lovely family. Nobody saw the kid with the dirty secret who was failing half of his classes and had no relationship with his parents. Nobody saw the insomniac who skipped dinner and hadn't seen much reason to take good care of himself in years. Nobody looked close enough to spot the circles under my eyes, or my nervous mannerisms, or my sour mood. Nobody reached out a hand to help, and I never asked for one.

All that they saw was what I projected on the outside. Or maybe that was all they wanted to see. Maybe they, just like me, didn't want to accept that I wasn't so beautiful.

I didn't even realize how frustrated I was until my fist shot forward and I heard a loud crack. My image in the mirror shattered as shards of glass clattered to the floor. I stared, shocked, at my hand. Blood streamed down my forearm from my knuckles and splashed against the wooden tiling beneath me. Small shards of glass protruded from the cuts along my fingers.

Several seconds passed until the awe evaporated and the pain settled in. I groaned and cursed as stabbing heat spread from my knuckles up to my shoulder and back down to the tips of my fingers, leaving my entire arm throbbing.

My door swung open, revealing the sleepy face of my sister. Her pajamas, bedhead, and annoyed expression told me she'd just woken up. Her eyes instantly found on my bloody hand, then darted to the broken mirror, and finally landed on my face.

"What the hell happened in here?" She demanded.

"What's it look like?" I said through clenched teeth. "I punched the fucking mirror. Where are mom and dad?"

"You punched the mirror?" Jenna exclaimed. Then she held up her hand. "You know what, on second thought, I don't wanna know. Mom and dad are in their room, ignoring us as usual. Come on, I've gotta get you cleaned up since I'm clearly the only responsible member of this household."

I let her lead me to the bathroom, wincing in pain and scowling bitterly at the notion that my little sister was the one helping me, instead of mom or dad. Their bedroom was on this floor, no farther from mine than Jenna's. If she'd heard me in her sleep, my parents, who I knew would be up at this time, had definitely heard me, too. They'd just chosen not to care.

Jenna sat me down on the toilet and shuffled through the cabinet below the sink until she found the first aid kit. Then she went to work.

Jenna and I were late to school that morning, but that was no shock. I was hardly on time on a normal day. We'd lost thirty minutes to picking the glass out of my hand and wrapping it. My right hand was pretty much useless, but I didn't care.

Everybody else did, though. All I seemed to hear all day was, "What happened to your hand?" I made up a story about accidentally hitting a spinning fan, and my peers were air-headed enough to believe it. When they realized I hadn't gotten into a fistfight, they lost interest and moved on.

At one point, I saw Lucas glance at me in surprise as I passed, and I watched his eyes land on my hand, but he didn't dare say anything.

The soccer team freaked out at first when they saw, thinking that I wouldn't be able to play at tonight's game, until I reminded them that I didn't need my hand to kick ass at soccer. After that, they didn't care.

Not a single person asked if I was okay.

I felt like shit all day. I was tired, my hand hurt like hell, and I hadn't had time to eat breakfast or pack lunch in the morning, so I was hungry.

Needless to say, I was irritable. Maybe that was why I snapped when Cameron Schetwaldski made me stop on my way to physics just to harass Lucas Morgan.

"Hey fag, wassup?" Cameron goaded, smirking like the pure-blooded American douchebag he was. "Suck anything good lately?"

Lucas raised an unimpressed eyebrow. He met my eyes as if to ask 'is this guy serious?' before saying, "Yeah, you want me to give you his number?"

Cameron snarled and put out his arm, stopping Lucas as he tried to walk past. "Listen up, fairy—"

"Grow up," I snapped. Cameron whipped around to stare at me incredulously. Lucas took the opportunity and winked at me before casually strolling past us, whistling. I stared after him for a moment, glaring and blushing at the same time, before turning back to my 'friend' who, judging by his expression, was not happy with me.

"The hell are you defending him for? You on his side now?" Cameron seethed. I shrugged.

"I'm not. You're just being immature."

Cameron glared at me but said no more.

A lot of people showed up for tonight's game. It must have been a pretty anticlimactic experience for them, because the game was one-sided the entire way through. The team we were playing was nothing short of terrible. When the final whistle blew, I felt as if I'd just been warming up for ninety minutes.

I wasn't the only one. Nobody on the team seemed particularly winded. I could hardly tell the starters from the kids who'd benched most of the game.

Still, it was the first game of the season, and that came with inevitable enthusiasm, no matter the team. Finally, the season was kicking off. And for seniors like me, who relied entirely on soccer to get into a decent college, this year was imperative. That alone brought a rush of adrenaline and put everybody in high spirits. The excitement was more necessary than ever, because it drowned out the negative mood that had been floating above our heads when we saw the starting lineup, with none other than Lucas Morgan as our center defender.

I glanced over at where Lucas sat on the bench, away from the rest of the team. The coach was hovering over him, saying something that I couldn't hear. Lucas was smiling and shaking his head, but coach's eyes were narrowed in suspicion. I wanted to know what they were talking about, but before I could move closer to eavesdrop, Tyler Fiero wrapped his arm around my shoulders and turned me away from the scene.

"How come you're staring at Lucas?" Tyler asked. I tensed at first, before I saw his grin and realized he was messing around. "You going gay on me?"

That wasn't how it worked, but I wasn't about to tell him that. "Hell no," I grimaced. "He's all yours, stud."

Tyler laughed and shoved me away. "Beyond gross, man. I don't even wanna think about that—oh god, I just thought about it. Traumatizing. Let's never have this conversation again."

I faked a laugh—I'd become quite good at that over the years. "Agreed. C'mon, let's go fuck with Morgan to take your mind off it."

Tyler's grin turned mischievous. "I'm always down to fuck with Morgan. Unless you're talking about Lucas—I wouldn't touch that punk with a ten foot pole."

"Me neither, dude."

The field didn't clear out until two hours after the game ended. Everybody was hanging out and talking and teeming with excitement for the first few players left, it started a chain reaction, and almost everybody was gone within fifteen minutes. A few, like me, stayed to shower first. I knew that Lucas Morgan was one of them when I saw him enter the locker room several minutes after I had, but I paid him no attention.

When I was finished showering, the room was nearly empty. Other than Lucas Morgan, only two freshmen remained, and they were walking out. For what felt like the hundredth time, I was alone with Lucas.

He was dressed and gathering his things to leave, but he looked up when I glanced at him. "Good game," he said as he shouldered his bags. I turned away without responding, and I was almost sure Lucas was rolling his eyes. "Well, great talk. I'd love to stay and chat, but I've got a rather long walk ahead of me."

"You could've caught Shawn if you hadn't come here," I told him, remembering that Shawn hadn't been one of the players to come shower after the match. He'd been one of the first to leave, but not too quickly to join if you tried. "So this is your fault."

"You're right," Lucas affirmed, surprising me. "But he had some very unkind words for me before the match, and honestly I'd rather walk than be in a car with him right now."

I knew what he was talking about. Before the game, Shawn had cornered Lucas and thrown just about every rude, offensive word I knew, along with some I'd never heard, at him. He'd made sure that the whole team was watching as he told Lucas that if he screwed the game up, he'd wish he was never born.

Lucas made to leave, but I said, "You already know I'll give you a ride, so cut the theatrics."

He stopped mid-stride and turned to face me. "Actually," he said slowly, "I really didn't know you'd . . . I thought it was just a practice thing. I'm surprised it even is a practice thing."

I shrugged and grabbed my things. "Whatever," I grumbled, strolling past him. "Come on."

Halfway to the car, Lucas looked over at me and asked, "Do you still expect me to believe you're not nice?"

"You fancy walking home?" I asked threateningly.

"I reckon you're too nice to make me," Lucas challenged. I laughed darkly at that.

"You really wanna make that bet?"

Lucas faltered and shook his head, which gave me a strange sense of satisfaction. "That's a strong no from me."

"Awesome," I said. "So shut up."

Lucas did shut up, at least for a little while. We were nearing his house when he decided to be annoying again.

"So, are we ever going to talk during these rides?" He asked.

"You keep talking and there won't be any more rides," I told him. He didn't listen.

"What happened to your hand?"

"None of your business," I grumbled. "But I hit a ceiling fan. You done?"

"Not quite," Lucas said, to which I huffed in annoyance. "I call bull on that, but whatever; like you said, none of my business. Are you, like, okay, though?"

I blinked in surprise. Funny how the first person to ask was the last person I'd have wanted. "Do you actually care?"

I felt Lucas's eyes on me and glanced sparingly at him. His expression was something like disbelief. "Would I have asked if I didn't? You might be an asshole, but you're not as bad as your friends, and you drive me home. So yeah, I care a little."

My left hand tightened on the steering wheel as butterflies erupted in my stomach. I didn't answer his question, instead asking my own. "What were you and Larmon talking about?"

Lucas hesitated for a moment, then said, "What?"

I resisted the urge to roll my eyes. "Don't play dumb with me, Morgan. I saw you and coach talking after the game. What was it about?"

Lucas smirked. "You watching me, Jean?"

"Don't change the subject," I snapped.

"He was just asking if anyone on the team had been giving me issues lately," Lucas admitted. "That's all."

That wasn't surprising. Coach Larmon hated conflict within the team, and he knew that the boys didn't like Lucas. "What'd you tell him?" I asked.

"I told him no," Lucas said. My eyebrows shot up in disbelief.

"That's a lie," I said.

"I'm aware."

"Why would you do that?" I asked incredulously. I didn't take Lucas Morgan as the type to lie for other people.

"I didn't do it for them," he clarified, as if he could read my mind. "I did it for me. If I tell coach that they give me shit every damn day, he'll just punish them, which would be great if it didn't mean they'd turn the harassment up to eleven."

I was surprised by the hint of anger in his voice. When I glanced at him in the corner of my eye, I noticed his jaw was clenched. I was so used to seeing him indifferent, I was surprised to see any signs that he could even get mad. "You're not as stoic as you make yourself out to be, are you?" I said. "They get to you."

Lucas turned to me, and though I wasn't looking at him, I could feel the heat of his glare. I'd struck a nerve.

He didn't say another word for the rest of the drive. He didn't even thank me or say goodbye like he usually did.

Lucas' behavior was back to normal when I drove him home after practice on Tuesday, but something seemed off. Not necessarily in him, but in me. I was half expecting him to say something, to try and start another conversation, but he was silent the entire drive. Each day, I waited for him to say something so that I could tell him to shut up, but he didn't so much as look at me until he said goodbye. The weekend came quickly, and I found myself strangely agitated at his silence.

I wasn't sure why I was so annoyed. Lucas had only spoken while I drove him home a select few times, so it wasn't as if his behavior this week was abnormal. Yet I couldn't shake the frustrated churn of my stomach, even as I ran down the field at Saturday's club game.

The truth was, as much as I hated to admit it, I wanted Lucas to talk to me. Even though I tried to cut him off whenever he spoke and wasn't very nice to him and kind of hated him, I still had feelings for him. Deep down, I liked his attention. The thought made me feel like a schoolgirl with a crush, and I didn't want to be that at all.

Still, I couldn't help myself; I did something about it. Monday evening, when Lucas sat down in the passenger seat of my car, I turned to him and said, "You've been quiet."

Lucas looked at me, puzzled. "Usually when I talk, you threaten to leave me on the side of the road," he pointed out.

"I know," I said, wishing I'd planned this interaction more thoroughly before I dove in. "I'm just saying."

Lucas flashed his lopsided grin. "You inviting me to talk more, Jean?"

Yes. "No."

"I think you are," Lucas said. "You miss my voice."

Yes. "No."

"How sweet," he cooed.

"You're insufferable," I groaned. "Forget I said anything."

Lucas hummed smugly but otherwise was quiet after that, and the drive soon become awkward. Then, just as I was pulling into his driveway, he randomly said, "We could be friends, you know."

"Not a chance," I scoffed without hesitating. "You must be high."

"Damn," Lucas whistled. "Rejected."

A memory from my childhood emerged suddenly, and I had to suppress a grin. "You ever see that episode of Zoey 101? With the rejected cheer-song-thing?"

Then I remembered who I was talking to and shut my mouth. "God," I muttered, "What am I saying?"

Lucas snickered and I shot him a harsh glare. Unfazed, he starting chanting under his breath. "Rejected, rejected, you just got rejected! R-E, J-E, C-T-E-D rejected!"

I refused to acknowledge that he'd gotten my reference and, turning fix him with a dry look, said, "We're here. You can go now."

He made no move to leave. Instead, he stared right back at me and smiled. I didn't smile back, but I discreetly took the chance to look at all of his features at once and was reminded of just how beautiful he was. His nearly-black hair was always in a sort of styled mess that suited him perfectly. Pale cheeks were speckled with faint freckles, and his light green eyes were framed by long, dark eyelashes. His smile showed off the single dimple in his right cheek. He was definitely a sight for sore eyes.

"I'll see you tomorrow," he said, like he always did. "Thanks for the ride. Try not to miss my voice too much."

With that, he left the car. I glared after him, but when he turned his back, a small smile danced on my lips.

You've been quiet. Three words that I quickly found I would regret.

Over the rest of the week, Lucas Morgan made a point to talk as much as he possibly could over the course of our car rides. For fifteen minutes each day, I listened to him blabber nonstop about anything and everything he could think of. I thought that he'd rest it come the new week, but Monday evening brought another one-sided conversation. No matter how many times I threatened to push him out of my car at 45 miles an hour, he wouldn't shut his mouth.

I didn't know one person could find so many things to talk about. The few times I stopped tuning him out and listened, I found myself learning things I never thought I'd need to know about him. His favorite musical, his hatred for sushi, and his fear of small fish were among the list.

"Oh my god!" I exclaimed finally, cutting off Lucas' story about the time he fed a toad Doritos. I pulled over and stared at him in utter exasperation. "What do I have to do to make you shut up?"

Lucas' expression dropped in an instant, becoming dead serious. Then, in a low voice, he said, "Kiss me."

His words took several moments to process in my head. When they did, my jaw went slack and my face paled. I stared at Lucas, wide-eyed and mortified. He stared right back. Seconds of silence passed between us.

Then he burst out laughing. He bent over in his seat, clutching his stomach and trying to form sentences through his guffaws while I blinked and tried to understand what had just happened.

"I've . . . I've been waiting . . . " He wheezed, "To do that . . .since you . . . Holy shit you should have seen your face!"

I stared, utterly confused and blushing wildly, as Lucas roared with laughter. He noticed my stunned expression and laughed even harder, though it looked like he was trying to calm himself down. As I recovered from the shock, I felt embarrassed and agitated and somewhat tempted to actually push Lucas out of the car. I grudgingly pulled back onto the road and ignored him to my best ability while he sobered.

"I'm sorry," he breathed; he was still chuckling. "I'll stop talking your ears off now. I've been waiting for—what's today, Wednesday? I've been waiting for a week and two days for you to say something like that so I could see how you'd react. I half thought you'd punch me, but that was way better."

"I could still punch you," I grumbled.

That night, I did a lot of reflecting. Reflecting was never good; it usually ended with several pillows chucked at my wall. Tonight wouldn't be any different.

My rough night started wit Lucas' laugh. Whenever I closed my eyes, it insisted on echoing in my head, over and over. It was a beautiful, happy sound. Another item to add to my growing list of reasons to like Lucas Morgan.

Moments like this were dangerous. Moments where I let go of my fear and anger for a short time and just thought about Lucas. Moments where I admired his optimism and confidence, where I thought about his bright smile and pretty eyes, where I appreciated his appearance and his personality. Moments where I was almost a normal kid with a normal crush. Moments that only led to more fear and anger when I remembered that I wasn't supposed to see Lucas that way. These were my best moments.

The moments that followed were always my worst. They were moments of self deprecation and abhorrence. Moments where I told myself, again and again, that if I had to be the way I was, I wasn't allowed to love, or even like, myself for it. Moments where I told myself that it didn't matter anyways, because Lucas Morgan wouldn't see me romantically if I was the only other gay man on earth. Moments of absolute despair. Then I responded to they despair with anger, because anger was easier to manage, and I had a lot to be angry about.

In my dark room, I was alone with my thoughts, and my thoughts were my ruin.

4: Nathaniel Jean's Burning Question

"It's because what you are is permanent."

Lucas turned to face me slowly, blinking rapidly as if something had taken him aback. He narrowed his eyes in obvious confusion and I stared back at him, silently asking why he was looking at me like that. "Um, what?" He said.

For a moment, I felt as confused as he did. Then I realized what must have happened and I mentally cursed myself over and over; I had said that out loud, hadn't I?

"Nothing," I said, too quickly. "Never mind. Get out of my car."

We were parked in front of Lucas' house. I silently prayed that he would let it go and get out. No such luck. He glanced at the car door, then back to me, and said, "No. what did you mean?"

"Lucas, get out of my car or I swear I'll—"

"You'll what?" Lucas challenged. "Leave me here? Push me out of the car at 60 miles per hour? I'm already home, Jean, and the car's not moving. Spill."

I hesitated for a moment, racking my mind for some sort of distractor. I blurted the first thing that came to mind. "Tough game tonight, huh?"

I wanted to slap myself. If the earth opened up and swallowed me right now, I'd be grateful. That had to be be the worst, least convincing subject change I could have gone for. Lucas stared at me with one eyebrow raised; we both knew that I would never willingly start a casual conversation about soccer with him.

"You're kidding, right?"

I felt more than a little embarrassed. I'd been thinking out loud, and I didn't want to admit that I was still pondering Lucas' words from weeks ago. There was no going back now, though. Lucas had his arms crossed and wore a determined expression. "You're really not leaving until I tell you?"

Lucas shook his head. "Unless you want to unbuckle my seatbelt and haul me out of the car yourself—which I can promise I will not make easy—you might wanna tell me what you were talking about."

I sighed in defeat. Lucas obviously wasn't budging, and I definitely didn't like the idea of dragging his screaming ass onto the driveway. "Remember when you talked about how everyone in this town is really hypocritical?" Lucas opened his mouth to respond, but I held up a silencing finger and spoke first. I wanted to get the embarrassment over with. "You asked why people stopped giving Katy Holman crap for what she did but still give you problems for being who you are. I think it's because your sexuality is, you know, a part of you. It will never go away or end. But Katy got her abortion and it was over with, so once it was done everybody had time to recover and move past it. There's no opportunity for that with you, because your . . . situation, is constant."

Judging by his expression, I'd taken Lucas by surprise. "I didn't know you were actually listening when I said all that."

That was what he took out of my spiel? That was in equal parts annoying and reliving.

"Yeah, well there're a lot of things you don't know," I grumbled. "You ready to leave now?"

He pursed his lips and stared at me in the analytical way he sometimes did. "One question, then I'll go," he promised. His intense gaze made me uncomfortable. "Do you think that that's . . . okay?"

I blinked. "What?"

"What you just told me," Lucas elaborated. "The reason people treat Katy Holman different than they treat me. Do you think it's okay?"

I didn't say anything, mostly because I didn't know what to say. I wasn't sure what I thought. Lucas didn't seem surprised, or even irritated, by my silence. He didn't ask again, but his eyes searched my face as if looking for the answer.

I tried to remain solid and unfazed, but I wavered under his gaze and looked away. The next thing I heard was the car door opening and closing behind me, and when I turned back, Lucas was gone, walking toward his front door.

I'd just put the car into reverse when I saw Lucas turn back. He hurried back to the car and tapped on the window.

"By the way," he said when I rolled the window down, "I won't need a ride after practice tomorrow."

I wanted to ask him why, but I bit my tongue. I didn't want him to know that I cared, even slightly. "I have auditions tomorrow," he explained nonetheless, and I wondered if he'd seen the question in my expression.

Once again, curiosity pricked my tongue, but I hesitated. Then I gave in and asked, "Auditions for what?" because I was beginning to realize that he could read me like a book. What I didn't say aloud, he saw anyways. I would have to work on that.

"The school is doing a production of Heathers this year," he said. He must have realized that I had no idea what Heathers was, because he added, "It's a musical, based off of an 80s movie. You should come when we perform it."

"I won't," I said, though I probably would. If Lucas had anything else to say, I didn't hear it, because I winded up the window and drove away.

The drive home on Wednesday evening was surprisingly lonely without Lucas. I didn't exactly miss him—or at least that's what I told myself—but I missed the company. I was so used to his annoying, amazing presence in my passenger seat, driving without him felt somewhat wrong.

The entire soccer team was buzzing with energy when Thursday came. We had another game, and it was going to be a toughie. Our team was rivaled by few in the state, but the school we were opposing was part of that small percentage. Their defense wasn't the best, but their offense always posed a challenge. Our record with them seemed to change every year—we'd win one year, then they'd win the next, then we'd win the next, then they'd win the next. Last year, we'd beat them 2-1, and this year we were determined to break the pattern.

One step into the locker room told me that adrenaline and testosterone levels were already high. Excited chatter echoed off the walls and the air seemed thick with tension. This promised to be the first difficult game of the season, and how we did tonight would reflect our team as a whole.

Trevor Cazamn and Cameron Schetwaldski stood to either side of me, deep in a conversation about offensive strategy that I pretended to engage in. Every now and then I would nod or hum, but I couldn't focus on their words. It was unlike me; I loved talking strategy and plays, and I knew them better than anybody on the team. Yet I felt distracted. My eyes kept darting around the locker room, my ears listened in on passing conversations, and my hands wouldn't stay till. I'd never been diagnosed with ADHD or anything even close, but I wondered if all of the stress I'd been under lately had somehow left me with distracted, nervous tendencies.

My attention drifted to Damien Diggory—which wasn't hard, since he towered over everyone. He stood in a huddled triangle with Tyler Fiero and our starting right defender, Bruno Sanctos. I couldn't hear their words clearly, but I picked up on enough to guess that they were discussing defensive strategies.

What bothered me, though it probably shouldn't have, was the absence of Lucas Morgan in their conversation. He was, after all, also a defender—and a damn good one at that. The team had, in some ways, grown to accept him. At least, they respected him enough not to give him trouble while we were on the field, and they played with him just as they played with any other teammate, because nobody could deny that he was a strong player. The moment we set foot on the grassy turf, whether it be during practice or a game, he was one of us. He was Lucas Morgan, our center defender.

Yet he still couldn't find his place on the team otherwise. Before the game started, and the moment it ended, he was back to being Lucas Morgan, the gay kid that nobody on the team wanted to be within three feet of, as if he was contagious. Then again, these boys were so air-headed, they probably believed that he was.

The instant Lucas came to my mind, my eyes began to search for him. I spotted him quickly enough; he was leaning against the brick wall, away from the rest of the team. That was no surprise. What did surprise me was the sight of his brother moving towards him.

Shawn Morgan usually ignored Lucas' very existence unless he wanted to give him trouble, so I assumed that he was harboring some choice words. It wouldn't be the first time Shawn had approached his brother before a game just to curse him out. He normally had an audience, though—Shawn seemed to find it absolutely necessary to make sure that everybody knew he hated Lucas, time and time again. As if he hadn't already made it clear.

Now, though, Shawn wasn't bullying Lucas at the front of the locker room, where everybody could see. They were in between two locker rows; if I wasn't so abstracted, and if I hadn't been standing where I was, I wouldn't have noticed them.

Lucas glanced up as Shawn approached and raised an expectant eyebrow at his brother. I couldn't see Shawn's face, but his crossed arms and tensed shoulders told me enough about how he was feeling. The two were the same height, but I'd noticed over the years that Shawn always stood straighter when he was around Lucas, trying to make himself taller. There was a constant battle for dominance between the two, but Shawn was the only one fighting. Lucas remained impassive, always.

Then Shawn spoke, and at first I was confused as to what he was saying. Then Lucas responded, and when realization hit me, my mouth fell open in surprise.

I had to strain my ears to hear them, but it made no difference. They weren't speaking English.

I'd known Shawn Morgan for years, and I'd had no idea he could speak another language. I couldn't help but gape as they had a lengthy, hushed conversation in a tongue I couldn't even recognize. It definitely wasn't Spanish, or French. I thought for a moment that it was German, but that didn't seem right either. Russian, maybe?

The conversation couldn't have been friendly, because Lucas looked beyond annoyed and Shawn's posture grew more rigid each second. After a minute or two, the latter stormed off. I should have looked away then, but I hesitated for a moment too long and Lucas caught me staring. I scowled at him, and he smiled.

I averted my gaze just as a horribly loud, high pitched sound pierced the air, leaving my ears ringing for several seconds after it ceased. I couldn't see Coach, but I knew he must have entered the locker room, because only his "lucky" whistle could make such a horrendous sound. He insisted on blowing it whenever he wanted the team to, and I quote, "get your punk asses onto the field and start warming up!"

Our coach was an interesting man.

I made a mental note to ask Lucas about the Russian later. Then I pushed all other thoughts aside; this was an important game. Every game was. I had no way of knowing when scouts would be in the bleachers, and making a name for myself was more important than ever this year. I could get away with being distracted in the locker rooms, but once I stepped outside, I needed to focus.

"That was a great shot," Lucas complimented, flashing his dimpled smile. "I thought it would bounce off the post for sure. Also, your friend isn't funny."

Trevor Cazamn had just left the locker room, leaving Lucas and I as the only remaining two. As he passed, he'd "whispered" loud enough to be heard throughout the entire room, "Might wanna get out fast before he starts trying to touch you."

I silently agreed—Trevor's comment wasn't funny in the slightest. That hadn't stopped me from fake-laughing at it, though. "That's your opinion," I remarked.

"I'm pretty sure it's yours, too," Lucas mused. When I glared at him, he raised his hands defensively. "But hey, that's none of my business."

I rolled my eyes but said nothing. In seconds I was out the door, with Lucas following behind as I headed toward my car. There were still people milling around in the parking lot—families chatting about the game, teammates celebrating the win. I didn't want anybody to see Lucas getting into my car with me, but I didn't have to tell him that. He knew the drill: keep your head down, and if anybody looks at you, pretend you're not with me.

It had worked well so far, but each time I stepped into the parking lot after a game, I still felt anxious. It probably would have been simpler to just let Lucas walk home, but I wasn't sure I could do that. Not because it was mean, but because he was Lucas Morgan, and that bastard unknowingly had me wrapped around his finger.

"So you speak Russian?" I asked as soon as we were on the road, driving away from Listrougth High School. I couldn't help but get straight to the point; the curiosity kept nagging at me.

"Romanian, actually," Lucas said. "Our mom is from Romania, so she taught us the language alongside English."

"And you're fluent?"

I caught Lucas' shrug in the corner of my eye. "I'm sure there's a lot I still don't know, but I'd say so."

"I never knew . . . Shawn never mentioned it," I said.

"Yeah, well, there're a lot of things you don't know," Lucas said. I glanced at him and he smirked smugly back at me, looking very pleased with himself for using my own words against me.

"What'd he say to you?" I asked. "You looked mad."

Lucas huffed, as if the mere thought annoyed him. "He saw a brochure for the club team on my desk, thought I was trying to join and apparently thought it was the start of Ragnarok."

I had no idea what Ragnarok was, but I didn't bother to ask. "Were you?"

He snorted. "As if. I don't have the time or commitment for that. My dad left it there because he wants me to join. He's been bugging me about it since I joined the school team. He loves soccer—he's the one that taught Shawn and I how to play."

Lucas was right; there was a lot that I didn't know. It was difficult to imagine Shawn and Lucas kicking a ball around in their backyard with their father, laughing and playing together like a real family. I had to remind myself that the Morgans once were a real family. A perfect family.

Now I knew why Lucas was so good at soccer. It was no secret that Bruce Morgan had once played professionally, and if he'd trained Shawn so well, it made sense that his other son would also be skilled.

"You would make the club team," I admitted. "Easily."

The school team and the club team had the same coach—Lucas wouldn't even need to try out. He'd be on the team in a heartbeat. However, he shook his head, and I realized that he didn't want to be on the club team, and his reasons extended beyond time and commitment.

"If I wanted to play for the club, or the school, I would've done so years ago, before . . ." he trailed off, but I knew what he meant. He would have tried out before everybody found out he was gay and turned against him. "Soccer has always been a hobby for me. Dad, Shawn and I would practice in our backyard for hours. Sometimes Shawn would bring some friends over and we'd scrimmage. For me, that was enough. Shawn was always the one with the passion. The one who wanted to play for his school and, eventually, his country. I didn't want any of that."

"Then why now?" I asked. "Why go for it all of a sudden?"

Lucas sighed, as if he'd been expecting the question but hoping I wouldn't ask it. "Because Shawn said I couldn't," he said simply. "After word got out that I'm gay, we stopped playing in the backyard. Shawn thought that I wouldn't be able to pick up where I left off two years later, so . . ."

"So you proved him wrong," I completed. Lucas hesitated, running a hand through his nearly-black hair.

"Not totally," he said honestly. "It was really hard. I did a lot of running over the summer to condition myself, and I practiced with Dad a little, but two years is a long time. I guess I did show him up a little though, huh?"

My lips twitched, but I forced down my smile. "If you don't want to play soccer professionally, what do you want?"

Lucas seemed to perk up at the question. He didn't hesitate before saying, "Theater. The second I'm done with this shit-hole of a town, I'm buying a one way ticket to New York. It's been my dream forever to act and sing for a living, to go to Juilliard, to be on Broadway. That's what I want."

I shouldn't have been surprised by Lucas' answer; after all, I'd seen him in countless school productions throughout the years. He could sing, he could dance, he could act. Yet somehow, I hadn't been expecting drama to be his aspiration. I'd always thought that theater was a hobby of his, but then again, perhaps that's what he thought when he looked at us soccer-players.

His dream was ambitious. Even I knew that Juilliard was incredibly diffi-cult to get into. Making it to Broadway was even harder. When I thought about it, though, I couldn't see him doing anything else. I'd watched him live. He was meant for the stage. I had no doubt in my mind that if he worked hard, he could be performing on 5th Avenue some day.

Maybe I was more surprised by how much his aspirations resembled mine. We had completely different interests, but we both wanted to leave this town in the dust as soon as we graduated. We shared the same destination, too: New York City; the Big Apple.

"You missed the turn."

I blinked, focusing my gaze, and cursed under my breath when I realized I had, in fact, missed the correct turn. I would either have to make a U-turn or take a five minute longer route to Lucas' house, and given that I sucked at U-turns and didn't want to risk my precious car, I reluctantly settled for taking the longer route.

"Since you just asked me a ton of questions, do I get to ask you one?" Lucas asked, although I'd spent enough time with him by now to know he would ask whether or not I said yes. With that thought in mind, I stayed silent and allowed him to continue. "You've got club practice on Mondays and Wednesday's, right? And before you accuse me of stalking you and throw me out of your car, remember that my brother is on your club team, too."

I rolled my eyes. We both knew that I hadn't been about to accuse him of stalking me and throw him out of my car, but he was clearly teasing. I wasn't sure how I felt about that.

The question seemed rhetorical, so I stayed silent. Several awkward seconds passed before I realized that Lucas hadn't continued yet. He was waiting for my answer. "Oh, yeah," I stammered. "I do. Why?"

"Because you still drive me home on those days," Lucas said. I blanched. "Practice ends at six, we usually don't leave until six-thirty, it's a fifteen minute drive to my house, and club practice starts at seven."

He'd backed me into a very tight, very uncomfortable corner. "Your point?" I asked, even though his point was very clear.

"I'm just surprised you give me rides on those days," Lucas shrugged. "Seems like more trouble than it's worth."

"Your house is on the way to the field," I told him. That was completely untrue—the club field was ten minutes in the opposite direction. Lucas didn't need to know that, though.

Thankfully, he believed my lie and didn't press the subject. "What about the showering? You shower after practice just to go get sweaty at another practice?"

"Listen, I've got leather seats," I said, and that was the truth. My parents had "made up" for their constant absence by buying me a very nice car, and I refused to sit my sweaty, muddy ass on its slick leather seats.

Lucas seemed amused by that, or maybe something else had caught his attention. "Would you look at us?" He chuckled. "Having a civil conversation."

After that, I was quiet.

Monday morning came with the panicked frenzy of students who just realized that the first quarter of the school year was coming to an end, and report cards would be given out that Friday. Students all day were begging teachers to bump up their grade or give them extra credit assignments. Trevor Cazamn told me he was thinking of seducing his math teacher into giving him a B.

I, on the other hand, wasn't fretting. Firstly, grades had been finalized last Friday, so the oblivious students still trying to amend their scores were wasting their time. Secondly, I'd need more than a small bump to have even moderately decent grades. My GPA was barely even enough to keep me on the soccer team, but that was nothing new. School wasn't my thing; never had been, never will be. That wasn't something I was particularly proud of—it wasn't comforting to think that soccer was my only way out of this town. It was a bit late to turn back now, though, and it wasn't as if I really could. Even if I put more effort into maintaining my grades, they wouldn't be spectacular. I just wasn't school smart.

"Everyone's going crazy now that report cards are coming out," Lucas commented as he pulled a shirt over his head. "Sae said her mom is threatening to pull her out of theater if she doesn't get her grades up."

Saeyoung Park was Lucas' best friend—one of his only friends. Unlike the rest of the school, the theater kids didn't care that Lucas was gay. They made up his small but loyal friend group, and sometimes I envied how they seemed to always have each other's backs.

I didn't respond, but, as usual, that didn't discourage Lucas. "How's yours looking?"

My only answer to that was a scoff, but I figured it got the point across. I was right, because Lucas chuckled and said, "You bartering for extra points?"

I shook my head, half hidden under the hood of my blue hoodie. "Nah," I said as I tossed my cleats into my duffel bag. "I don't see the point."

Lucas walked over and tossed his bags onto the bench in front of me—his way of telling me he was ready to go. "Me neither," he agreed. He sat down on the bench and looked up at me, his wet hair falling in messy black waves all over his forehead.

"You probably don't need to," I grumbled. Lucas was good at soccer and theater, no doubt he was good at school, too.

Lucas made a face. "I wouldn't be so sure about that, Nathaniel Jean. I'm too creative to be smart."

I covered my surprise by pretending to look for something, then realized I didn't have to pretend, because I actually was missing something. There was only one sock in my bag.

"Sounds like an excuse," I told him as I searched the locker row for my sock. How the hell do you lose a sock you were wearing thirty minutes ago?

"Sure is," he admitted with an affirming nod. "What's yours?"

I checked the adjacent locker rows, but I saw nothing. I looked under the bench, but no sock was in sight. I had club practice tonight, and I couldn't very well go with only one sock. I wouldn't have enough time to go home and get a replacement after I dropped Lucas off. "That I don't care enough," I answered distractedly. Where the hell was my sock?

Lucas chuckled. "I like it."

I took a brief break from my sock hunt to glance at Lucas. He was standing now, staring at me with an amused expression. His lips were quirked up in his lopsided smile and his eyes were twinkling. He looked happy.

I didn't understand that. I didn't see how he could ever be so full of happiness and laughter when people were constantly tearing him down. Sure, I'd seen him annoyed, and upset, and even angry. But when he was in a good mood—when he was happy, or excited, or amused—it was genuine. I could tell just by looking at him.

I felt annoyed a lot. I felt angry a hell of a lot. But I couldn't remember the last time I'd been genuinely happy, or excited, or amused. Just knowing who I was—what I was—I found it impossible to be content with myself.

Lucas didn't only have to deal with knowing who he was. He also had to bear the weight of everyone else knowing who he was, and treating him horribly for it. Yet he could still be happy, and excited, and amused. I simply didn't get it.

"How are you so happy the way you are?" I asked. I didn't even feel embarrassed for saying that out loud—I'd intended to. I trusted Lucas to be honest in answering, because he almost always was, and I wanted to know. The question wasn't new. It had been slowly simmering at the back of mind for weeks, waiting to be ignited. Now, it was burning.

Lucas pursed his lips and chuckled. "You mean gay?"

I nodded, albeit a little shyly, and said, "I don't . . . I don't understand how you can be so pleased with yourself all the time. How you can be so sure that you're right, and everyone else is wrong. How you can carry yourself confidently and not give a damn that you're gay, or that people have a problem with it."

In a heartbeat, the amusement fell from his expression. Lucas became serious but not surprised, as if he'd known this was coming. He ran a hand through his damp hair and scanned my expression, and I silently wondered if I'd ever feel comfortable under his scrutinizing gaze.

"It's not too hard," he said eventually. "You just haven't tried it yet. With the way this town is, it's not easy to know what's law and what's belief. They make everything so black and white, but life isn't a matter of rights and wrongs. At least, it shouldn't be. The fact is, I'm gay. I can't change that. And it's not like there was never a time in my life where I wanted to. I spent a whole year wanting to. But there's a moment when you have to realize that you can't change it, so you can choose either hate that part of yourself or love it.

"You think that you have to hate yourself for who you are, because that's what this town has trained you to believe. You think it's the right thing to do. But this town is just a tiny, insignificant spec on a map. Eventually you realize that life goes on beyond this town, and there are so many places you can go where nobody gives a rat's ass if you like boys or girls or both or anything in between. Set your sights on a place like that—a place like New York City—and it'll help you stay afloat. I know it's easier said than done, but I think you should try. You deserve to be happy with yourself, Jean."

I stared, dumbfounded, at the boy in front of me. I hadn't expected him to have so much to say on the subject. I certainly hadn't expected him to directly address me. As seconds of silence passed and it sunk in that he hadn't been answering the question for himself, he'd been answering it for me, a hot bubble of panic rose in my throat.

He knew.

"I—" I choked on my words as every fear I'd built up over the years crashed over my mind like a tsunami, destroying everything in its path. "I never said—"

"You didn't have to," Lucas said. I couldn't see his reassuring smile, or hear the comforting tone of his voice. I couldn't think enough to realize that with Lucas, my fears of exposure and exclusion, of being hated and cast aside, were irrational.

"It's okay that you're—"

In my panic, I lashed out, grabbing a fistful of his shirt and pushing him roughly against the lockers behind him. He hissed in pain as his back slammed against the metal. "Don't fucking say it," I snarled. My brain was on overdrive, and with so many things running through my mind, I was only half-aware of what I was doing. Terrible images of what could happen if Lucas uttered a word to anyone flickered through my head. I saw my parents telling me to pack my things and never show my face again. I saw my entire town turning their backs on me—their golden boy gone wrong. I saw the doors of my church, opening for my mother and father and sister, then slamming shut and locking before I could enter. I saw the boys kicking me off the soccer team as if we were never friends. I saw myself with no friends, no family, no home, and no way to escape Nowhere, Nebraska.

Lucas raised his arms submissively, and for the first time maybe ever, I saw fear in his eyes. "It's okay," he said. "I won't tell anyone. You don't have to—"

"Shut up!" I yelled, and I flinched as a loud crashing sound pounded against my ears, pushing against my brain until I felt lightheaded. My heart was beating so painfully against my chest, I felt as though any second now it would rip through my flesh and I'd be dead.

I lowered my voice to a deep, dangerous growl. "Don't you ever make shit like that up again. I'm not a fucking fag like you, and if you tell a single goddamn person that you even thought that for a second . . . I'm not like your brother, Morgan. I'm not afraid beat you into the dirt. So keep your mouth shut and stop pretending to know so much, because one day you're gonna talk yourself to death."

Lucas' eyes were wide and intimidated. I gave him a final push against the lockers and then let him go. I grabbed my bags and didn't remember how to breathe again until I was seated in my car, alone. When I grabbed the steering wheel, pain shot up my left hand. I turned it over and stared at my palm, shocked to see four bloody, crescent shaped wounds. My fist had been clenched so tight, I'd cut into my skin with my fingernails.

By the time I arrived home, my lip was bleeding from how hard I'd been biting it and my knuckles were white from gripping the steering wheel so hard. I'd forgotten about my missing sock, but it didn't matter. I wasn't going to practice.

I rushed up the stairs and stumbled blindly into my room. The moment the door was shut behind me, I collapsed against it and fell to the floor. Something was wrong with me. I didn't know what was coming over me, but I'd never felt it before.

My heart was beating irregularly, pounding hard and fast against my ribs. My entire chest felt tight, and no matter how I tried, I couldn't catch my breath. My stomach clenched painfully and bile rose in my throat. Sweat coated my skin, but I was freezing. There was a tingly, uncomfortable sensation dancing across my hands, but when I tried to lift them, I couldn't; I felt completely weak. My head was spinning so fast, I felt like I would pass o ut.

Then I did.

5: Nathaniel Jean's Downfall

The next day after practice, I was showered and out of the locker room before Lucas Morgan could so much as look at me. And the next day, and the day after that.

A small part of me wanted to talk to him, to make sure that he knew he couldn't say a word to anyone. A smaller part wanted to apologize for the way I'd acted. A third part, bigger than the other two combined, wanted to pretend nothing had happened and simply cut Lucas out of my life, just like I had in the seventh grade. That seemed like the easiest method. The path of least resistance.

It wasn't.

Destroying Lucas' image was hard when he was all I seemed to think about. It was as if he'd somehow claimed a sector of my brain and dedicated it to himself. The worst part: the thought of Lucas came with the thought of what Lucas knew. I wasn't stupid, I didn't think he'd bought any of my "I'm not gay" speech. He knew. He had that information, and he could use it however he wanted.

That thought alone hadn't allowed me more than six total hours of sleep since Monday. It was Friday now, and halfway through practice, coach pulled me aside.

"Jean, you look like you're gonna pass out on me," he said in his deep, coarse voice. "You sick?"

"I'm fine," I all-but snapped. It was never a good idea to be rude to Marcus Larmon, but lack of sleep was making me irritable. Of course, he was right. I felt queasy and dizzy, constantly somewhere between throwing up and passing out. But I wouldn't stop until my legs gave out. If I overworked myself, so be it. I desperately needed the distraction.

"No, you're not," Larmon insisted. "It shows. You were all over the place at last night's game, and you look green now. You need a break."

I'd been playing for Coach Larmon for years, and I knew him well. The tone of his voice now told me that arguing would bring me nothing but trouble. His decision was final.

"Fine," I said. "I'll take five minutes."

I thought that was fair. Coach, however, shook his head. "Practice is almost over. You're done for today. Go back and—"

"Coach!" I whined. He held up a hand, efficiently silencing me.

"You're done. Now go back to the locker room and freshen up. Drink a lot of water. And get some sleep, Jean. Skip the club game tomorrow, that's an order. And if you're not looking better by Monday, I'll bench you all g ame."

My eyes widened in disbelief. Coach had never made me skip a game, or threatened to bench me for so long; he rarely ever benched me at all. I was one of his best players, maybe his best. He needed me on the field.

Especially next Monday—the team we were playing was no pushover. But Coach didn't bluff. If I didn't catch up on sleep, he wouldn't let me play. If only he knew that I tried to sleep. I couldn't. Not while anxiety and paranoia made me restless.

Nevertheless, I hummed in grudging understanding and headed for the locker rooms, grabbing my water bottle on the way. Teammates glanced at me as I passed, confused. The only one who didn't turn to look was Lucas.

When I sat down in the locker room, my entire body seemed to sag. I was so tired and anxious and angry and sad. That wasn't exactly abnormal—I spent most of my time feeling tired and anxious and angry and sad. Never to this degree, though. If I didn't get it together soon, I would become my own downfall. Or perhaps I already was.

So many things were wrong. Physically, that was obvious. I looked horrible. My hair was stringy and messy, my face was caved in with exhaustion, and coach was right—I was starting to look a little green.

The problems I faced below the surface were so much worse, though. I was so anxious, my hands were constantly trembling. My mind was so chaotic, my vision seemed blurry and unfocused. Fear gripped and twisted my stomach, like cruel hands kneading dough, leaving me perpetually sick. So much could go wrong. So much would go wrong if Lucas said anything.

He wouldn't. Somewhere, I knew that. But he could, and that thought was enough to make me shiver.

What made everything worse: I missed Lucas. I was furious with him for finding out my secret, for igniting my deepest fears, but the car still felt empty without him. I missed his lopsided smile and his twinkling eyes and his deep dimple.

Suddenly, I was gagging. I rushed to the bathroom and into a stall. For minutes I stood, bent over the toilet, heaving and coughing. There was nothing to throw up, though. I hadn't eaten since breakfast yesterday morning. So I was left heaving, dry and painful.

I wasn't sure how long I remained there, coughing up nothing at all but unable to stop. Soon enough, I heard the sounds of the locker room doors opening and voices filling the area. I hurried away from the toilet and into a shower stall before anybody could catch me at such a low point. Maybe a shower would clear my head.

I pulled off my sweaty practice uniform, hanging it on the hook against the shower wall. I tossed my cleats, socks, and shin guards under the shower curtain, and turned on the water.

I stayed in that shower for a long time, thinking about everything and nothing. I wasn't even quite sure where my mind was going, I just knew it was nowhere good. My head spun relentlessly, and for a quick moment, I could've sworn my vision went red. I felt like I was going insane. Maybe I was.

I hated this confused, blurry state of mind even more than I hated the paranoia, or the fear, or the anxiety. I felt as if I was outside of my body, separated by a glass barrier, watching from a distance as I lost myself more and more.

I wanted to destroy the glass wall. I wanted to reenter myself and regain control. I wanted to break through and see clearly agin. I shut my eyes and tried to calm my mind, just long enough to picture my fist crashing through the glass, destroying any barrier between me and myself.

I cried out in pain. My eyes shot open to see the wounds I'd gotten when I punched my mirror, now open again. I'd thought they'd healed fully after so many weeks, yet my knuckles seemed to be cut in the exact same places. Blood was smeared against the wall, painting the white tile scarlet. Water washed over the cuts with a violent stinging and dragged my blood to the floor until I was standing in a puddle of diluted red.

I heard a series of footfalls. "Who's there?" A voice—Lucas' voice—called. "Is everything okay?"

I spat out a curse. Lucas' footsteps drew nearer and stopped in front of my stall. "Who's in there?"

"I . . . I need a t-towel," I stammered. In seconds, a towel was tossed over the curtain. I caught it and clumsily tied it around my waist, getting several splatters of blood on it in the process. Then I pulled back the curtain, immediately met with Lucas' concerned expression.

"Nate, what happened?" He gasped when he saw my hand.

"Doesn't matter," I grumbled; I tried to step past him, but he maneuvered in front of me. "Move."

"You need help," Lucas said. "I'll go find coach."

My left hand shot out and grabbed his wrist before he'd even turned. "No," I said. If coach saw me like this, I'd be on the bench on Monday for sure. "Don't, he'll just pester me."

Lucas looked like he wanted to argue, but he sighed and gave in. "Fine. But you have to let me help you."

I let go of his wrist and his eyes darted to the thin bandage wrapped around my palm. "What happened there?"

"Nothing," I said. "And I don't need your pity."

I stepped around him again, and this time he didn't try to stop me. However, he spoke up as I passed. "It's not pity, Nate; it's support. There's nothing wrong with needing someone to lean on every now and then. And if you don't let me help you, I'm going to get Coach. Your choice."

He had the same final tone to his voice as Coach Larmon. I turned to face him, glaring harshly, and said, "Fine."

Lucas led me, still clad in only a bloody towel, to the office at the corner of the locker room. I sat on the desk chair as he rummaged through the drawers for a first aid kit. When he found it, he knelt in front of me and extended a hand. I realized with a nervous jolt that he was waiting for me to give him my own.

I hesitated, then laid my hand over his. He held it delicately, examining the wound, before opening the kit with his other hand. He pulled out a small packet and tore it open with his teeth, pulling out a wipe. I winced when it touched the lacerations in my skin, but remained still as he gently cleaned the wound.

My knuckles were turning a deep, ugly purple. When Lucas disinfected the wound with alcohol, I hissed, but other than that the process was silent. In only a few minutes, my hand was almost entirely wrapped in bandages, just as it had been weeks ago.

"Thank you," I said; not because I felt like I should, but because Lucas had somehow managed to soothe the turmoil in my head, if only temporarily. Something about his composed expression and tender handling made me feel as if I was supposed to be calm, and my mind responded accordingly. He didn't know it, but he'd helped me mentally more than he had physically. Lucas glanced up at me and offered a small smile. He still hadn't released my hand.

"You're welcome."

Lucas stood up then, so I followed his lead. "I can drive you home, if you want," he offered.

I didn't try to cover my surprise. "What?"

Lucas shrugged. "No offense, but you don't look too good—even without the mummy hand. I don't want you driving like this. I can drive you to your house and then walk back to mine."

I shook my head. "You don't have to do that."

"No shit," Lucas chuckled lightly, and I could tell he was trying to lighten the mood. "I want to, Jean."

I didn't bother refusing after that; I was too tired. Lucas gathered all of my things while I got dressed, and then he drove me home.

We got out of the car at the same time. Lucas smiled at me from across the hood, and before my brain could catch up to my mouth, I said, "Do you want to stay for a while?"

If I didn't feel so horrible, I would have laughed at the pure shock on Lucas' face. "Would I . . . What?"

It wasn't too late to go back. Yet, strangely, I didn't want to. Perhaps my tiredness was slowing my normal thought process, but I couldn't bring myself to care. After days of avoiding Lucas Morgan like the plague, a large part of me—the part that cared for him—just wanted to be near him again. Chances were, I'd be back to almost-normal after a decent sleep and a few meals, and I would never make a decision like this. Might as well take advantage of my sluggish, slightly-deluded mind.

"You heard me," I said. "Stay over, hang out for a bit."

Lucas hesitated. "Aren't you scared your family will see me? I know they know who I am, and they don't like me very much."

"My parents are on a business trip," I told him. "And my sister is sleeping over at her best friend's house."

Jenna spent more time with her closest friend, Emma Lee Gardner, than she did in her own home. I didn't blame her—Emma Lee's parents treated her more like their daughter than our's did.

Lucas looked like he was struggling to accept the fact that I was really inviting him over. "You. Want me. In your house?"

I shrugged. "I'm a little high on exhaustion right now," I admitted. "Or else this would never happen. But you did a pretty good job taking care of me back in the locker room, and I think . . . I think I need to let myself be taken care of for once. For some reason, you're still nice to me after all the times I've been shit to you, so I might as well stop pushing you away, at least for t oday."

Lucas still looked utterly confused. His eyes searched my face for the truth, but before his gaze could lock with mine, I put my hands over my face. "Stop doing that," I whined.

"Uh, what?" Lucas asked. I peeked between my fingers and, when I was sure he'd stopped analyzing me, dropped my hands to my sides.

"That thing you do," I said. "Where you like stare into my soul. It's weird, stop doing it."

Lucas chuckled, rubbing the back of his neck sheepishly. "Oh, sorry. I like to read people, I guess."

"Well I, for one," I said, "Do not like to be read. Now, we gonna stand out here all day or what?"

The moment we stepped inside, Lucas asked me where the kitchen was.

I blinked in surprise. "Uh, on the other side of that wall. Why?"

"You need to eat," Lucas said pointedly. I rolled my eyes.

"I can make food for myself."

"Good for you," he said. "Now go sit on the couch while I make you something. I'm taking care of you today—or did you forget that already?"

I gave up on arguing and did as he said, stretching out on the big leather couch in the center of the living room. "You cook?"

Lucas paused on his way to the kitchen and turned back to me with a snort. "Not at all." With those last words, he disappeared into the kitchen.

He emerged five minutes later, carrying a glass of orange juice and a plate with a bagel on it. "I present to you," he said, handing me the items, "My most exquisite meal yet, consisting of classic orange juice, squeezed not-so-fresh and adorned with artificial preservatives, and a moderately burnt bagel, lathered in too much cream cheese."

"You're a loser," I said as I took the 'meal', but there was no malice in my words. Lucas pushed my legs off the couch and sat down, earning a grunt of protest that was muffled by the bagel—which was, as described, slightly burnt.

Lucas leaned back against the cushions and crossed his hands behind his head. He stared at me for a few seconds, not analyzing or smiling or frowning, just watching. I held his gaze, and several moments seemed to pass slowly. It dawned on me then that Lucas Morgan was in my house, and we were alone. I had no idea whether or not he was interested in me at all—he probably wasn't. But if he was, things could happen.

If I let them. Somehow, though, I didn't think I could handle that.

I definitely couldn't handle that.

"You punched a wall," Lucas said, breaking the silence.

I shrugged, trying to hide my embarrassment. "It happens," I said.

Lucas furrowed his dark eyebrows. "Um, not really, no." I shrugged again, and Lucas huffed in frustration. "I thought you said you were going to stop pushing me away."

"I never said I'd tell you all of my secrets."

"Well maybe you should start with one," Lucas suggested. I averted my gaze.

"I'm not talking to you about my sexuality," I muttered. I didn't bother to deny anything, because there was no point. He knew.

Lucas didn't say anything. I brought my eyes back to his face and could tell right away that he didn't like my answer. He didn't push it, though. "Fair enough," he said. "But can I talk to you about it? I just want—I need to make sure you know that I would never tell anybody. Even if you did something terrible to me, I'd keep your secret. Being out in this town isn't easy, I would know. I'm not imposing that burden on anyone."

I didn't say anything. Lucas stared at me expectantly, but when he realized that I had no response, he continued. "You've been shaky since Monday. Do you feel better now that I said that?"

"Yeah," I admitted. At that, Lucas smiled. "Yeah, I do. I was freaking out."

"I could tell," he said. "I'll leave you alone on that now. Do you wanna watch a movie or something?"

"Sure."

We decided on watching the Avengers; I insisted when I found out he'd never seen it. He seemed to like it a lot—he was on the edge of his seat during the intense scenes, smiling during the cute ones, and laughing at the funny ones. I noticed something I hadn't before: when he laughed, his nose scrunched up the smallest bit. It was devastatingly cute.

We hardly talked aside from a few stray comments, and we were sat on opposite sides of the couch, but it was nice. Two and a half hours later, when the movie was over, I felt a lot better than I had over the last few days. Lucas had told me out loud that he would never, under any condition, tell my secret, and I realized that that was what my brain needed in order to calm down.

Of course, I still felt pretty crap. I was absolutely exhausted, and Lucas could tell, because when the movie ended he said, "I should get going."

"You don't have to," I said without thinking. "You could, uh, stay longer."

Lucas smiled, a little awkwardly, and shook his head. "You need sleep."

I groaned, but didn't argue. Just because I was being friendly with Lucas didn't mean I was about to start acting desperate, no matter how much I wanted him to stay. "I'll walk you out."

I ended up walking with Lucas all the way to the end of our driveway. The sky was dark, and I didn't like the idea of him walking home alone, but he insisted. He made the point that I shouldn't be driving so drowsy, and I reluctantly agreed.

I was halfway back up my driveway when Lucas called out, "Hey, Jean?"

I turned back to face him. "Yeah?"

"I was just at your house for a few hours."

Confused, I shrugged and said, "Er, yeah."

"We talked about stuff."

"Yeah."

"We watched a movie together."

"Yeah."

"I made you a five-star meal."

I had no idea what he was getting at, but I chuckled. "Yeah."

"Doesn't that sound an awful lot like something friends would do?"

"Oh." I said stupidly. That's what he was getting at. "I don't know."

Lucas shoved his hands into his pockets. "I guess I just want to know what I should expect the next time I see you," he said.

"I don't know," I said again, and I meant it. I had no idea how I would feel when the weekend ended, or where Lucas and I now stood in terms of friendship. I didn't want to promise anything, because I was almost sure I would let him down.

Lucas didn't press the subject, but I caught a shift in his expression. "Goodnight, Nathaniel Jean."

As Lucas walked away, I knew with absolute certainty that I wouldn't even have the chance to be my own downfall. He'd long ago claimed that role. Lucas Morgan would be the end of me.

6: Nathaniel Jean's Link

The next Monday marked the beginning of the second quarter of the school year. Report cards were handed out in fourth period; I watched as students' faces lit up or fell, as friends high-fived or tried to offer each other comfort.

I didn't dwell too long on mine. It sucked, but I'd been expecting that. Besides, I had other matters on my mind.

Like the fact that I had absolutely no idea what to do about Lucas.

Our eyes met once, when I was heading from lunch to sixth period. He smiled at me. I'm not sure what I would have done—smile back, scowl, avert my gaze—had Tyler Fiero not opened his big mouth to loudly say, "Yo Nate, the queer's got his eyes on you! Ha!"

Lucas looked away then, and so did I. Tyler nudged me with his elbow, as if he was waiting for me to acknowledge his joke. So I chuckled half-heartedly and said, "Nah, man, I think it's you he's got eyes for."

Tyler laughed and made a face. "Dude, that's, like, nightmare fuel."

Late October temperatures were perfect for soccer—the summer's heat and dryness subsided, making practice more refreshing than torturous.

The cold stung a bit, but it was better than melting into a nasty, sweaty puddle.

That said, anytime Lucas Morgan looked at me, the temperature in the air turned to 100 degrees Fahrenheit on an arid day. Extremely torturous.

I was half-dreading our conversation in the locker room, because I still had no inkling of a clue how to approach him. He wanted to be friends, and though I wouldn't admit it, I did, too. But could a guy like Lucas and a guy like me ever really be friends? We were in two different worlds.

Nevertheless, the time eventually came when the boys finished their chatter and the locker room cleared out, when I was alone with Lucas. I didn't so much as look at him—I was trying and failing to formulate some sort of game plan in my mind—until we were both ready to go and I had no choice.

He leaned against the wall next to the exit and raised an eyebrow at me as I approached. "You're being weird. Stop it."

"I'm not being weird," I said defensively, pushing open the door and stepping past him.

Lucas snorted. "Oh, you're being so weird. C'mon, I thought we were past this."

I sighed and ran a hand through my hair, frustrated with myself. "I did, too," I admitted.

Lucas used to be someone I both genuinely hated and really liked at the same time. Over the first quarter of my senior year, he'd managed to dissolve any traces of the hate I'd felt, leaving me with only the sweeter, much scarier feelings for him that I'd spent so long trying to avoid. Now, I just really, really liked him. Here he was, trying to be friendly with me. And I was acting like a freak.

Lucas seemed to realize that something real was bothering me, because he smiled reassuringly and said, "Whatever's freaking you out, ignore it. The world won't end if we're friends. You don't have to commit social suicide and, you know, talk to me in front of your dude bros or anything. Just relax."

Maybe I should have felt guilty for it, but his words did make me feel better. I didn't know what I'd do if the boys starting asking questions about why I was suddenly friends with Lucas, if they began spreading rumors.

"Sorry," I said remorsefully. Lucas shrugged.

"S'okay."

We climbed into my car and he glanced at me as he pulled on his seatbelt. "You going to Shawn's party Saturday?"

I rolled my eyes—I'd nearly forgotten about the Halloween party that Shawn was throwing at his house that weekend. Their parents were away on a short vacation to Alaska or something; it was bound to be a shit-show. "Do I have a choice?"

Lucas chuckled and offered his lopsided smile. "You know, I'm starting to think that you don't like my brother much more than I do."

I shifted my car into drive with a scoff. "That's because I don't."

Who would have ever guessed that Nathaniel Jean and Lucas Morgan would spend their drive home that Monday bonding over their shared hatred for Lucas' brother? I don't know, but it felt good to rant.

Lucas and I kept it up like that for the next few days. Talking while I drove him home about whatever came to our minds. The conversations were no longer one-sided or reluctant. I finally gave in and let myself talk to Lucas Morgan like a friend without feeling as though I was doing something wrong. Guilt sometimes found me during the nights, sometimes didn't. Occasionally, I even let myself try to think his way; to tell myself that I didn't have to hate who I was, because I was right, and the rest of this hell-town was wrong. Those moments never lasted too long.

Still, I was starting to find less and less excuses to push myself away from the amazing boy who was so whole-heartedly offering his camaraderie.

And if I thought I'd liked him before, I was in deep shit now.

Saturday rolled around pretty uneventfully. I didn't bother buying a costume for Shawn's party; instead I showed up in jeans and a leather jacket. All I brought was a twelve-pack of beers that I stole from my parents' "off limits" cupboard and the hope that no girls would try to advance on me tonight. I just wanted to get shit-faced and not worry about where I woke up in the morning.

I could hear the music from nearly a block away, which meant that this party was probably gonna be cop-crashed eventually. I'd have to remember that and get out early.

The house was packed, but nothing less was expected of a Shawn Morgan party. All around me, girls and boys in slutty costumes grinded against one another, whether they knew each other or not. The music was deafeningly loud and about as vulgar as music could get. Just about every underaged teen here—aka everyone here—was holding a red solo cup or a shot glass. I knew from Shawn's past parties that there was beer pong being played just a room away. There were a couple of dudes in one corner smoking weed, some girls in another doing lines of cocaine, and several people throughout the house were vaping, making the air around them foggy.

It was funny to think that pretty much everybody in this house was Catholic. Lucas was more right than I'd realized before—we were so hypocritical, it hurt.

Not that that would stop me from getting wasted and having a shit-ton of fun.

I navigated through the mass of sweaty bodies into the kitchen, where I knew all of the hard stuff was. I was greeted by the sight of Shawn Morgan himself, between the legs of a girl sat up on the counter who I was almost positive was a freshman. "Yo, Casanova!" I called.

Shawn pulled away from the girl, who groaned in protest, to look over his shoulder at me. His mouth was smeared with her crimson lipstick. He grinned and left her entirely to stumble over and give me a high five. "Heyyy man! Almost thought you weren't gonna show!"

I laughed and gave him an incredulous look. "Me? Do you even know me?"

Shawn laughed way too hard and slapped me roughly on the back, half-stepping, half-tripping past me towards a cooler on the floor. "Whatcha lookin' for, bro? Beer?"

"Something that'll fuck me up," I told him. His grin widened.

"I like the way you think, Jean. Tequila good for you?"

"Hell yeah, pour it up."

Shawn clumsily grabbed a red solo cup and a half-empty bottle of tequila. "You gotta drink this shit slow, man," he said as he filled the cup with so much tequila that liquid splashed onto the floor with every movement. "Don't die on me."

I laughed and took the cup, raising it to my lips and took a small sip that left my throat burning. This was strong shit. "If I do, take some artsy-ass pictures for me, alright?"

Shawn chuckled and nodded. "Will do. Now go get out there and get fuckin' wasted! And laid, dude. You don't get laid tonight, I'll be disappointed."

The party was intense, and by the time an hour had gone by, I couldn't tell my right foot from my left. Hell, I couldn't tell my foot from my hand.

I didn't know how or why, but I was dancing with Madeleine Montgomery, the deacon's daughter. Her body was pressed against mine and her lips were on my neck, her hands going anywhere and everywhere. It wasn't exactly a pleasant experience on my part, but I had to admit, Madeleine was gorgeous. She was tall for a girl—model height, for sure—with long brown hair and tanned skin and cute freckles. Her body was the kind that straight boys ogled at in porn magazines and insecure girls looked to with awe and jealousy, wondering what workouts and diets and waist-trainers they could use to achieve it. Madeleine had a soothing voice, deeper than most girls', and her hair smelled intoxicatingly good.

She was everything I wished I was attracted to. If I wanted a girl like Madeleine, I could have her. But I didn't want her, and that was the tragedy of it all.

Dancing like this with her, in a way that was anything but innocent, was what I needed to uphold my reputation. It was girls like Madeleine, who saw me as rich and hot and figured that was all that mattered, that kept me on top of the high school food chain.

She kissed me, and I let her; I always let them. No amount of alcohol could make me like it, though. Even now, as drunk off my ass as I was, the kiss was gross and sloppy and made me want to recoil into myself.

When her hands went to my jeans and her lips to my ear, whispering that we should get away and find somewhere more private, I drew the line. I wasn't sure why—it wouldn't be my first time—but I really didn't want to sleep with her. I didn't want to spend my Halloween pretending to enjoy something that never gave me the slightest bit of pleasure. For some reason, the idea seemed especially appalling tonight. I told her I needed some fresh air and I bolted.

Before I could reach the front doors, Trevor Cazamn appeared out of nowhere, a blunt between his fingers in one hand and a beer bottle in the other, and punched me in the shoulder in greeting. Except he was so fucked up that me missed, and the momentum would have carried him off his feet had I not held out an arm to catch him. I realized too late that I was just a screwed as he was, and we both crashed to the floor in a laughing, drunk heap.

"Fuck," Trevor groaned, making no move to get up from on top of me. "Dude, this party is so fucking lit. Jessica . . . Jessica wants me to meet here somewhere. I forgot where. Fuck."

I tried to push him off, but he stayed limp like dead weight. "Better go find her before Shawn does," I joked, because Shawn was notorious for snatching a girl right from your fingertips.

Trevor just groaned again. I called his name, and he snored in response. The bitch had passed out on me.

I inwardly rolled my eyes and struggled to get him off. He rolled onto the floor and I left him there, only half-caring if he got stepped on or choked on his own puke. His weight on top of me had left me feeling sweaty and more claustrophobic in the crowd than ever. I had no recollection of which part of the estate I was in—there were so many useless rooms in this big-ass house, I could get lost in it sober. Drunk, I stood no chance.

So I made a beeline for the only feasible escape I could see—the stairs. I pushed past people and couples and a few guinea pigs, which I decided was a question better left unasked, until I reached the spiral staircase leading to the second floor. I stumbled at least seven times on my way up, despite my tight grip on the railing, and nearly fell back down once trying to step over the bodies of two oblivious teens with their tongues so far down each other's throats they were poking out of their asses.

It was a journey, but I managed to trek the incline, only feeling slightly nauseous afterwards. There was a second staircase leading to the third floor of the huge house, but I wasn't sure I could scale another one and stay in one piece.

I barged blindly into rooms, finding a bedroom, a laundry room, a bathroom, and some kind of movie room, all of which were occupied by people who were really enjoying their night. With a final, somewhat desperate hope, I pushed open the last door in the hall. To my relief, there were no naked teenagers.

The room wasn't empty, though. Staring at me from the queen-sized bed, looking very amused at my current state, a thin paper book in his hands, was my sort-of-friend, Lucas Morgan.

"Woah, you live here too," I breathed, as if it were some sort of revelation. Lucas held back a laugh and nodded.

"That I do," he agreed.

"Well whatreyoudoinguphere?" I asked with a pout, my words slurring together to create one big mess.

Lucas raised an eyebrow. "I don't think I'd be exactly welcome downstairs."

"Stop with the big words," I whined, although it processed in my brain two seconds later that he hadn't said any big words. I shrugged to myself and stepped into the room.

"Shut the door," Lucas said. I narrowed my eyes suspiciously, and he rolled his. "Calm your shit, I'm not gonna rape you. But that trash music is really loud and really annoying."

"Hey, I like that music!" I protested, but I shut the door nonetheless and stumbled into Lucas' room. It was a big room, with posters and records on the walls of plays and musicals that I'd never heard of. My eyes were set on the bed, though, so that's where I went. Collapsed is a better word, really; I let myself fall face-first into the comfortable mattress, and giggled at the way it bounced underneath me.

"I'm drunk," I said intelligently.

"Your face is in the mattress, I can't hear you," Lucas informed me. How kind of him. I rolled over onto my back. "Dumbass."

"That's offensive!" I exclaimed to no one in particular, my eyes focused on watching the ceiling fan revolve around and around, until it made me dizzy and I turned my head to look at Lucas.

He was sitting cross-legged, the paper book still in his hands, and his shoulders were shaking with suppressed laughter. "You're funny when you're fucked up," he said. "Also, there's lipstick on your neck. Don't get it on my bed."

"Blah, blah, blah," I mocked. "I bet you wish it was your lipstick."

"I don't wear lipstick," Lucas deadpanned.

"Let's talk," I suggested randomly. He stared down at me rather quizzically, but his eyes sparkled with amusement.

"About what?" He asked. I shrugged.

"Normal stuff. Politics, the weather, GTA."

"Don't you have a party to get to?"

I groaned. "And get more lipstick on my neck? Let's not."

"You could just tell whatever girl did that to stop, you know," he said as if it were obvious; I guess it sort of was.

"I've got a reputation to uphold," I reminded him. "Straight douchebag player who gets all da ladies."

Lucas rolled his eyes. "God forbid people find out that you're not a douchebag."

"Dude, that's probably the most accurate part of my description."

He laughed at that, which made my brain feel kinda fuzzy. Apparently, drunk Nate was extra sensitive to Lucas.

I pointed vaguely at the book in his hands. "Watcha readin'?" I sing-songed, like that one girl from Ferbeas and Phin. Phinerb and Feas? Phinerbas and Ferbean?

He lifted the book so I could see its cover. Through my slightly wonky vision, I managed to make out the words: Heathers: The Musical. "It's a script," Lucas explained.

I could've sworn I'd heard that name before. Had we already had this conversation? Or was this just deja vu? Was deja vu even real? We covered it in the memory unit two years ago . . .

"What are you thinking about?" Lucas asked with a chuckle.

"Sophomore year psychology," I said honestly. Lucas must have thought I was kidding, because he blinked several times before his mouth made an 'o' shape. "Anyways," I changed the subject, because poor Lucas looked lost, "So why are you being a nerd and reading scripts?"

"It's for the school musical," Lucas told me. "Gotta learn my lines."

"Ohhhhhhhhhhhh," I said, as if I'd just learned something life-changing. We'd definitely gone over this already. "Lines for what?"

Lucas sighed and pinched the bridge of his nose. "The school musical, Nate."

We'd had this conversation already, too. Like, two seconds ago.

I gave another prolonged 'Oh' and asked, "Who are you acting? I mean playing. Who are you placting? Playing! I'm drunk? Please tell me you're playing Heather, whoever Heather is."

Lucas chuckled and bit his lip, which was very unfair to me because my tummy did a thing and it was not nice. "I'm playing Jason Dean," he answered, "Though Heather Chandler was my second choice for sure."

"And when's the act? Play, when's the play?"

"God, you're such a mess," Lucas laughed. "And it's a musical, by the way. January twentieth; but rehearsals start next week."

I furrowed my eyebrows; Lucas was forgetting something very important, something that even I, in my screwed-up state, could remember. "What about soccer?"

Apparently, he'd been expecting the question. "Rehearsals don't start till 6:15," he explained. "So I'll just have to leave practice a couple minutes early to get ready and be there on time. And I guess I'll have to miss some rehearsals for games."

If Lucas was going straight from practice to rehearsals, that meant. . .

"No more rides home?" I gasped. "You're leaving me alone?" Okay, even drunk me had to admit that that sounded needy. The difference between drunk me and sober me: drunk me didn't care.

Lucas's lips quirked. "You can still take me home on Fridays, so it's not a total loss."

I rolled my eyes so over-dramatically hard, I was surprised they didn't get stuck in the back of my head. "That's ugly."

"You're ugly."

"I bet you don't think so."

Lucas shrugged. "Objectively speaking, you're right, I don't."

I blushed way more than I should have at the sort-of-compliment. Apparently drunk me was also bold me, because then I asked, "And what about subjectively speaking?"

Now we were both blushing, though Lucas significantly less than I, and he looked away. "I mean . . . Yeah."

"Yeah?"

Lucas hid his face in his hands. "Fucking hell, Nate," he chuckled awkwardly. I'd never seen him flustered before. Naturally, it was adorable. I took in the sight, hoping that I would still remember it in the morning. "You're backing me up into a corner, here. But no, you're definitely not ugly. Very not ugly. Gah, that makes no sense."

I gave Lucas a toothy grin, and made a silent vow to myself to remember this moment when I woke up. There was a certain warm validation in hearing it from him, a feeling different from any girl telling me I looked hot or sexy, or any parent gushing about how nicely I've grown. Somehow,

Lucas Morgan saying that I was "Very not ugly" had to be the best thing I'd heard in a while.

"Well, if it's any consolidati—" I hiccuped, "Consolidation, I think you're very not ugly, too." And then I giggled, because Lucas was even more red now.

"Thanks," he laughed, still staring at his lap. We were silent after that, and it was a comfortable silence. I would sneak a glance at Lucas every now and then. He'd gone back to looking over his script; his dark hair fell over his face as he read, and every few minutes I'd hear him mumbling lines under his breath. He was so pretty.

I was content to stay like that for a while, just relaxing in his company and looking at him whenever I could get away with it. The minutes helped me to sober down, if only a little. Eventually, though, I got bored. I pondered for longer than necessary over what I should say—something that would start a lasting conversation—and found myself asking a question that I would never ask sober.

"You know that time you told me how you cope with the gay thing?"

Lucas looked up at me, and the expression on his face told me that he remembered that day all too well. "You mean the time you shoved me against a locker and threatened me?"

He didn't look or sound angry, but that didn't stop me from feeling guilty. That certainly hadn't been my best moment. "Er, yeah," I said sheepishly. "Sorry about that."

Lucas shook his head. "No harm done. What about it?"

I was starting to think that I wasn't drunk enough for this. I was setting myself up for a conversation that would probably bring me a lot of restless nights in the future. Nevertheless, I continued.

"I wanna try it."

His eyebrows quirked up and his lips parted in surprise. "You . . . Really?"

I nodded, swallowing. Drunk or not, it was true. Part of me, a part that had been there for years but had grown exponentially since I started talking to Lucas, was sick of hating myself. That part of me wanted to just be happy with who I was. "It's just . . . It's so fucking dumb, you know?"

"What is?" Lucas asked; I knew that he knew the answer, but he wanted me to say it myself. He was staring at me intently now, giving me his full attention, and I felt like the only person in the world.

"I don't know . . ." I trailed. Except, I did know. I knew too well. "I look at you—once one of the golden boys—and the way this place tossed you aside like you were nothing and I just think: that could happen to me. And that scares me shitless, because I genuinely can't afford that. You've got your parents, who stuck by your side through all of it, but me . . . And the more I think about it, the more fucking idiotic I realize it is. You never hurt anybody, never said anything mean or hit anyone or stole anything, and that's more than can be said for half of the snobs downstairs, yet they're just fucking perfect, aren't they?

"It's so ridiculous and it makes me think—damn, were stupid. We're so stupid, to put so much hate into something so simple as love. And it makes me want to rebel; I wanna screw over what everyone believes—what I've always believed—and love who I wanna love and shit. But then I remember what could happen if anyone ever found out; I've got so much to lose. And I think about what this goddamn town has wired me to think about and I hate myself even more for even considering that what I am is even close to okay.

"But then I think about you, and I wonder if I could ever be there. If when I blow this town and find my way to The Big Apple, I could actually be happy. And then I get mad at myself again for ever thinking that. My brain is so back and forth man, I'm going fucking crazy. Actually fucking crazy."

I finished with a sigh. I hadn't expected to say so much, especially in my wonky state of mind, but once I started, each word escaped my mouth like water from a leaking dam. I couldn't stop, and I was glad I didn't.

Lucas regarded me for a long while, but I didn't feel uncomfortable under his inspecting eyes for once. Maybe I'd gotten used to him. Or maybe I was just finally opening myself up, letting him look into me freely.

When he finally spoke, he seemed to pick his words carefully. Like they actually meant something, like he genuinely wanted to help me. "It's called internalized homophobia, what you've got. It's been trained into you, and it's hard to shake. And it's not going to go away until you realize that what these people around you think means nothing. I know it's easier said than done, and I'm not telling you to go shouting from the rooftops that you're gay. You'd be an idiot if you did that. Wait it out until you're out of here—they don't need to know, it's none of their business. And in the meantime, work on your mentality.

"I'm not Catholic anymore, but I know you are, and I think that one of the things holding you back is this crazy idea so many have that you can't be gay and believe in God at the same time. Get this into your brain now—that is utter and absolute bullshit. Also get this into your brain—being gay isn't a flaw. It's not defining. It doesn't make you better, and it doesn't make you worse. It's just another part of what makes you, you, just like your eye color and your voice and your blood type. Things that are defining are the things you decide for yourself—whether you're going to be a good or bad person, whether or not you'll follow your dreams, whether you're dedicated or slacking. Those are things that define you.

"You think that being who you are is bad because it can't bring you any good in a place like this. Look to your community, Nate—they're everywhere, people like you and me, and they'll support you even if they don't know who you are. And you know I'll support you. Anytime you need a little pep talk, I'm here. This place is so isolated, so lacking when it comes to LGBTQ+ people and supporters—so I'll be your link, okay? I'll connect you to that great big world out there, because it's pretty damn awesome."

I merely nodded, because I was at a bit of a loss for words. My mind was working in overdrive to preserve what he'd told me, every last sentence. I never wanted to forget it. Lucas Morgan would be my link to the rest of the world. He'd keep me grounded, he'd help me learn. And god, I wanted to learn.

"Okay."

7: Nathaniel Jean's Struggle Within a Struggle

I was surprised by how excited I was when Friday came around, when Lucas didn't have rehearsal and I would get to drive him home.

When he saw me approach him in the locker room, he shouldered his duffel bag and grinned, flashing that goddamn dimple. "You miss me?"

"No," I lied.

He didn't say a word to me as we walked through the parking lot to the car—he never did. The moment we were sat down, though, he turned to me and asked, "How are you feeling? Not in general—I don't care about that. I just mean about the conversation we had Saturday night, if you even remember it."

I remembered it clearly. Parts of that night had fallen from my mind, lost and unimportant. Lucas' words, though, had stuck. I'd made sure of it.

"I'm . . . I'm trying," I said, and I really meant it. When I started feeling down, right as I climbed into bed, I would repeat his thoughts like they were my own. Sometimes it helped; sometimes I actually felt better. Some-

times I fell asleep with a smile on my face, and on those nights, I got a good r
est.

Other times, the second side of me won, and I felt shittier than ever. I didn't
sleep well, sometimes I cried, sometimes I punched pillows. Those nights
made me want to give up on ever finding what Lucas had.

"Good and bad, huh?" Lucas said, and I mentally cursed his uncanny
ability to look into my mind. "You'll have a lot of that. Just don't lose hope,
alright? Remember you've got a friend."

I nodded, and Lucas smiled. He changed the topic after that, to trivial
things like weather and picture-lighting and white shoes.

The big surprise came when I pulled into his driveway and he said, "Come
inside."

I hesitated. A part of me—a really big part of me—wanted to go in with
him. To spend time with my one real friend and talk about real-friend shit.
But if Shawn ever saw me voluntarily hanging out with his brother . . .

"Nobody's home," Lucas added. "Shawn started these overnight soccer
camp things right outside town, from Friday after school to Saturday
morning before your club games. And my parents both work really late on
Fridays. The house is ours for the taking."

He sounded kind of nervous, like he was afraid that I just didn't want to
go inside with him at all. His insecurities didn't show often, but when they
did, in moments like these, he seemed so much more human.

"I'm in," I told him.

We ate first, because soccer practice was a bitch. Lucas, thank god, found
leftover lasagna in the fridge—no more burnt bagels. We shared the meal
over more casual conversations. Small-talk usually bored me, when it was

Trevor or Damien or Cameron talking. With Lucas, though, everything was interesting

"Okay, first thing's first," he said when we made it to his bedroom. He kicked off his shoes and went straight for his laptop, tossing it gently onto his bed and climbing on behind it. He laid stomach-first, propping himself onto his elbows, and I stood awkwardly in the doorway for a moment before he patted the spot next to him and I realized with some embarrassment that he wanted me to join him. When I did, he turned to me, head in his hands, his eyes sparkling, and said, "It's time I introduce you to your fellows."

He opened his laptop, and the first place he went was a website called Tumblr. I knew what it was, sure, but I'd never used it. Tumblr was for a certain group of people, and I'd never thought that I was a part of that group.

Turns out, I was.

He went from blog to blog, and for the first time, I truly understood that I was a part of something big. Pride rallies and parades, speeches, essays, artwork, rants, people—all displayed on the screen before me, showing me what I never knew I needed to see. Gay men and women, holding hands, kissing, putting "boyfriend tags" and "girlfriend tags" on YouTube together. Proposing, getting married. Transgender teenagers and adults, talking about their struggles and triumphs to an audience that wholeheartedly supported them. And whenever there was even a glimmer of hate—a mean comment, a protest, the words and actions of this town and others—they were snuffed out. Attacked with a vengeance.

We didn't just stay on Tumblr. He took me through social media sites, across support pages, everywhere he thought I needed to go.

This group of people treated each other like family. When someone insulted a brother or sister—or someone who identified as neither—they defended them with all of their might. Complete strangers fought for each other because they—we—were all connected by this invisible cycle of love that tolerated no hate.

As in every family, there were fights. People discrediting others, deciding who is or isn't accepted into the group. Words I'd never even heard before—asexual, demisexual, non-binary—were suddenly written clear as day in front of me. And some people, hypocrites to their own cause, started civil wars that were fought just as fiercely.

We spent so long in front of that computer screen. I couldn't look away. I was captivated and mesmerized and maybe a bit horrified, but I'd get over than soon enough. When three, maybe four hours passed, and I realized that I needed to get home, I had to drag myself away.

Lucas walked me to my car. "So?" He prompted, leaning against the hood. "Did that change your perspective?"

"Like you wouldn't believe," I breathed; I couldn't wipe the smile off my face. Finally, I had something to look forward to. If that was what I would meet when I left Nowhere, Nebraska, then graduation couldn't come fast enough. "Thank you, Lucas. So much."

He smiled, a little bashfully. "Hey, I told you I'd be your link, didn't I?"

He opened his arms, and I was too giddy to be surprised when, for the first time since seventh grade, Lucas Morgan and I hugged.

He was warm, and he smelled nice—kind of fresh.

It became a routine of ours. On Fridays after school I would go to Lucas Morgan's house, eat his leftovers, and he'd show me things that made me smile. Things that made me feel a lot less worthless.

As with everything, there was a downside. It seemed like the more happy I became with myself and my identity, the more that dark, angry part of me tried to rip that away. I found my restless nights matching my peaceful ones in number and tripling them in intensity.

God, it was frustrating. I just wanted to be happy, and yet I couldn't seem to let myself have that. That second part of me screamed that I didn't deserve it, and sometimes, I screamed it too.

It was hard. A struggle within a struggle. But now, I didn't give up, didn't even think about it. I told myself every day that eventually, that other part of me would be dead, and I would have the sense of pride that was so often written and sung about. I just had to be patient, and remember that it wouldn't be an overnight process.

I didn't tell Lucas about all of this, but I had a feeling he knew. He always knew.

The third time I went with him to his house, that thirteenth week of senior year, he shut his computer one hour in. I stared for a moment at the blank wall where the screen had just been, then I turned to Lucas, confused.

"Is it time to go already?" I asked, not even trying to conceal my disappointment. The time couldn't have gone by that fast. I checked my phone; it was only 7:48.

Lucas shook his head. "I just thought maybe a change in scenery would be suiting. You down to watch a movie?"

I could tell by the mischievous glint in his eyes that we wouldn't be watching an ordinary rom-com. I said yes, though, because he was Lucas Morgan, and he could ask me to wash my hair in barbecue sauce if he wanted; I would probably do it. Thank God he didn't know that.

The movie he chose was called Brokeback Mountain. I'd never heard of it, but I understood pretty quickly why he'd looked so cheeky as he took it out.

"You little shit," I muttered. Lucas laughed.

I didn't mind too much until the tent scene came. As soon as I realized where it was going, my face lit up red and I looked away, mortified. Lucas found my embarrassment hilarious, and he got a kick out of my refusal to look at the screen. He even played into it, using one hand to cover my eyes and telling me that I was "too young".

When the scene was over and I still refused to look, Lucas's task switched from shielding my eyes to trying to convince me to open them.

"You're such a baby, Jean," he laughed, giving up in his attempts to pull my hands away from my eyes.

"Sticks and stones," I chanted.

The sound of the movie stopped. "Did you pause it?"

"Yup."

"Why?"

"Open your eyes."

"No."

"Yes."

"No."

"Yes."

"Please?"

"No."

I felt Lucas' fingers wrap around my wrists again, and we were back to pulling. It was a battle of brawn, and though Lucas was strong, I was stronger. I could see him through a tiny crack in my fingers, his lips pressed together with effort, and it was that sight that made me lose. I cracked up, and Lucas easily won the upper hand, pulling my wrists away from my face with a triumphant cheer.

I didn't care that he'd won, though, because pretty soon we were both laughing. The situation wasn't even that funny, but we were laughing at nothing and everything. We were laughing at the movie and my embarrassment and his futile attempts to out-strengthen me and each other's laughs and that one vase over there.

Then, out of nowhere, I sneezed, and Lucas stopped laughing entirely. I looked warily at him as he stared at me with doe eyes and a weird, sort of adoring smile. "Uh, Lucas?"

"You have such a cute sneeze," he said. "Oh my god, you have such a cute sneeze. Sorry if the word cute makes you lose macho-dude-bro points, but oh my god. Like a kitten!"

I scowled; I hated when people said that. It was, as much as Lucas would roll his eyes at me for thinking this, super emasculating. Lucas cooed at my pink cheeks and sour expression. "Nathaniel Jean, you're fucking adorable."

I wasn't sure if he was being serious or making fun of me, but either way, my cheeks only got pinker.

"Shut up and play that damn movie," I grumbled, and he did.

By the time the movie was over, it was around the time I would usually go home. Lucas walked me to the door, but no further, because "It's kinda cold and my coat is up in my room and I don't like you enough to go out there and freeze."

"How'd you like the movie?" He asked as I took down my own coat, which I'd wisely left hanging on the coat rack that was on the Morgans' front door.

"It was good," I said vaguely, because I felt sort of awkward going into great detail. Then I made the mistake of turning around; Lucas had been right behind me, and I'd just managed to deplete any space between us. "Super gay," I added, though the words came out tense and nervous. Lucas looked just as uncomfortable as I felt, but he didn't step back.

"Yeah," he laughed awkwardly. I could feel his cool breath on my face. Absolutely clueless as to how to get out of this awkward situation—and not totally wanting to—I occupied myself with counting his freckles. "Super gay. Like us."

"Like us," I shakily agreed. He still hadn't moved back. His proximity was definitely clogging my mind, and I was reminded once again that Lucas Morgan had a crazy effect on me. Now I really, really didn't want him to move back. And I was pretty sure he didn't want to, either.

I inhaled sharply when I realized that he was doing the opposite. He was closer now than he was seconds before, I was positive. I could feel the tips of his feet against my shoes, and a few stray hairs against my forehead. Then his nose against mind. His chest. His thighs. Everything except his lips.

Then his eyes fluttered shut. I forgot how to breathe as mine did, too.

And then the contact was gone, and they flew back open. The change was so quick, my lips parted in a silent gasp at the loss. Lucas was a foot away from me now; still so close, but the moment was over. He wouldn't meet my eyes.

"Sorry," he muttered. "That's was dumb."

I swallowed the disappointed lump in my throat. "Not that dumb . . ."

Lucas finally looked at me, and I could tell he was disappointed, too. Guilty, even. "I know, I just . . . We should wait."

"Waiting sucks," I said, because I really really wanted him to kiss me. There was no point in being subtle and hiding how I felt now—clearly he felt the same way, at least a little. There was something between us, something more than friendship, and now that it was so close, I wanted it more than ever.

Lucas chuckled humorlessly. "Yeah, it does; but you're not there yet."

I opened my mouth to protest, to ask him how he would know whether or not I was ready, but he held up a hand and continued. "You've still got shit to deal with. You don't have to admit it, because I see it. I don't want to enter the equation before you've even figured yourself out. I want to help you, and I think that would do more harm than good."

I absolutely hated that he was so smart. "And how will you know when I'm ready?"

Lucas' lips quirked up the slightest bit, the left side just a little higher than the right. Then he said, "Because you'll kiss me."

The idea alone made my stomach erupt into angry, excited butterflies. I knew what Lucas was getting at, though he didn't say it out loud—he didn't want anything to happen between us if I wasn't sure I could handle it. He was afraid, though he wouldn't admit it, that he would kiss me and I would regret it the next morning, after I'd had time to think. I had to make the move. Then he'd know I was sure.

"And what if I'm ready now?"

Lucas looked unwaveringly into my eyes, green meeting blue. "Then kiss me."

I wanted to. I really, really wanted to. I'd been wanting to for what felt like so long now, and I never thought a moment like this would present itself. Lucas Morgan was standing before me, proposing that I kiss him. He liked me—he had to. These crazy, horrible, wonderful feelings I'd been harboring weren't unrequited.

I'd dreamed about this, more than once. All I had to do was lean forward, maybe take an extra step, and . . .

And I couldn't. I wasn't ready.

"Goodnight, Lucas."

His expression didn't falter. If anything, his smile got bigger. "Goodnight, Nate."

As I stepped into the frosty November air, regret and dread settled over me like a cloud. Had I just made the wrong choice? What if Lucas moved on, found someone else or simply lost interest before I was ready? What if I never was ready?

But what if, some day, hopefully soon, I was ready? And I would kiss him, and it would be perfect—not rushed or anxious or regretful?

I didn't sleep much that night. Not because I was upset or angry or stressed, but because I was too pumped and anxious and giddy to close my eyes. I had a new goal now, something to strive for, and I couldn't wait to achieve it. The thought filled me with a newfound excitement that I didn't want to let go of.

The Monday that followed brought the first snow of the season. It was light and pretty—the type of snow that made you want to go outside. Perfect to start off Thanksgiving break.

Despite there being no school, soccer practice would still be held every day except Thursday and Friday, so my schedule wasn't entirely free.

The locker room was booming with cheers when I entered, and, curious, I walked over to the center of the room to see what the action was about.

As it turned out, there was no action at all. Most of the team was gathered there, either sitting on the long wooden benches that lined the lockers or stood in a wonky circle. They were chatting like the fratboys they were destined to be, punching each other in the shoulder, overusing the word bro, and talking about their "conquests".

"Lauren was so fucking easy, dude," Damien Diggory was saying. "I barely had to do any work."

"But bro!" Duke Lawson, one of our back-up midfielders, laughed. "She's a freshman!"

Damien raised his eyebrows and shrugged suggestively. "You'd never know by looking at her, if you know what I mean."

Shawn Morgan smacked him on the shoulder. "You should see her sister, man. Now that's a chick you wanna get with."

"Oh, she was there, too!"

Boys erupted into howls and wolf-whistles, some slapping Damien on the back as if he'd won the lottery. I guess in their eyes, he had.

"Yo, but have you guys seen that new chick?" Tyler Fiero piped up. "The one from Switzerland or Sweeden or one of them?" Several boys hooted in agreement. "Have you seen the ass on that one? Damn!"

"She was totally eyeing me at the party," Cameron Schetwaldski said smugly. "And what can I say? I don't blame her!"

"Aw hell yeah!" Shawn cheered. "Dude, I fucked with her a couple nights ago—she's freaky as fuck! It was so epic."

"Maybe it's a Swedish thing," Trevor Cazamn laughed.

There was only one other boy in the room who was anything but engrossed in the conversation. Lucas Morgan was leaning against the end of a locker row, looking uninterested and moderately disgusted.

Trevor looked at me, and I silently begged him not to drag me into the conversation. "Yo Nate," he called, and I sighed. "Have you seen Lucy Conwick lately? Talk about a glow up! Her body got so fuckin'—"

"They're women, not pieces of meat," Lucas spoke up suddenly. I admired his bluntness—it was a trait I wish we shared—and mentally thanked him for saving me.

In an instant, conversation died. All eyes turned to him. I could already sense an argument coming, could already see the boys ready to throw their sticks and stones.

"I swear to fucking god," Shawn cursed. "Do you have to be such a cunt all the time?"

"Chill, Shawn," I said with a roll of my eyes. I agreed with Lucas, though I'd never say it out loud. Besides, I didn't want to deal with another gang-up-on-the-gay-kid party, not when that gay kid was my friend and entirely right. "You're whinier than my sister."

I could tell the guys were pissed at me for opening my mouth. I tried not to care too much, even as they continued to be angry and petty throughout practice. None of them wanted to talk to me, but then again, talking to them usually cost me brain cells, so maybe the change was good.

"Stood up for me, huh?"

I jumped a foot into the air and nearly fell on my ass when Lucas' voice startled me as I walked out of the showers. I'd thought I was the only one left.

"Fucking hell, Lucas," I groaned. "Don't do that."

He laughed as I began to dress, and I tried not to blush when felt his eyes on my back as I pulled a hoodie over my head. "Sorry."

"Shouldn't you be at rehearsals?"

"We don't have 'em over break," Lucas said. I tried to hide how happy that made me—the daily car rides would resume, at least for the week. "But don't change the subject. You totally shut them up for me back there."

I couldn't help but grin. "Yeah, well, it felt pretty good."

Lucas chuckled, shaking his head disbelieving. "Do you like any of your friends?"

"Including you?" I said. "Yes"

"And not including me?" He prompted. I scoffed and made a face, and he laughed. "Aww, I feel special."

I made another, somewhat less sour, face. "You're gross."

"I'm awesome."

"Wanna come over?"

I hadn't meant to ask so suddenly, but now seemed as good a time as ever. Lucas, however, hesitated, and I could read in his expression why. "I want to hang out with my friend," I added, and he grinned.

Things were kind of awkward at first. After last Friday, Lucas and I didn't quite know how to act around each other. There was a lot of awkward stuttering, and even more awkward flirting, and even more awkward blushing. Still, it was fun, because it was Lucas, and things were never not fun with him.

"I didn't mean it like that!" I exclaimed, burying my red face in my hands. Lucas laughed, leaning his head back against my pillows, but his cheeks were just as bright.

"You are really killing it with the innuendos today," he said, and I just blushed more, because he was right; this was the fourth time in the last hour that I'd embarrassed both of us by saying something very—unintentionally—sexual. "You know, you used to say shit like that all the time in seventh grade. I think you genuinely had no idea, though."

I paled. "Did I really?"

Lucas laughed. "Oh, it was so bad."

I slid my hands down my face and groaned exaggeratedly. "That was not my best year."

Lucas pursed his lips playfully. "Aw, c'mon, it couldn't have been that bad. We were friends back then, after all."

I scoffed. "Yeah, that was the problem. You fucked me up big time, Morgan."

He raised an eyebrow, obviously curious. "Oh yeah? How so?"

I wasn't even embarrassed to tell him. At this point, I'd told him more about myself than anybody else. This seemed like such a small, insignificant secret compared to the things we'd talked about before. If anything, it was something to laugh about.

"You were my first crush."

Lucas' jaw dropped. He was silent for several seconds, before he half-whispered, "Seventh grade Lucas is shaking right now. I was obsessed with you."

I half-laughed, half-choked. "No."

"Yes."

"You're serious?"

Lucas nodded fervently. "I'd been crushing on you from a distance like a creepy school girl since like fifth grade. When we started talking I thought I was gonna explode."

I couldn't believe what I was hearing. Lucas Morgan had liked me back then, too, just as much as I'd liked him—maybe even more. At the time, I'd thought there was no way—I'd had no idea that he was even gay, let alone interested. And now, six years later, we were back to the same exact feelings.

"Holy shit," I breathed.

Lucas grinned. "It's crazy how things go full-circle, huh?"

8: Nathaniel Jean's Project

"**A** diós Hermano!"

Jenna was out of sight before I'd even found a parking spot. You'd think she'd at least walk into the mall with me after I'd driven her all the way here, but nope. Gone like the wind to meet her friends, leaving me to fight through the Black Friday crowd and hope a spot would open up.

Then again, driving alone was better than listening to my little sister rant about celebrity couples and millennial pink.

It took thirty minutes. Thirty minutes, in which I followed a bunch of people to their cars like a stalker, almost got into a fight with a middle-aged mom, and probably wasted all of my gas.

The mall was one of the few places I went regularly where I didn't recognize almost everybody present. There were no big shopping centers in my little town, so I had to drive a few extra miles to get here, and once I left Nowhere, Nebraska, I felt as if I were in a new world. The Midview Square Mall was always full of unfamiliar faces, which was more than a little refreshing compared to my day-to-day.

After I parked, it didn't take long to find the boys. Trevor texted me a few minutes ago that they were in Adidas—surprise, surprise—so I just needed to navigate the mall to find it.

I would much rather be hanging out with Lucas right now, as he'd proposed, but raiding sports stores on Black Friday was a tradition among my friend group. I would have to be puking blood to get out of going—to not show up was, in their eyes, nothing short of blasphemous.

I heard a voice hollering my name and turned around to see Cameron Schetwaldski beckoning me over. In his hands was a pair of neat looking cleats. "Watcha think of these, Jean?"

I joined him, nodding approvingly. "Sick, man. How much are they?"

Cameron scoffed. "Who the fuck cares?"

"Where is everyone?" I asked, raising my voice over the noise of the crowd. Cameron waved his hand dismissively.

"Around. Tyler's right there."

He pointed behind me, and I glanced over my shoulder to see Tyler Fiero approaching, joggers slung over his shoulder. "Don't you already have those?" I asked, because I was pretty sure that just about every member of the boys soccer team had the basic adidas joggers. Lucas looked really good in them, by the way. Just saying.

Tyler, however, shrugged. "Yeah, but those are a few months old now. Time for a change, dontcha think?"

And this, everyone, is why people hate rich white boys like us. Nevertheless, I nodded and said, "Yeah, 'course."

Tyler looked around for something, then turned back to me with a disappointed pout. "Yo, where's the better of the Jeans? I thought you said you were bringing Jenna, too?"

"I did, but she's off with her friends," I explained. Tyler's frown deepened.

"What a shame . . ." He said. "I was looking forward to seeing her. She's grown up so . . . nicely."

My eyes widened at the suggestive glance he exchanged with Cameron. "What the fuck, man?" I exclaimed. "She's my sister! Better yet, she's fourteen."

Cameron hummed. "She sure doesn't look it."

He and Tyler high-fived, and I had to refrain from punching them both.

We were at the mall until it closed, and we went to every athletic store and section it had to offer. I spent way too much money, but it wasn't as if I couldn't afford to. And I wasn't as bad as Shawn. I'm pretty sure he dropped quadruple digits.

Everything seemed pretty much normal all day, until we were walking through the parking lot to find our cars. We'd spotted mine, and I'd just dropped my load of bags into the backseat when Shawn turned on me. Before I could say my farewells, he leaned against the driver's side door with his arms crossed and said, "Care to explain?"

I blinked, partially because I had no idea what he was talking about, and partially because I was really tired and only half-processing what he was saying. Listening to these guys talk for hours was mentally draining, and shoving past crazy soccer moms trying to buy cleats for lil' Timmy's first game was physically exhausting.

"Uh . . . Huh?"

Shawn narrowed his eyes into a glare. "You think I never noticed your car dropping Lucas home every day?"

Well, shit.

"It's actually only every Friday now," I said, which probably wasn't my smartest move. Shawn only looked more aggravated.

"Who the fuck cares?" He snapped. "I wanna know why you're doing it."

The other boys nodded in agreement, and I realized they'd planned this conversation. At some point when I wasn't around, Shawn had shared this information with them and told them he'd confront me about it. They were his back up. Bunch of snakes.

I shrugged. "Because it's the nice thing to do."

Tyler Fiero scoffed and got in my face—at least, as well as he could without getting on his tip-toes. Then he, as usual, said something stupid. "So you stand up for him because it's the nice thing to do too, then?"

I blinked at him, waiting for him to realize that what he'd said had a pretty obvious answer and didn't make him sound any tougher. He just kept staring at me, though, his chest puffed out like one of those frigate birds. "Uh, yeah," I said, maybe a bit condescendingly. "It is."

Shawn rolled his eyes and nudged Tyler out of the way. "You know I'm startin' to think you're a fairy too, Jean. Always taking his side. You his friend or ours?"

His. I huffed impatiently, wishing I'd just faked sick and ditched them for Lucas instead of coming here. "Being a decent human being and being gay aren't the same thing, Morgan. Not that you would know."

I tried to push him away from my car door, but he just took this as an invitation to shove me back, way harder. I stumbled at the force, my back hitting Damien's hard chest. "Dude, what the hell?" I snapped. "Get over yourself and move!"

Shawn stepped away from my car, only slightly. "I'm watching you, Jean. All the time. I don't want two fags on my team."

I rolled my eyes and scoffed. "Watching me all the time, are you? All the time? You sure Lucas is the only queer in the family?"

Maybe I was spending too much time with Lucas. That was definitely more something he'd say than I, with that smart mouth of his.

Shawn snarled at the implication and surged forward. In all of his petty glory, he probably would've punched me had Trevor Cazamn not put a hand on his chest to stop him. Still, his shoulder nudged mine roughly as I stepped past him, and I felt his glare even as I pulled out of the spot.

I was the last person to get back to the locker room after practice the following Monday, because I'd stayed a few extra minutes to discuss strategy with coach. I only heard two voices when I finally entered, which was never a good sign. Even worse, I recognized the voices as those of the Morgan brothers, and there was yelling.

"You shouldn't even fucking be here!"

Lucas and Shawn were in the center of the locker room, where commotion seemed to always take place. Shawn was red in the face and Lucas was, as usual, acting aloof.

"Yeah well if you hadn't opened your mouth, I probably wouldn't be," he said with a shrug. Teammates were gathered around them, watching silently and not even pretending to be subtle about it.

"Do you have to take everything so fucking seriously?" Shawn yelled. "It's hard enough having to call you my brother, let alone my fucking teammate!"

Lucas' jaw dropped, and I saw a sudden shift in his demeanor. His eyes flashed angrily and for a moment, he lost his cool. "It's hard for you? You? You think I wanna be known as the fucking gay kid? You think I came out willingly? Newsflash, brother: I was outed. If it wasn't for whatever son of a bitch started spreading shit, you wouldn't think twice about having me here! You would never fucking know!"

It was strange to think, but it was true. Nobody would ever assume that Lucas was gay if it wasn't a known fact. He didn't fit the stereotype in physique or personality or even the clothing he wore. Everything about him, from the messy style of his hair to the deep tone of his voice to the Nikes on his feet, fit the straight boy prototype pretty well.

Someone in one corner of the room snickered obnoxiously loudly, and Lucas snapped his head toward the sound. His eyes landed on Damien. "Something funny, Diggory?"

Damien sniggered again. "It's just, I thought you knew."

Lucas was regaining his composure now. His shoulders had relaxed and he put on his signature I don't care about anything you all have to say face. "You thought I knew what?"

"Who told everyone you're a fag."

Lucas raised an unimpressed eyebrow. "Do you know?"

Damien smirked. "'Course I do, he said with a snort. "I'd have to, since I did it."

Lucas didn't seem to process this for a long moment. He just kept staring at Damien, shaking his head slightly and looking as confused as I'd ever seen him. Finally, he blinked, looked our goalie in the eyes, and said, "You?"

Damien crossed his arms over his chest and leaned against the wall, his eyes twinkling maliciously. "Yeah, me. That a problem?"

Lucas still seemed to have trouble accepting the fact, though I couldn't understand why. Damien was the tool of all tools, it made sense that he'd do something like that.

Lucas approached him, stopping a few feet away. He looked up at Damien, studying his face, maybe trying to gauge if he was telling the truth or not. "Why?"

"You remember Katrina Jarrows?" Damien asked. A few boys whistled appreciatively. "Yeah, she was one hell of a girl. I really liked her. And she really liked you. So I told her you were a fag."

Lucas' eyes widened. "How did you—"

"I didn't," Damien admitted. "It was just a rumor. Never thought she'd spread it so much, definitely never thought it would be true. It's your fault for admitting it, dude."

Lucas' fists clenched at his sides, and I unconsciously scooted closer, afraid that he would do something stupid. He didn't strike me as the violent type, but Damien was at least half a foot taller than him—he was at least half a foot taller than everyone—and picking a fight with him would be suicide. Then again, with the shit coming out of Damien's mouth, I wouldn't blame Lucas for trying.

"Let me get this straight," Lucas said; the low tone of his voice wasn't one I recognized, and it was alarmingly furious. The air seemed to crackle with tension around him, but Damien refused to be affected. "You told people

I was gay in a place where being gay is beyond intolerable because you were jealous of me?"

Damien shrugged. "Guess so."

I watched Lucas carefully. He was seething, and Damien's nonchalant tone clearly wasn't helping.

"Are you fucking kidding me?!" He shouted, surprising everybody in the room. An uneasy murmur went up among the boys—Lucas Morgan never raised his voice.

His eyes glimmered with a rage I'd never seen on him before. He looked like an entirely different person like this, stiff and stressed and angry.

"Do you have any fucking idea what you did to me, out of jealousy? This whole fucking town treats me like a goddamn criminal! I get so much shit every day, and not just from you assholes! My own brother—the one person I used to count on for everything—doesn't even want to be seen with me!"

I saw Shawn flinch then, and for the first time ever, something like guilt clouded his expression.

There was something threatening about Lucas' gaze, and for a moment he seemed to bite his tongue—also rare for Lucas. Damien stared back at him challengingly, as if daring him to say whatever it was he was thinking.

"All because one fucking girl—" Lucas growled instead, "who doesn't even live here anymore—liked me?!"

Damien shrugged again, and it was clear that he didn't think much of his actions. "Pretty much," he said, still smirking. There was a cruel satisfaction in his eyes that made me want to punch him.

Turns out, I didn't have to, because Lucas did.

The locker room erupted with excited chatter and shouts of surprise as Damien cried out in pain and gripped his nose. Blood dripped between his fingers.

He recovered quickly, though. He threw his weight at Lucas, sending them both crashing to the ground, and punched him square in the jaw, the impact making a horrible thud. I thought Lucas was done for, but before Damien could get another blow in, Lucas kicked at his chest so hard, the other boy went tumbling off of him.

I rushed in before matters could get worse, dragging Lucas to his feet and away from Damien, who was already standing again. He lunged forward, but came to a choking stop when Shawn Morgan grabbed his collar from behind and pulled him back.

"Pull yourself together!" Shawn yelled at Damien, which was in its own way more surprising than anything else that'd happened in the last ten minutes.

"Let me go!" Damien demanded, accompanied by some interesting curses. He tried again to run at Lucas, and I feared that Shawn would let him, but instead he grabbed Damien's arms and held him in place. "Who's fucking side are you on?!"

"I said pull yourself together!" Shawn repeated firmly. He whipped his head towards Lucas and I, his glare intensifying. "Get him out of here."

Lucas was leaning against the lockers, holding his jaw. I listened to Shawn—as tough as Lucas was, this was a fight he wouldn't win—and took his brother by the arm. I hadn't showered yet, and my car seats would not be happy about it, but I figured that was the least of my problems.

Lucas didn't protest as I pulled him through the crowd of sneering boys and out of the locker room. He was silent the entire car ride, despite my attempts to talk to him. He kept his head pressed against the window, his eyes glaring heatedly outside. His fists kept clenching and unclenching in his lap, as if he needed something else to punch. I was still reeling from surprise—never in a million years would I expect Lucas to lash out and hit somebody. And all of those things he said . . . they just proved that the way he was treated hurt him more than he let others see.

I took him to my house instead of his, because I was pretty sure neither of us wanted to deal with Shawn when he got home.

Lucas sat wordlessly on the couch and I went to the kitchen, coming back with a bag of frozen cauliflower—we didn't have peas, okay? I sat next to him and pressed the bag to his jaw, which had turned an unpleasant shade of purple.

"So . . ." I said awkwardly. "What's going on up there right now?"

Lucas didn't say anything. He took the bag from my hand and held it to his face himself. His gaze was still burning, and I could feel the heat of his anger and grief just by sitting next to him.

"Lucas," I tried again. "Talk to me."

Once again, his lips stayed shut. He turned away from me, but I still caught his fingers brushing just beneath his eyes. He was crying. "Lucas."

This time, he shook his head, and I couldn't help but feel frustrated. It was so rare for him to be closed of like this, and I was so used to him being open and honest. I knew he wasn't mad at me, but with his tense posture, his uncharacteristic lack of words, and his angry glare, I couldn't help but feel like I was the one who'd upset him.

It was like this for a while. Me, sitting awkwardly, unsure of how to handle the situation and Lucas, glaring at nothing and everything, trying to pretend he wasn't crying.

Then, something snapped. I saw it in the twitch of his lips right before he shot to his feet, the frozen cauliflower falling, forgotten, and yelled out, "I can't fucking believe him!"

Lucas' hands ran frustratedly through his hair, then dropped to his sides in angry fists. I had a feeling that if this was his house, not mine, he would have kicked the coffee table by now.

I reached up and took his wrist in my hand, gently pulling him back to the couch. He didn't protest.

"It's fucking rich, coming from him!" he snarled to no one in particular. "Fucking rich!"

"Why is it rich?" I asked tentatively.

He looked at me for the first time since the incident in the locker room. His eyes were still angry, but they were sad, too, and regretful. Mostly angry, though. More angry than I knew he could be.

"There's only one guy in this town I've ever hooked up with. Can you guess who it was?"

My jaw might have hit the floor. Now, I knew that Lucas hadn't merely been living without any sort of intimate contact his whole life—he'd told me once that sometimes he had quick flings on vacation with boys in other places, some just outside of Nowhere, Nebraska. But the fact that he'd hooked up with someone inside the town—Damien Diggory, no less—was enough to make me question life as a whole.

"Damien's gay?" I exclaimed incredulously. Lucas shrugged.

"Maybe bi, maybe pan, maybe curious. Who the fuck cares? That son of a bitch ruined my life!"

"Why didn't you say anything?" I asked. "You could've gotten him back! Picture the look on his face if you'd—"

"I told you," Lucas cut me off. "I don't out people. I don't care what he did, I'm not gonna . . ."

Lucas stood up then, his face in his hands. I wanted to understand how he felt so I could help him, but for all of the times Lucas had wanted me to open up about my feelings, this was one conversation for which he refused to do just that.

I stood up, too; if I couldn't talk to him, I could comfort him in other ways. But when I tried to hug him, he pushed me away.

"I don't want your pity," he spat, and just as quickly as he'd stood, he sat down again. I followed his lead, sitting close enough for our shoulders to touch. He looked away stubbornly, reminding me of . . . Of me.

"It's not pity, it's support," I said. "It's something you've given to me too many times to count, so let me repay the favor."

Lucas sighed. He rubbed his eyes, suddenly looking exhausted, and said, "Sorry."

He leaned his head against my shoulder and I put my arm around him, pulling him into my side. We were both still in our practice uniforms for soccer—socks and cleats and all—and we probably smelled like sweat, grass, and snow. Lucas picked up the frozen cauliflower and pressed it against the bruised side of his face. Every few seconds I'd see him blink, or wipe at his cheeks.

Lucas was so much more complex than I'd realized. He wasn't all that he made himself out to be. Suddenly, I felt like I was working on a semi-impossible decoding project; I wanted to understand him, every single great and horrible aspect. I wondered if he saw me that way, too. If maybe that was why he ever took an interest in me in the first place.

I decided to distract him with a very un-subtle subject change. "How's Heather's going?"

He smiled slightly. "It's gonna be so great," he said. "Lilliana Rogue is playing Veronica, and she's so talented it physically hurts."

I smiled; Lucas' eyes always lit up in the most infectious way when he talked about theater. Even now, when he was so distressed. "And what about that theater school place? How's that?"

Every Saturday and Sunday, Lucas spent most of his day at a huge, expensive, exclusive theater academy about an hour out of town. He'd told me about it during the week when he wouldn't shut up in the car rides home. It was a place he'd been going to since he was in elementary school, and if it weren't for soccer and rehearsals, he'd be going at least four times a week.

It was one of the few times I'd actually listened to what he said during those car rides. I actually really liked listening to him talk about theater, because he was just so damn incredible and he didn't seem to realize it. He'd been training in the massive school's junior high classes in fourth grade, its high school classes in eighth grade, and its adult classes since sophomore year. Lucas could get his college degree there if he wanted, and they'd be more than happy to have him. I was in love with his talent, and even more so with his passion.

Lucas glanced up at me, looking surprised that I'd even brought it up. "So you were listening when I told you all that stuff after all, huh?"

I blushed a little, but nodded nonetheless. "You were pretty damn hard to ignore."

Lucas chuckled, albeit a bit half-heartedly. "We actually have a major musical theater competition coming up in December. So yeah, that's exciting."

He was playing it off as a casual occasion, but I could tell from little details—the shift in his posture, the determination in his eyes—that it really was exciting for him. I wasn't sure how important this competition was, but it didn't matter; Lucas was a performer in body and at heart. This was the stuff he lived for.

"Is it something critical?" I asked. Lucas huffed and nodded.

"Oh, you have no idea. Especially this year, for me at least. Scouts love to show up at things like these."

"Oh shit," I breathed. "Scouts from Juilliard?"

"If I'm lucky," he said. "Maybe, maybe not. Either way, I can't fuck up."

He was getting into the conversation now, forgetting Damien Diggory as I'd hoped. "What are you performing?"

Lucas pursed his lips. "I found out yesterday that I've got a solo, a duet, and a group number. For the solo, I'm singing a song called Michael in the Bathroom, from Be More Chill." Naturally, I had no idea what that was. "I'm doing the duet with one of my friends in the class, Mark. We're going a gender-bend performance of Take Me or Leave Me from Rent." Never heard of it. And what the fuck is a gender-bend? "And for the group number, we're doing Seize the Day from Newsies."

Now that, I'd heard of. Jenna was in the middle of a major Broadway phase, and she'd convinced me to watch the live Newsies performance on Netflix with her a while back. I was half asleep while it was playing, but if I remembered anything, it was the dancing. That wouldn't be easy to pull off.

"You're gonna do that?" I said disbelievingly. "With all the jumps and spins and flips and shit? Can you even do that?"

Lucas laughed. "Yes, we are—with a lot of training—and yes, I can."

I didn't doubt it. After all, he was Lucas Morgan. He was talented way beyond his years.

And the school was made for people like him; people who were too good for their high school drama classes. The performance was bound to be impressive. And I wanted to see it.

"Where's this competition gonna be held, exactly?" I asked. "Just, you know, out of curiosity."

Lucas stared at me, eyes wide. "You would come watch?"

I couldn't help but grin at his puppy-like excitement. "Hell yeah! I wanna know what all the hype is about."

Lucas was beaming. "Well you're in luck, Jean. The competition's held at the academy this year."

"So I don't even have to go far?"

"Nope!" He popped the 'p'.

"Dude," my grin widened. "That's sick!"

Lucas groaned and rolled his eyes. "Don't you dare talk fratty to me, Nathaniel Jean."

I laughed and pulled him closer into me, until he was practically on my lap. He cuddled into my chest, chuckling with me and seeming like an entirely different person from the angry, brooding boy he'd been just minutes before. I knew then that I would have been more than willing to travel far to see his competition, just because it made him so damn happy.

9: Nathaniel Jean's Exciter/Inhibitor

Another update so soon? Am I feeling inspired or am I procrastinating on hw?

I'm procrastinating.

***

"Who the fuck invented December," Lucas grumbled as he climbed out of the warmth of my car into the frosty winter air. I suppressed a chuckle at the way he shoved his hands into his coat pockets and all-but ran to the front door of his house.

I followed leisurely behind him, watching as snowflakes floated down from the sky without a rush in the world and joined their companions on the ground. The scene would have been peaceful, had it not been for Lucas fumbling with his keys and cursing like a sailor.

The moment the door was open a crack, his body disappeared inside. Lucas Morgan liked a lot of things, but the cold wasn't one of them.

I walked in slowly after him, shutting the door behind me, while he occupied himself with furiously rubbing his hands together in a futile attempt to warm them.

"Here," I said. I took his hands between my own and held them together; his fingers were freezing. Lucas let me, and I wasn't sure if the pink color of his cheeks was due to the cold, or if I'd made him blush. "Better?"

Lucas shook his head. "My hands, yeah. The rest of me could use the same treatment, though."

He didn't wait for my response. He rested his body against mine and I complied to his unspoken wish, wrapping my arms around his shoulders. His own arms circled my torso, and his head leaned against my shoulder. I could feel the poor boy shivering, and it only compelled me to hug him tighter.

"This is so gay," he muttered, and I chuckled.

"No homo."

It was moments like these when being friends with Lucas Morgan was really great. Really, really great. And really, really, really confusing. Because we didn't act like friends.

Lucas was a naturally cuddly person, I'd learned. He liked physical affection; holding others and being held by others. And I sure as hell loved to hold him and he held by him. Why watch a movie sitting on opposite ends of a couch when you can be snuggling in the middle?

I liked the way we were. I liked the fact that I could rest my head on Lucas' shoulder and not feel weird about it. I'd never had that kind of relationship before. Where touch sometimes held more value than words. Not with my parents, or my sister—definitely not with my friends.

The only problem?

It was excruciatingly frustrating. To sit so close that our shoulders bumped, or to feel his hair brush my cheek. So many times, I could've kissed him. I wanted to. He wanted me to. Perfect moment after perfect moment seemed to be thrown at my face in big, bold, highlighted font to ensure that I wouldn't miss them. The opportunities were strangely infinite, and I knew Lucas saw them as clearly as I did. He held back, though, and I hesitated. Every damn time, I hesitated, and then the moment would be gone.

The fact was, I still had no idea if I was ready to offer Lucas a legitimate relationship. He'd helped me so much over the past several weeks, and my mental state now was drastically different than it had been at the beginning of the school year, or even the beginning of last month. I was finally learning to be almost satisfied with myself. The good nights were starting to outnumber the bad.

I still had all of my insecurities and fears, though. And they still drove practically everything I did. I still wished I could be someone other than the person I was. I would change to make things easier without much thought. As long as I carried that mentality, how could I be enough for Lucas?

But at the same time, I really wanted to just fuck it and date him.

"I saw Beth Crampton reject Damien in the halls today," Lucas said out of the blue, his voice a muffled murmur against my shoulder. "It was really satisfying."

"You fucking sadist," I laughed. "Details?"

Beth Crampton was one of those girls that just about every guy at school had wet dreams about. She lived in what was probably the biggest home in Nowhere, Nebraska; she was crazy smart; she was super athletic; and she was ridiculously sexy—at least from a different viewpoint. I'd hooked up with her once last year—ugh—and she and Shawn Morgan had a sort of on-again-off-again thing going on. I knew that she'd at some point gotten with Trevor and Cameron and Tyler, leaving Damien Diggory as the only one of us who hadn't tasted Crampton. The boys loved to make fun of him for it, so I'd known it was only a matter of time before he made a move.

"He sauntered up to her like he was the shit and did the creepy jock thing where he put his hand on the locker behind her and got all in her face. She told him to fuck off before he even opened his mouth."

Okay, he was right. That was really satisfying. "Bitch deserved it," I grumbled. Lucas huffed.

"Amen to that."

"Beth dodged a major bullet. Damien probably gave her an STD just breathing on her."

Lucas snorted, but a thought hit me then. Lucas had hooked up with Damien Diggory. That was a fact. Damien Diggory loved sex. That was another fact. Lucas wasn't a virgin. Fact number three. So . . .

"Hey Lucas?"

"That's my name."

"How many times did you and Damien—"

Lucas cut me off with a loud groan. "We are not having this conversation."

"Humor me," I pleaded. "How many times?"

I felt him shrug. "A few, I don't know. Four or five, maybe. I've blocked out those memories."

Jesus Christ, that was more than I'd been expecting. "Oh . . . Okay. When?"

"Nate."

"Lucas."

"Sometime last year. You done?"

"Not quite. Did you guys, like . . ." I felt myself blushing at even the thought of asking. "Did you . . . Have sex?"

"Oh my fucking—"

"Answer the question."

Lucas sighed. "Yes. I had sex with Damien Diggory. More than once. You happy?"

I most certainly was not happy. As curious as I'd been, hearing him say it made my stomach drop. I couldn't imagine that pair ever happening. Damien with a guy, Lucas with a guy as dumb as Damien . . . It didn't seem right at all. Or maybe that was just jealous-Nate talking.

"You surprised Damien would have sex with me?" Lucas asked, one eyebrow raised.

I scoffed. "I'm surprised you would have sex with Damien. What happened to standards, Morgan?"

He laughed. "I'll admit, they were rock bottom back then. I'd say they've improved since, though."

I tried not to feel too giddy at what he was implying.

The next Friday was the last before winter break. The poor teachers were growing gray hairs trying to get their excited students under control, but to no avail. Teenagers were buzzing about their plans and gifts. They caused the teachers even more headache by bombarding them with questions about their marks, hoping for that extra 0.13% to bring them from a C to a B, or for extra credit work that they should've asked for a week ago to fix their sucky grades.

I, as usual, was ignoring my not-so-awesome scores and praying that some college would look past my grades and accept me purely for my skill. That was the game-plan. Albeit, it was a very suck game-plan, but a game-plan no less.

I wasn't excited in the slightest for Christmas or presents or vacations. Those were family events, and I would need a real family to take part in them. My parents had come home from a three-week trip last night, momentarily gracing us with their distant presence and the sounds of them yelling at each other all night, and left for another trip this morning. Family wasn't my forte.

That wasn't to say that I had no excitement for winter break, though. Winter break meant no soccer for me—aside from club—and no rehearsals for Lucas. Which therefore meant a lot of time for he and I to wade in our deafening sexual tension. His competition would be next week, and I was way too excited to go and watch him perform.

Before any of that could happen, though, I had to get through the remainder of the day. All I had to do was pretend to listen to Trevor on our way to the locker room and play footie with the fuckboys, and then I would be done. It would be me and Lucas again.

I got more excited than I should have over the prospect of spending a few hours alone with him. Maybe I was starting to like him a little bit too much. A lot too much. That doesn't even make sense.

"Duuude," Trevor's voice whined in my ear. "Can you quit doing that?"

I blinked and shook my head. "Uh, huh?"

He rolled his eyes. "Don't act like you don't know. You've been all gross and smiley lately. And you keep doing that thing where you just like space out and smile and it gives me the creeps. The hell is up with you nowadays?"

I subconsciously touched my lips. Had I been smiling more recently? I didn't think I had. At least, I never noticed.

"I don't know what you're talking about," I said, which was half-true. I didn't doubt that he was right—after all, I'd been feeling exponentially happier lately—but I didn't think I made it that obvious.

Trevor scoffed. "That is total bullshit and you know it. There some girl messing with your mind or something?" He grinned suggestively and elbowed my side. "That's it, isn't it? You're totally whipped! Dude, what happened to your game? Too many babes out there to tie yourself down to one right now!"

Sometimes, he made me genuinely want to throw up. As in bile legitimately rose in my throat. This was one of those times.

"Nah, man," I played it off. "You're crazy. I'm just like I've always been."

That was about as far from the truth as it could get.

Trevor shrugged and elbowed my side again, and I gritted my teeth in annoyance. "Fine, don't tell me. S'long as you keep scoring goals, I don't care where you put your dick."

No, that was about as far from the truth as it could get. Because I knew very well that if I put my dick where I wanted, it wouldn't matter how many goals I scored.

"Your home screen is the Statue of Liberty," Lucas pointed out.

We were laying on his bed, being your stereotypical teenagers who spent their time together using their phones and barely paying attention to each other. My head was on his chest while he rested against his pillows, one arm crossed behind his head.

I nodded. "That it is."

"Is that where you're going?" Lucas asked. "New York, I mean. After you graduate."

The thought alone of escaping this town in a few months made me smile. "Yup. I've got my sights set on NYU."

"Brooklyn or Manhattan?"

"Manhattan's the dream."

Lucas shifted onto his side, forcing me to lay my head down on the mattress. His lips were pursed, quirked up just a little bit. "Like Juilliard."

I swallowed the sudden lump in my throat. "Yeah, just like . . . Juilliard."

If Lucas and I ever did happen, our futures were already intertwined. I knew it was too hopeful to picture us sharing an apartment in New York City, but I sure did like the image. We would never have to deal with the long distance induced separation—and ultimately, end—that college often brought couples.

Which was ridiculous to think of now, because we weren't even a couple.

"What do you want to study?" Lucas asked, fracturing the silence.

"Engineering," I said, which was true. Physics was one of the very few subjects that I was genuinely good at. Science in general came easily to me. "Though I'm really gonna focus on soccer. If I get in, that is."

Lucas groaned. "Don't remind me. There's just a few months before we get our acceptance—or rejection—letters."

I stared at him, a bit incredulously. "You're not seriously worried about whether or not you'll get in. You."

Lucas made a face. "Juilliard has a seven percent acceptance rate. I should be worried."

"Nah," I dismissed. "You're gonna get into every college you applied for, including Juilliard. That's a fact. Me . . . I'm not so sure."

Despite the casual tone of my voice, there was nothing casual about the fear. It plagued me constantly, especially now that those letters were getting closer. Yeah, I was good at soccer. Really good, even. But so were thousands of other boys my age. With my grades, if I didn't get into a school for soccer, I wouldn't get in at all. And then I'd be stuck, rotting in Nowhere, Nebraska for an eternity.

I had a feeling Lucas could sense my distress, simply because he had an uncanny way of doing so. He reached out and played with my hair, twirling the blonde tips between his fingers. "You're as good as they get when it comes to soccer," he said sincerely; I loved how I could always tell that he was being genuine. There were so few people like that in this town. "You'll have free rides thrown at you from every direction."

I offered a grateful smile. "Thanks, Lucas. I hope you're right."

"I am. I always am."

I snorted at that, but continued seriously. "Do you ever . . . New York is the center of America—figuratively. It's where everything happens. It's massive. There are so many people there with so many talents and . . . and it would be so easy to go there imagining success and end up at the bottom with everyone else. Do you ever wonder if we're ridiculous for thinking that we, out of the millions like us, can just pack up and leave and actually, you know, succeed and achieve that All-American Dream?"

Lucas' expression told me that he'd considered this before; many times, even. He regarded me thoughtfully. "Maybe we are ridiculous," he mused. "Who knows, we might crash and burn. We could be completely, utterly stupid for aiming so high. But like you said, that's the All-American Dream;" Then he grinned. "And we're All-American idiots, baby."

I pondered that for a minute. All-American Idiots. I liked it.

"Complete idiots," I said. "You and me."

He reached for my hand, intertwining our fingers, and said, "We might fuck up."

I nodded in agreement. "We could totally fail."

"Or," Lucas said, "We might not. It's a big what if, but hear me out. What if one day, I'm attending Juilliard? What if one day, you're playing soccer at New York University? What if one day, I'm opening on Broadway, and you're moving onto the pro league? What if one day, I'm accepting a Tony, and you're scoring goals at the World Cup?"

The idea made me smile. It was far-fetched, but it wasn't impossible. "What if when you win your Tony, I'm there in the audience?"

Lucas bit his lip. "What if when America wins the World Cup thanks to you, I'm cheering from the bleachers?" He smiled. "I'd make a big sign; it would say—in red, white, and blue of course—Nathaniel Jean is an Idiot."

I chuckled. "Sounds pretty perfect to me."

"How about you help me with my lines?" Lucas prompted. A few hours had passed, and we'd reverted back to antisocial teen behavior.

He reached over to his nightstand and picked up his thin script of Heathers: The Musical.

I groaned as he waved it in front of my face. "I'm no actor, Morgan. This will not be pretty."

Lucas grinned. "Even better."

"If I do this you're not allowed to make fun of me," I said, sitting up cross-legged.

"No promises."

Lucas soon learned that I wasn't lying when I said I couldn't act. Two lines in, I could see him holding back his laughter. It didn't help that I was reading for Veronica, the female main character. Not to mention, I made the mistake of reading her name as a part of the dialogue at least seven times in the first five minutes.

Lucas gave up pretty quickly on trying not to laugh. I ended up laughing with him, because his laugh was just so damn contagious, and pretty soon we were snorting out lines.

"Okay, wait wait wait," he said, putting his hand up. He took a deep inhale to calm his breathing. "This is a serious scene, we have—we have to be serious."

"Oh god," I grumbled, then looked down at the page.

"JD, are you okay?" I read.

"Yeah. Yeah, I'm fine," Lucas—JD—said. Of course, he actually sounded like a normal human being. He was staring straight into my eyes, and I found myself annoyed with how damn convincing he was. "How about you, are you okay?"

"Yeah, yeah, I'm fine. I'm awesome." The script said I had to cry next, so I tried my best at a fake cry. Lucas, like the little asshole he was, burst into laughter.

"I fucking hate you," I grumbled. Lucas pressed his lips together, but his shoulders were still shaking, and a strangled noise sounded from his throat.

I pouted grumpily and threw the script aside, not unlike something I would do as a toddler. I would never admit it, but I was blushing a little. Maybe even pouting.

To my surprise, Lucas stopped laughing altogether and groaned. He leaned his head forward onto my shoulder and said, "You gotta stop with the cute shit, Jean. God, I could kiss you right now."

My stomach did a somersault and I had to purse my lips to avoid choking on air. "You should," I said.

He shook his head, which made his hair tickle my neck. "I stand by my word."

Here it was. Yet another moment that I could take. I ignored it.

"Your word is ugly," I whined.

"You're ugly."

"We've had this conversation."

"Yeah, when you were shitfaced."

"I'm cute drunk."

"You're always cute."

"Someone's feeling extra flirty today, huh?"

Lucas chuckled. "Honestly, I'm as surprised as you are. I don't think you know what you're doing to me, Jean. What you do to everyone."

Unsure of what exactly he meant, I furrowed my eyebrows and asked, "What do you mean? What do I do?"

"You've got this effect on people, you know?"

"No, actually, I don't," I said honestly. "Enlighten me."

"Think about it," Lucas said. "Everyone looks up when you enter a room, right? And not just because you're the town's golden boy. Or because you're rich and sexy and one of the best athletes in Nebraska." My cheeks went bright red at the 'sexy' part, and I was more than a little glad that he couldn't see me with his forehead against my collar.

"You've got this presence about you, though I don't think I can really describe it. You're just . . . You're a stunner, Jean."

Now, maybe more than ever, I really wanted to lift Lucas' face and plant one on him. The moment was strangely raw, and I couldn't ignore the way my heart swelled at his words. Still, something big and ugly was holding me back, and we both knew it.

I wanted to be with Lucas. That much was unquestionable. But I also wanted to be good for Lucas.

A kiss was something so small, but we'd put so much meaning behind it that it had become something much larger, and it terrified me. If I made that move, I was telling him that I was ready to be whatever he needed. I was scared that I would jump in too soon and hurt him. He'd been burned so many times, and I didn't want to be another item on the list of reasons why he hated this town.

It was weird to think that he was at the root of both my excitement and my inhibition. He was—obviously—the reason I wanted to be with him. But he was also the reason I wanted to stay away from him.

"Yeah, well," I said finally. "I don't deserve the attention."

Lucas lifted his head from my shoulder and quirked an eyebrow. "Then who does?"

The answer seemed obvious to me. He deserved the praise much more than I did. "You."

He didn't bother to argue. "Maybe, but," he shrugged. "Things are how they are, and I can't change that. But as soon as I'm out of here, I'm out of here for good, and things will be different."

"Yeah," I agreed. "Really different. And really good, I think."

10: Nathaniel Jean's "Something Good"

Video on the side of the duet performance. Warning: gay

Also I have such a bad headache rn but I'M POSTING ANYWAYS YAY

The theater was huge. Hundreds of seats fanned out from the center stage. I was sat in the mezzanine, in a nice spot where I could see everything clearly. The lights were dim, and I felt as if I was about to watch an actual play on broadway.

A line of old, pretentious looking people—judges, I assumed—were sat along the front of the stage, their backs to us. The closed curtains displayed the projected words: Nebraska State Theater Competition. All around me, excited parents, siblings, aunts, uncles, cousins, grandparents, and friends bragged about the competitor they were supporting. Occasionally, I listened in on conversations, or even got engaged in them. The family sitting next to me was apparently here for a girl named Dejá, and they had high expectations for her.

When they asked who I was supporting, and I told them Lucas Morgan, the mother's eyes lit up in recognition.

"Oh, that's that North Company boy!" She said. Her husband and son stared at her cluelessly, and she turned exasperatedly toward them. "He's the one who won best male solo last year, don't you remember?"

"Do you know him?" I asked curiously. The lady shook her head.

"No, but he's at just about every competition in Nebraska. I swear, I've never seen that boy walk away without a top three award in at least one category. He knows what he's doing, that's for sure."

Realization dawned on her husband's face. "Oh, I know who you mean." He smiled kindly at me. "Is he your brother?"

"Best friend," I said, because I figured it sounded better than something-between-friend-and-boyfriend. And it was true—Lucas was by far the closest friend I had.

"You should be proud," he said. "That kid's gonna be a star."

I returned his smile and nodded whole-heartedly. "He sure is."

Here, over an hour away from Nowhere, Nebraska, things were so different. People saw Lucas as a prodigy, not a problem. Nobody cared that I was friends with him—they probably didn't know he was gay, but it wasn't as if they cared regardless. I was fairly certain that several of the boys here were, and no one judged them for it. Simply being surrounded by people like this, who were all here to support each other and appreciate this form of art, made me want to hop on the first train to New York. This was just a tiny sample of my dream, and actually being immersed in it made that dream seem all the more sweet.

It wasn't long before the competition began. I had no idea how the whole operation worked, but I understood once the host explained. Young adults from different schools would perform, with and against each other, each being scored on a point system. At the end of each round, individual people or groups were ranked first, second, and third based on how many points they recorded. And at the very end, all of the points would be added to determine which school had done the best overall, and that school would be the winner.

Okay, maybe the scoring system was slightly more complicated than I was making it seem, but I didn't care to learn the details.

I watched as pair after pair performed the first round—the duets. I quickly realized that this wasn't some high school talent show—this was on an entirely new level. These were young adults who'd worked their entire lives to be as great in this art as they could be, and it showed. Each one of them was crazy impressive.

Three of the competing pairs were from Northern Nebraska Theater Company, and Lucas' duet fell somewhere in the middle. I unconsciously leaned forward in anticipation as he walked onto the stage, clad in a tight, black, graphic muscle shirt; leather boots; and jeans that hugged him so snugly, I was surprised he could breathe at all. He had the body to look really damn good in them, though—just putting that out there.

His partner was another boy, named Mark Glenwald according to the host, a little older than Lucas. He was a cute, insanely tall African-American boy, and he was wearing a white blazer and matching khaki pants. The look seemed very professional, especially next to Lucas'.

Their set was very simple. A white table with a chair pushed into it at either end was positioned in the center of the stage, and that was it. Mark was trailing behind Lucas, looking aggravated. The scene began, but with dialogue rather than singing.

"The line is 'Cyber Arts and its corporate sponsor, Grey Communications, would like to mitigate the Christmas Eve riots.' What is so difficult about that?"

Lucas pursed his lips. "It just doesn't . . . Roll of my tongue. I like my version."

Mark rolled his eyes and scoffed. "Right. You, dressed as a ground hog to protest the ground breaking."

"It's a metaphor!" Lucas insisted.

"It is less than brilliant!"

Lucas' eyes narrowed, and he snapped. "That's it, Miss Ivy League!"

"Uh," Mark gave Lucas a weird look. "What?"

Lucas stormed towards him, stopping only a foot away. "Ever since New Year's, I haven't said boo. I let you direct; I didn't pierce my nipples because it grossed you out; I didn't stay and dance at the Clit Club that night because you wanted to go home."

"You were flirting with the woman in rubber!" Mark exclaimed. Lucas' lips parted in a silent "oh".

"That's what this is about?" He chuckled. A piano tune started up behind him, soft at first but slowly growing louder. "There will always be women in rubber flirting with me, give me a break."

He began singing then, his voice as smooth and melodic as ever—even a bit sultry now. The entire scene was very homo-erotic, and I felt an uncomfortable pang in my gut whenever Lucas put his hand on Mark's chest, or got close to his face. It was dumb to feel jealous—we weren't together in the slightest, and he was playing a character for God's sake—but I couldn't help it. The mind does what the mind does.

Nevertheless, I loved the performance. Lucas was, as expected, amazing to watch—he hit every note and performed the role so well, he seemed to me more like Maureen Johnson than he did Lucas Morgan. And I would admit that watching him play a somewhat seductive character wasn't the worst way to spend the first Saturday night of winter break.

There were a few more duets before that sector of the competition was over. Lucas' duet ended up coming in third, behind two girls who'd done a song from Spring Awakening (whatever that was) and a boy and a girl who'd performed a duet from Grease. Maybe I was biased, but I thought that Lucas and Mark deserved first place. Still, judging by the sheer number of competitors and the celebration that went up among the NNTC kids, third place was pretty damn good.

The next round of the competition was the female individual numbers. There were several impressive performances, but I couldn't help but wait impatiently for their competition to end so I could watch Lucas perform his solo.

As luck would have it, even when the male individual numbers came around, Lucas' was the second to last. Every time I heard the words, "Coming from Northern Nebraska's Theater Company . . ." I would sit forward in my seat, only to recoil in disappointment when some other boy's name was called.

Lucas' time came eventually, though. He walked calmly onto the stage, dressed much more normally now—he wore gray shorts and a geeky graphic tea, and wide-rimmed glasses were perched on his nose.

I found myself smiling to myself as he confidently introduced himself—he was so in his element here, so unlike how he was at school. This was, in every meaning of the phrase, what he was born to do. When the music began, his expression shifted, and he was no longer Lucas Morgan.

One verse into the song, I knew I was screwed. The music itself was cute and sort of happy, but the lyrics were the opposite. Lucas immersed himself into the character so well, I genuinely felt bad for him. There was one point in the song, nearer to the end, when the music became urgent, and his words and gestures changed to match it perfectly. His expression was a mixture of anger and fear and sadness, his movements became frantic and frustrated. He was sweating, his body was visibly shaking. Tears rolled down his cheeks. He—or at least the character he was playing—was having a panic attack. I just wanted to run up onto that stage and give him a hug.

When he was done, the mother from before turned to me, shaking her head, and said, "He really is something special."

It was no shock that he won first place. His vocals were great, yeah, but it was his performance that left the other competitors in the dust. Nobody else had the stage presence he did, nobody even came close.

The group performance round was much shorter than the others, because each school could only have one participant. That said, it was by far the most exciting and diverse. Groups of three or more would go onto the stage and give their absolute best as to not let down their team.

Some had eccentric numbers with wild dancing and flashy costumes. Others had massive kick lines and wild hairstyles. Some of them were much more minimal, but they made up for the lack of fast-paced movement and eye-catching clothing with belting and harmonies that made me want to go watch something gay like Les Mis. There were instruments on stage in some, too—pianos, guitars, drums.

I was teeming with excitement by the time Northern Nebraska's Theater Academy was called. A flood of young men swarmed the stage, each wearing worn brown trousers and old-school cabbie caps. My gaze found Lucas first, in a striped white shirt, suspenders, and glasses. Jenna could probably take one look at him and tell me which Newsie he was, but I just knew him as The Guy Who Made My Heart Do Annoying Things (And Looked Really Cute In His Costume).

Somehow, despite the giant crowd, his eyes met mine for a brief moment, and I smiled encouragingly. Then the music began, and Lucas Morgan was a Newsie.

And fuck, he could dance.

The entire performance was fantastic. Every man on that stage knew what he was doing and did it well. They managed to do all of this exhausting-looking dancing and still sing, and that on its own was a phenomenon to me. They deserved every bit of the standing ovation they got. NNTC really did produce good students.

As great as they were as a whole, I could hardly stop focusing on Lucas. I'd had no idea that he could move so fluidly, or jump so high, or do flips like that. There was a point where he was center stage, doing those spinny-things that dancers do. He did so many, and so damn fast, I felt dizzy just watching. The audience went crazy for him.

After that number, the rest of the performances didn't matter. Their score had been so high, it would take a miracle of nature to beat them. Nobody was surprised when they came in first.

There was also little surprise when North Nebraska's Theater Company won the entire state competition. Their scores had been consistently high throughout, and they'd won for the last several years. They were the best, simple as that.

The event had taken the entirety of my day, but it was more than worth it. At a text from Lucas saying that he would meet me as soon as he could, I left the theater and made my way down to the lobby of the building, where I found a comfortable chair and relaxed.

"As soon as I can" turned out to be an hour and a half later, but I wasn't too annoyed. Being the impatient guy I was, I didn't love the wait, but it wasn't unexpected. He had to celebrate with his school and his family, and I was sure he'd been approached by several different scouts along the way—hopefully one from Juilliard.

It was nearly midnight when he found me, still waiting in the lobby. I was looking at my phone screen, headphones plugged into my ears, so I didn't know he was there until he tapped my shoulder. I may or may not have jumped when he did, but that detail wasn't important.

When I realized it was Lucas and not some creepy old man telling me to stop loitering, I hopped eagerly to my feet and threw my arms around him in a congratulatory hug. "You were so fucking good, oh my god!"

Lucas laughed and wrapped his arms around my neck. "Thank you," he said. "And thank you for coming. You didn't have to."

I pulled back and beamed at him. "I'm so glad I did. So fucking good, man. Those spinny things you did? So cool!'"

Lucas smiled wide, dimple and all, and said, "Let's go for a walk, yeah? Also, they're called pirouettes."

The air outside was frigid, and I knew Lucas must not have liked that too much. Still, he didn't complain. He'd changed since his last performance into proper winter-wear, gloves and beanie and all.

We walked in silence for a long while. The Company building was in the middle of a rather rural area, and soon the sidewalk turned to a dirt path and the buildings turned to trees. A very light snow fell, the kind that melted as soon as it landed on the ground but clung to the leaves of trees, creating a winter wonderland-esque picture. Between gaps in the clouds, a crescent moon luminesced, soft but bright and surrounded by scatters of stars.

Lucas' skin was nearly white in the dim glow. His cheeks and nose were dusted with pink from the cold, and flakes of snow dotted his shoulders, his eyelashes, the tips of his hair that peeked out from underneath his beanie. Beauty came so naturally to him, it was unfair. He didn't even have to try.

He turned to look at me, caught me staring. "What?" He asked.

I looked away from him and tried not to feel embarrassed. Then I felt something curl around my pinkie finger, and glanced down to see his own intertwined with mine.

We were utterly alone, yet I still, idiotically, felt bubbles of stress rise in my stomach. There was literally no chance that anybody we knew would see us out here, hidden in the trees an hour from home, but something in my brain refused to accept that. The mere fact was that we were in sort-of public, sort-of holding hands, and that made me sort-of anxious. I tried to shrug off the nagging feeling, tried to tell myself that it was ridiculous, but it persisted.

Lucas must have noticed the shift in my atmosphere, because his pinkie began to slip away from mine. I made a last second decision and flipped my pessimistic mind the bird, taking his entire hand in mine.

***

what do u mean ur sick???? -Shawn M

I rolled my eyes. What kind of question was that?

Sorry dude it just came out of nowhere -Nate J

can't you just come anyways? -Shawn M

Bro I'm puking enough without tossing booze down my throat -Nate J

that's lame -Shawn M

ur missing out -Shawn M

I highly doubted that. If Shawn's New Year/birthday party was anything like it was last year, I was only missing out on alcohol poisoning and a one-night-stand I would seriously regret the next day.

These parties had been going on for years. On Shawn and Lucas' birthday, their parents would take them to do whatever they wanted. Then, on the day after, they would book a hotel room and let the boys have their fun at home. Of course, the booze was a more recently added element.

I left him on 'read' and moved on to text the better of the Morgan twins.

Come over? -Nate J

A few minutes later, my phone buzzed with his response.

Don't you have a party to attend? -Lucas M

Yeah, actually, I do. Come over-Nate J

Okay, so maybe I wasn't exactly sick. But I needed some excuse to get out of going to Shawn's shit-fest.

It's like ten at night -Lucas M

Is that a no?? -Nate J

I'll be there in twenty -Lucas M

When Lucas arrived, I could tell right away that he wasn't in a good mood. His eyebrows were furrowed ever-so-slightly, and he didn't greet me with his usual smile.

"Someone looks happy," I joked. Lucas stepped past me into my house, apparently unamused.

"Wouldn't you be if your brother kicked you out because he doesn't want you around during a birthday party that's supposed to be yours, too?"

I frowned. What a prick. "You could've just said no. He doesn't control you. Or tell your parents about what a dick he's being."

"What's the point?" Lucas asked tiredly. "I wouldn't be wanted there anyways. And I don't drag my parents into his petty shit. They know he's not nice to me. They try to fix it, but he doesn't listen."

I wished I could argue, or give him some comfort, but it was pretty obvious that he was right. And how would I comfort him? Hey, it's okay that your brother makes your life a living hell, man. You'll be fine. Yeah, no. I settled for saying, "Good thing I hit you up then, huh?"

He offered a half-hearted smile, which was at least an improvement. "Yeah, it's better than driving around aimlessly. I hope you plan to entertain me."

I grinned. "Oh, I do. You hungry?"

Lucas shook his head. "Not really."

Dammit Lucas. Work with me here. "Well we're getting food anyways. Come on."

Lucas shot me a questioning look, but followed nonetheless as I led him to the kitchen. I flipped the light switch, illuminating the room, and he gasped softly.

"Nate . . ."

The kitchen was decked out from floor to ceiling with obnoxious, brightly colored, birthday-themed decorations. Across the wall cabinets were rainbow streamers and a big, colorful Happy Birthday! banner. Helium balloons were just about everywhere—tied to chairs, touching the ceiling, fastened to drawer knobs, even hanging from the microwave handle.

Below the banner was a huge stuffed bear holding a heart-shaped Happy Birthday! sign (I saw it and I had to buy it). And perched on the kitchen island, with a single lit candle at its center—the sparkling kind—was a small orange cake shaped like a cat's head—why not, you know?—next to a bottle of whiskey, because what party would be complete without underaged drinking?

"Happy birthday!" I exclaimed, laughing at his awed expression.

Lucas kept looking back and forth between his surroundings and me, his surroundings and me. Finally, he said, "Nathaniel Jean, you did not."

He stepped further into the kitchen, examining every detail, and I followed closely behind him. He chuckled when he looked at the teddy bear. "Clearly, I did." I gestured to the cake. "Make a wish."

"I can't blow out that candle," he pointed out.

"Make a wish anyways."

Lucas caught me by off-guard then, turning around and throwing himself onto me. I stumbled back in surprise, but managed to regain my footing and returned the warm embrace.

I could feel his distress radiating in waves as I held him. The way his fingers curled tightly around the fabric of my shirt, the way he was leaning into me for support. This was yet another rare moment in which he let himself be vulnerable. He still loved his brother, though he never said it. Shawn hurt him, over and over again, every single day.

Lucas received so much hate and so little love. He had his parents, sure, and his close friends. But the imbalance took a tole on him. I hated that. I really, really hated that, because he was hands-down the best person I'd ever met. There wasn't a single other person in this shit town who was as genuine or caring.

Suddenly, my mind was racing, because I realized just how much I cared about the boy in my arms. He deserved the world, and I would give it to him if I could. He was so damn important to me.

And that was really overwhelming, because I'd never valued another person so much. All of a sudden I felt sick—legitimately sick to my stomach—of waiting around in this awkward zone between friendship and something more.

There was still so much shit going on in my head. I was closer to satisfied, but far from happy. I liked Lucas a lot more than I liked myself, and that wasn't a good thing. My mindset wasn't healthy for me, let alone for a relationship.

The smartest choice would be to wait. Bad things would probably happen if I didn't.

But I wasn't sure I could. Not now, not with the way my heart was pounding against my throat. If I did, it just might burst out of my body.

It was a reckless decision, too impulsive to be smart. A thoughtless thought. But I wanted it, and I didn't want to wait.

I abruptly pulled away from Lucas and turned my back to him, running my hands through my hair and wishing my mind wasn't so fucked up.

"What?" He asked. He sounded so concerned, it made me even more confused.

The defiant words ringing in my head as I turned back around were fuck it. The words that came out of my mouth, probably because I was too frayed to work right, were "Fuck you."

Then, before I could think better of it, I grabbed Lucas' face and I kissed him.

There were none of those classically-described fireworks you hear about in books and movies. The only sparks in the room came from the candle on Lucas' cake. What I felt instead was a cold rush of something that shot down my spine and made me shiver. It felt absolutely terrible and absolutely amazing at the same time.

The kiss was short; the moment I felt his lips respond, when his fingers brushed my waist, I pulled back. I wasn't sure I could've handled another second.

His eyes fluttered open and he stared at me, blinking in surprise. "Well . . . fuck you, too."

With a shaky exhale, I leaned back against the kitchen island, using my palms to hold myself up, and tried to organize my mind. That had actually just happened. I'd just done that. "That was weird."

"Not that weird," Lucas pondered, looking annoyingly amused. I felt really nervous and jumpy all of a sudden, and I had no idea why. This giddy, unsure feeling in my stomach was new to me. I wasn't used to being self-conscious, at least not about matters like these. Not about one little kiss.

"I guess not. But you're, like, tall. I'm used to kissing people who are, you know, shorter than me. So it was weird, you know? Well maybe it wasn't weird but different, definitely different, and I guess since it was so different that kind of made it weird for me. I'm used to one thing, and that was another thing, so my body's all like 'Woah what's this thing?' Weird."

I was speaking way faster than normal, and talking with hands a lot. Unfamiliar nerves chewed at me, making it hard for me to keep my eyes in one place.

Lucas' eyebrows lifted in concern. "Are you alright?" He asked, tilting his head slightly.

I nodded, though I wasn't sure that I believed it myself. I wasn't not alright . . . I just wasn't alright, either. "I'm okay, just . . ." My lips were tingling. I lifted my fingers to touch them. "Woah."

"Good woah?" Lucas asked. "Or bad woah?"

"Everything woah."

He was silent for a moment, looking just as confused as I felt. Then he asked, "Where's your head at right now?"

I could hear hesitation in his voice. With a pang of guilt, I realized that he was scared now, scared that I'd changed my mind. That I'd decided I didn't want this. I pushed myself off from the counter and shoved my hands into my pockets. "I don't know, Lucas. I don't know, but . . . but I really like it."

He visibly relaxed, the smile returning to his expression. "Good," he sighed, "Because I like it, too."

He leaned forward, gently pressing his lips against mine. It was so nice, kissing him. He moved slowly, cautiously, as if he was afraid he'd scare me away, but I didn't mind. Tenderness was what we needed right now.

My hands found his neck, his my hips. He stepped closer to me, his chest pressing against mine, and tilted his head. There was something so romantic about the simplicity and sincerity of it all. We were just two boys who had crazy feelings for each other, finally acting on those feelings. There was nothing wrong or weird about it. And god knows, it was worth the wait.

"Also . . ." He murmured against my lips. "How'd you know my wish?"

"That was so fucking cliché, oh my god."

Lucas laughed and wrapped his arms tighter around me, pulling my body into his.

Three hours, two movies, one entire cake, and a half a bottle of whiskey later, Lucas and I were sat against the headboard of my bed, watching Riverdale on Netflix. We were watching Jughead's birthday episode, because it only seemed appropriate.

"You know," Lucas said out of the blue. He was sitting against my pillows next to me—half on top of me, more accurately—and our legs were a tangled mess. We were a little tipsy, but nowhere near hammered. "You never told me when your birthday is."

"It was right before school started," I told him. Literally, it was the day before.

Lucas pouted. "Well fuck."

I shrugged. "I don't really care much for birthdays. I just stay home and shit." Lucas nodded in understanding, though he still looked disappointed, so I changed the topic. "What'd you do yesterday?"

His face lit up with excitement and he sat upright. "Wanna see?"

I stammered in surprise at his sudden drastic change in demeanor. "Uh . . . yeah?"

He turned his body so that he was facing me from the side and sat cross-legged. He pulled his hoodie off over his head, and I immediately understood just why he was so excited. "Holy shit," I muttered. He nodded enthusiastically.

On the side of his torso, starting at his hip, was an image of a fully-bloomed, blood red rose. Above it, written sideways all the way to the base of his arm in a pretty cursive script, were words written in a language I didn't recognize.

I reached out and touched the tattoo in awe. It was still a bit red and irritated, but it was beautiful nonetheless. "That's incredible," I breathed. "What does it say?"

"It's Romanian," Lucas answered. "It says "and rain will make the flowers grow"—a lyric from Les Mis."

I could tell, just from the way he said it, that the words meant a lot to him. And rain will make the flowers grow. It was lovely.

Despite how captivating the tattoo was, I couldn't help but let my eyes wander. I'd seen him shirtless plenty of times, sure, but never this close up. He had the body of a dancer—slender and light, but defined from years of hard work. Freckles dusted his shoulders. I wasn't sure which piece of art was more captivating—the tattoo, or him.

Okay, that's a lie. It was definitely him, hands down.

I heard Lucas swallow. My hand was still on his side, and I wasn't exactly being discreet in admiring him. "There, er, there's more."

I forced myself to look up at his face and blinked away my distraction. "Huh?"

He turned around so that his back was facing me, and I gasped aloud. Depicted across the upper part of his back, from shoulder-blade to shoulder blade, was a sketch-like, intricate image of a city skyline. New York City skyline, to be specific. It was mostly done in black ink, but there were undertones of blue and white, too.

My fingers ghosted across the image, as if I would smudge it if I pressed too hard. Lucas shivered at my feather-light touch. "Do you like it?"

"Of course I like it," I said, still tracing the buildings with my fingertips. "It's so pretty. And so detailed. And so Lucas."

It really was. It was a dreamer's tattoo, and if Lucas Morgan was nothing else, he was a dreamer.

He smiled gratefully and turned back around to face me. "Thanks," he said as he took fistfuls of my shirt in his hands, pulling me towards him. He closed any distance between us, and I had to try hard not to blush at the fact that he was still shirtless, kissing me. I let myself fall back into the pillows, pulling him down with me, and when his body merged with mine, fitting into every curve like a skillfully carved puzzle, I knew this was something good.

And so it begins

11: Nathaniel Jean's Biggest Fear

Video of the song Lucas sang for his solo above (it's really good just saying) (also the lady laughing can suck my ass)

For every moment that Lucas was with me that night, I was smiling. How could I not be, when I was finally experiencing a part of my life that I'd deprived myself of for so long?

The moment he left, so did my smile.

Because the moment he left, someone else surged forward to take his place. Someone I knew well and didn't want to see. Someone who brought all of his friends with him as well, because he was never quite alone. He kissed my cheek softly in greeting and whispered ruthless nothings in my ear. Then he rubbed my shoulder, consoling me, as his friends released their fury. He told me to listen to him, like a father speaking to his son; he told me that it would help. He would make things better—I only had to listen. His friends backed off then, retreating to softly supporting his sayings.

But they threatened me, too. He was an absent-minded fellow, and they muttered, when he wasn't paying attention, where I would end up if I didn't listen. With them, they said. On top of me, crushing me, suffocating me. They would kill me. Or at least, they would hand me the knife.

They were silent when he was focused again, though. They respected him—after all, they worked for him, not with him. Without him, they would not exist. Not within me, anyways.

His name was Paranoia. And his friends, his friends were Fear, they were Regret, and most horribly, they were Hatred.

I did have my own defense, yes. I had my new friends—I had Confidence, I had Acceptance, I had Bravery. But they were exhausted. They'd been fighting for so long now, without a break. Paranoia and his gang had rested recently, up until now. They were ready for a new war—my friends were not. My friends lost.

They fought bravely, though. They argued that we could do this—nobody but Lucas and I would have to know. Then we would be off to New York—just a few months from now—and it wouldn't matter who knew.

They said that this, even now that it had happened, was nothing bad. Nothing was wrong, or impure, about our actions or feelings.

They told me I would be good for him. That he really liked me, and in his own ways, he needed me as much as I needed him.

Paranoia and his buddies clapped back just as fiercely. I would get caught, they said. I would lose everything, all for one measly boy. I would be hated, I would never get out of here.

This was wrong, they whispered, sometimes yelled. Thinking and acting were very different, and acting would be my end. This was where my friends won, because I was past that mindset. I refused to fall into it again. I wasn't wrong, I wasn't dirty. Maybe I still struggled with that sometimes, but not enough to go back. I promised myself I would never go back.

Everywhere else, we lost.

I was bound to hurt him, they told me, over and over. I was toxic for him. I wouldn't be there for him. I didn't deserve to be there for him. I was selfish and needy and unsympathetic and mean, they shouted, so loud I felt my brain would explode. My personality was ugly, I believed that much without their verification. Their word made it fact.

And so I descended, with my enemies on my heels, into a restless, tearful sleep. I awoke to a painful day, filled to the brink with internal argument which I always seemed to lose. I was so screwed up, coach nearly benched me at Saturday's game.

I didn't want to get caught. I didn't want to hurt Lucas. Those two didn't seem to mix together well.

Paranoia didn't fully succeed, at least. I wouldn't stop what I had with Lucas, not so soon after it had begun. I would force a smile if I had to. I could pretend to be alright—I'd been doing it for years. I wanted this relationship, and I was determined to keep it.

If it costed me my mental health, so be it.

I was expecting that I wouldn't actually have to do much faking until the following Friday. At least not to Lucas. I faked okay in front of my peers all the time—it was the only way I could survive. Lucas was much more difficult, though. I'll put it like this: if my fellows at school looked at me and saw aluminum foil, Lucas looked at me and saw seran wrap.

However, Sunday afternoon was accompanied by a text from the one and only.

My house is empty, be here in 20-Lucas M

Which was succeeded by a follow-up.

Fuck that rhymed someone sIGN ME-Lucas M

It made me chuckle, which was refreshing. Even when he had no idea what the fuck was going on in my head, he still knew what to say.

You're such a dork-Nate J

Also I'll be there in 30 I'm not some kind of wizard-Nate J

I may or may not have been laying in bed since morning, doing absolutely nothing to prepare myself for the day ahead.

I was anxious as I drove to his house forty-five minutes later—oops—because I had absolutely no idea how I'd go about acting like everything was fine. I'd never been able to do it around him to begin with. And I was scared that once he realized how much I was freaking out, he would freak out and, like most normal people, not want to get involved with someone who didn't even fully know what they want.

That problem, for all the stressing I'd done, turned out to have a shockingly simple solution. The moment Lucas, with his pretty-boy smile, opened the front door, I didn't need to fake it. I was so damn happy just to be in his presence, it was almost scary.

Paranoia was still there in the back of my mind, that was for sure. In his gravely voice, he warned me that the moment I left, I would meet him again. He'd be back, rested and ready to fight.

But for the time being, I could hang out with Confidence and Acceptance and Bravery and Lucas.

There was a new obstacle now, though. It was called "the awkward tension between two boys who have no idea where they are or how to approach the situation but really really like each other and therefore are reduced to stuttering, blushing, horribly awkward piles of hormones".

"Hi," he breathed, smiling in greeting.

"Hey."

I wasn't even inside yet and the tension was already Kim K thick.

I expected Lucas to step aside and let me in, but he simply stood in the doorway, smiling at me.

"Can I, er, come in?"

Lucas' eyes widened as he seemed to realize that he was blocking the entrance entirely. His cheeks turned pink and he quickly shuffled to the side, sputtering out several apologies. As I stepped past him into the house, I accidentally stepped on his bare foot, causing him to yelp, and now I was the one furiously apologizing.

In other words, we were a mess.

"God," Lucas groaned, putting his face in his hands. "Why are we like this? Let's just, like, try to be normal, yeah?"

"Right," I coughed. "Normal is good."

Good, yes. Easy? Hell no. As it would turn out, being normal was much easier said than done. There was a strange formality in the air, as neither of us knew quite how to act around one another. Do we hug? Kiss? Or do we just act like friends? Are we just friends?

The first thirty or so minutes that I spent with Lucas in his room were full of uncomfortable silences and small talk. We seemed to be apologizing for something every other minute, and we used filler words such as "Um" and "Er" and "Like" every other sentence.

There was a different kind of tension, too. A less awkward but equally uncomfortable kind. The type of tension that arose every time we brushed shoulders, or when our hands touched on accident. Which was momentously stupid, because before today we spent our time together cuddling like lovers. Now that we actually were something along those lines, we were acting like strangers.

We were both starting to get frustrated with ourselves and each other, I could tell. But we were also too confused and suddenly shy to do anything about it, at least for a while. Lucas piped up eventually though, being the braver of the two of us.

"This is ridiculous," he sighed. "Why are we acting like we met on Grindr two hours ago?"

Confused, I asked, "What's Grindr?"

Lucas waved his hand dismissively. "The point is, we've gotta stop being dumb, because it's really freaking annoying. Let's do something . . . Help me practice my lines."

I didn't hesitate. "No way."

Lucas crossed his arms childishly. "Why not?"

"You're just gonna make fun of me," I whined. He shook his head insistently, but I could see him already holding back chuckles, and we hadn't even started yet.

"See?" I exclaimed. "You're laughing just thinking about it! No way, not in a million years."

"Please?"

"Fine."

Fuck. Why did that always work on me?

Lucas grinned triumphantly and grabbed the script from his nightstand. He shifted through it, scanning the pages before he chose which one he wanted to go over, and handed the book to me.

He didn't last four seconds before he laughed.

I decided to play into it, though. I was already a bad actor, so why not just be worse? It made him laugh, at least, and his laughter was probably the single best sound on the face of this planet.

I upped the antics, and was proud when he cracked up even more. I was exaggerating now, being much too theatrical—ironically—but Lucas loved it, so, by default, I loved it.

My drama display mellowed when I flipped the page and saw what was on it. A soft blush coated my cheeks as my lips curled into a grin. "You're sly, Morgan."

He didn't say anything other than his next line, but I caught his mischievous smirk. He'd thought this out all too well.

My eyes couldn't stop darting between the lines I was saying and the stage direction printed not far below. My stomach rose in anticipation as we neared it. Three lines away. Two lines. One.

Lucas' hand moved under my chin, gently gripping my jaw. He used his hold to pull me closer, until finally his lips met mine and the tension in the air seemed to dissolve, like a cloud blown apart by a jet of wind.

Then he leaned back, laying himself onto the bed and pulling me with him so that I was directly on top of him. The script fell, forgotten, out of my hand as I settled between his legs, filling any space separating us.

He bit down gently on my lower lip, and a sudden rush of heat surged through my body. As much as I loved Lucas' personality, I could never ignore the insane physical attraction I felt toward him. And now we were together, alone, as close to each other as we could possibly be. I'd be crazy not to make the most of the situation.

And so, I opened my mouth, and for the first time in my life, I was full on making out with a guy. Lucas' hand slipped along my jaw into my hair, and I could feel him thawing under me. I wasn't sure I could handle how soft his lips were, or how he pulled at my hair, or how his other hand gripped my lower back, just low enough to drive me mad. When my hands slid under the hem of his shirt, yearning to feel his soft, muscled skin, and he arched his back below me, I was sure I nearly burst into flames.

My body responded naturally; my hips grounded down against his, uncontrolled. I didn't have time to be embarrassed, because the sound that Lucas made in response spurred me on to do it again. And when I did, his hips rolled upward to meet mine.

There was nothing sweet or innocent about it anymore. It was rough and ardent and too hot for me stop and think of how fast we were moving. To hell with it—we were eighteen, we could do whatever the fuck we wanted, as soon as we fucking wanted.

But then Lucas was pushing gently at my chest, and I sat upright in fear that I'd done something wrong. Maybe this was moving too fast.

Lucas sat up, too, and I worriedly said, "Is everything alri—"

I never got to finish, though, because Lucas simply pulled his shirt over his head and took my face in his hands, smashing his lips against mine once more. A noise of surprise sounded from my throat, but I responded instantly and with equal fervor. My hands moved of their own accord to feel every inch of his chest.

It seemed like only seconds before my shirt was discarded, too. I grabbed his hips and pulled him onto me, his legs on either side of mine. I abandoned his lips to kiss along his jaw, down his neck, his chest. He groaned as I left indiscreet marks on his skin, all-the-while my hands sliding lower and lower, until I reached behind him. He had such a perfect body, it would be a crime not to appreciate it all.

He explored my upper half, his hands sliding up and down my chest, my back. Everywhere he touched, my skin seemed to burn for second after. "Jesus, Nate," he groaned.

I just about lost it. I found Lucas' lips again, and I kissed him hard. A sort of battle ensued—a messy clash of lips, teeth, and skin—as we both sought control of the situation. Lucas was the first to cave; he subdued and just let me kiss him, let me touch him and hold him and have my way with him him.

My body was ablaze with a new kind of heat I'd never felt before. My mind was a fuzzy blur, I felt entirely intoxicated—I was drunk on Lucas. And god, I never wanted to be sober. I wanted more, I wanted to get fucking wasted. They way his body curved into mine, chest to chest, sharing our heat, extinguished every ounce of rationality in my brain.

I'd thought for so long that I'd never feel this. Had sleeping with girls, when I knew I'd never be attracted to them, been stupid and dickish? Yes, but we already know I'm stupid and a dick, so there's no surprise there. I'd never felt anything though; not a thing. Nothing real, at least.

Now that I was here, meshing with someone who I was so attracted to it hurt, I finally understood what the fuss was about. I'd never been so turned on in my life—never even thought I could be—and I didn't want to miss a thing.

I dragged my face away from is, finding satisfaction in the way his lips chased mine for a brief moment. "Random thought," I said; my voice came out low and husky and practically unrecognizable.

Lucas pressed a kiss below my ear, one hand running absentmindedly down my chest. "Hm?" He hummed.

I decided to just say it bluntly. Why beat around the bush? "We should have sex."

Lucas backed up to look at me, his eyes rounded in surprise. In an awkward response to his silence, I added, "Just saying."

Lucas blinked. "Right now?"

"Unless you don't want to," I said, feeling my cheeks heat up in embarrassment.

Lucas' lip quirked up into a grin. My eyes followed his hand as it left my skin, moving down to the hem of his jeans. Unbuttoned, then unzipped. Looking down at him now, I realized that he was just as excited as I was.

"I've heard good things about you," he said, wrapping his arms loosely around my neck. "I've got high expectations."

I smirked. I was pretty confident in my abilities. "I don't think you'll be disappointed."

He leaned forward and captured my lips again. My pants were the first to come off, then his. There was so little clothing separating us now, and I fell in love with the way his body fit with mine.

"You better rock me, Nathaniel Jean," Lucas murmured against my lips.

"Fucking hell," Lucas breathed as he fell back into the pillows.

I grinned, maybe a little proudly, and scooted closer to him, placing an arm around his shoulders and pulling him into my side. "Did I meet your expectations?"

He softly kissed my neck, then my cheek. "You surpassed them by a ten-fold," he said, which made me feel giddy all over again. "But I'm sure you already knew that."

His fingers traced random circles into my chest. He rested his head against my shoulder and hummed contentedly. "How are you feeling?"

How was I feeling? Words couldn't describe. I was elated. And exhausted. And exhilarated. "Fucked up," I said. When Lucas furrowed his eyebrows, I added, "In a good way. I just feel really . . . Different. Good different. Awesome different."

Lucas smiled. He rolled away from me and reached over the edge of the bed, coming up with his underwear and mine. He put his on and tossed mine towards me; it landed, quite unpleasantly, on my face.

"Gee, thanks," I groaned as I peeled the underwear from my face and pulled it on, all the while making my disgust apparent in my expression.

Lucas scooted back next to me. "Seventh grade Lucas is pissing himself right now."

I laughed. "Seventh grade Nate is sprinting to confession with a tent in his pants."

Lucas snorted. His hair tickled my neck. "Sounds like twelfth grade Nate, too."

"Oh my god, too real."

I leaned over and kissed him for no good reason, and then pulled away with a smile as I realized that I could kiss Lucas Morgan for no good reason. This was too damn good.

"So we're, like, dating, right?" I asked. Lucas scoffed.

"That was the single least romantic way you could've asked me out, Jean. Is this how you woo all the girls?"

"No, but I don't actually like all the girls," I said, which succeeded in making him blush.

He smiled. "I'd never have pictured Nathaniel Jean as my first boyfriend, you know," he mused.

"No?" I didn't hide from my voice the satisfaction that I felt knowing I was his first real relationship.

He shook his head. "Nah." Then he pressed his lips against mine, just for a moment. "I'm glad you are, though. What kind of stereotypical high school gay would I be without dating the closeted fuckboy jock?"

The next week, it turned out, would be really fucking frustrating.

Seeing Lucas Morgan every damn day—in the hallways, eating lunch, at practice—without being able to do so much as talk to him, would be the death of me. To finally have him and be entirely unable to show it seemed horribly unfair.

On Monday afternoon, in the locker room before practice, Shawn had decided to speak up about something that caught his attention.

"Dude, what the fuck happened to you?" He'd asked Lucas, gesturing toward his brother's torso. Lucas had glanced down at himself, at the small bruises that marked his neck and collar and chest, and looked back up with a smirk.

"You wouldn't want to know."

Absolute disgust had entered Shawn's expression when he realized what Lucas had meant. He'd stormed past his brother, red faced and spitting homophobic slurs.

Lucas and I had locked eyes then. His smirk grew, and I may have been fostering one of my own, too.

But that was an exchanged glance. And that was all we shared for the next few days—glances. I hated that. I hated hiding. But hiding was all I'd ever known. And the idea of coming out of hiding . . . I didn't even want to imagine it. It was, by far, my biggest fear, and I didn't have a fourth of the Bravery I'd need to face it. I wasn't nearly as strong as Lucas, and I didn't t ry to be.

I'd originally planned to make them wait longer before they had any smexy times, but if I'm completely honest I can't see them waiting. It would be more romantic, yeah, but kinda unrealistic in my opinion. They're horny teenage (technically young adult) boys, and they've already spent so much time drowning in sexual tension. Maybe it would be different if either of them were virgins, but they're clearly not lmao. I can't imagine sex being a super big deal to either of them, but then again that's just me.

Also yes I know I didn't write smut. Why? Because I didn't want to. I'm really not comfortable doing it, and I haven't done it before, and that's all there is to it. Sorry y'all.

Also I know I kinda hinted at Nate topping but who do you guys think tops?? Just curious XD

12: Nathaniel Jean's Anxiety

L ast but not least, the group number from the competition. This is one of my favorite videos of all time bc cute boys + cute costumes + epic dancing = I feel desolate (in a good way)

When Friday finally came around and practice was over, I was practically bouncing with anticipation. In my excitement, I showered extra fast; which made no difference, since I had to wait for the locker room to clear out before I could leave with Lucas anyways. I ended up sitting on a bench, silently glaring at everything as the other boys took their sweet damn time in leaving.

The seconds lasted an eternity. When the last freshmen left, laughing about dick-jokes on iFunny, I couldn't have been more relieved.

I stood from the bench and walk around the lockers until I found Lucas, packing his bags to leave. "Ready to go?" I asked, my hands clasped behind my back.

Lucas hummed in response, shrugged his bag onto his shoulder, and walked over to me. "Let's get out of here," he said with his dimpled smile. He placed his arms loosely around my neck and leaned in to kiss me.

And I panicked.

Something in my brain clicked and my hands shot up to push him away, much harder than I'd meant to. He stumbled back, and would've fallen over had he not smacked the lockers for support.

"What the hell?" He exclaimed, his eyes wide and alarmed. "Are you out of your mind?"

I couldn't do it. Not here. Paranoia paid me another visit, and he didn't try to be friendly this time. His fear became my anger. "What were you thinking?"

Lucas gaped incredulously at me. "I was thinking I'd kiss my boyfriend hello! Why are you acting so weird?"

"You can't just do shit like that!" I fretted, glancing around nervously.

"Why the hell not?" Aggravation was in his eyes now. "You already having second thoughts?"

"No! God, no, but you can't . . ." I didn't even know what I was saying. I sounded crazy. I was crazy. "Someone could see us!"

"Nobody's here!" Lucas snapped. "Nobody's fucking here!"

"There could be . . . There could be cameras," I breathed. Lucas scoffed.

"Right," he said, crossing his arms. "In a locker room."

I knew he was right. I knew I was acting like a freak. But I couldn't control the flood of stress that had crashed over my body when he'd nearly kissed me. This locker room, as obscure as it was, still counted as a public space. Coach Larmon, or a player who'd left a shin guard, or a custodian, could walk through those doors any moment. Maybe there were cameras, displaying the image to a watching eye who would call my parents and share with them the awful news: their perfect son is a fag.

The idea was so incredibly unreasonable, and I knew. I genuinely knew, but it wasn't something I could push away. After so many years of being here and listening to the unkind words so many students and teachers had to offer, this school had become linked in my mind to homophobia and hatred and exclusion. I physically could not stand the idea of getting caught doing anything with Lucas here.

I was freaking out just thinking about it. My breathing wasn't quite under control, and my hands were shaking. I had so much fucking anxiety, and Lucas didn't understand that.

"Can you just back off?" I snapped at him. It made me angry that he didn't understand, because he'd been the one person I thought I could count on to understand.

Lucas' jaw clenched. "Sorry I don't wanna back off after you shoved me away like some kind of freak. That was so unnecessary!"

"You don't get it!" I exclaimed. "You don't get it at all, so you can't say jack-shit!"

Lucas laughed sardonically. "There is literally no way anybody could see us right now! You've got no reason to be acting like this!"

"Maybe you're right!" I was practically yelling now. Maybe it wasn't necessary, but my body didn't seem to know that. I was acting purely on freaked out, stress-driven impulse. "Maybe there is no way! But either way it freaks me the fuck out and you need to respect that!"

"Fine!" He raised his voice to match mine. Then, after a deep breath, he lowered it again."Whatever. But get it into your head that nothing gives you the right to push me around like that. I'm not like all of those girl you played, Jean. I've taken enough shit from other people, I don't need it from you, too."

I couldn't deal with this. I genuinely couldn't. My hands were shaking so violently now, I had to shove them into my pockets. I didn't even want to respond to him when he was like this, when I was like this. I wasn't sure exactly what was wrong with me, but we both knew well enough that I struggled with a lot of crap. Whatever the hell it was, my emotions were just as real as his, even if they made much less sense.

Fed up with the argument, I turned and stormed towards the exit. I was only a foot away from the doors when Lucas called out, "Don't leave." Poorly hidden frustration was still clear in his voice.

Scoffing, I turned around and said, "You scared you'll lose your ride home?"

He rolled his eyes impatiently. "No, I'm scared I lose you, dumbass," he said dryly. "This thing we've got is too new and too good to already crash and burn. We're both just really pissed right now, so how about we just seethe for a bit before we try to figure shit out, okay?"

That was how I ended up driving, as per usual, to Lucas' house that Friday evening. Except the drive was anything but usual. Not a word was uttered the entire time—we were both too damn stubborn to give in and say something. Lucas glared out of his window, his fingers tapping annoyingly on the dashboard until I snapped at him to stop. I didn't like the tension in the air; it was thick and angry and unpleasant.

When we got to Lucas' house, he muttered about needing to clean his room and rushed upstairs, leaving me alone in the living room.

I was calmer now, now that we were out of that locker room and I could breathe properly again. But it wasn't okay. I was still angry. Lucas was still angry.

We'd both been jerks, sure. I hated the way he'd made me feel as if my emotions were stupid. I'd always seen him as the kind to be mindful of others' feelings, even if he didn't fully empathize with them. But he wasn't doing that now, and it hurt like a bitch.

I figured that I'd be sitting there, fuming, for hours. I'd think of all the things he did wrong and ignore my own faults as he did the same up in his room. That was how my arguments usually went, at least.

What I hadn't expected was the sudden sensation of loneliness that overcame me ten minutes in. Being angry with Lucas while he was right there next to me turned out to be way different that being angry with him while he was up in his room, seemingly a world away.

And goddammit, I hated it.

I considered his point of view. I really shouldn't have pushed him like that.

Jesus, this fight was so dumb . . .

And before I knew it, I was taking the stairs two at a time, rushing down the familiar path to Lucas' room to find him and fix things. Right as I raised my fist to knock on the closed door, it swung open.

Lucas jumped a little in surprise at my sudden appearance. "Nate!"

"I'm sorry."

My voice mingled with another, and after a moment, I realized it had been his. We'd spoken the exact same words at the exact same time.

We both opened our mouths to continue, but I was the first to speak. "I shouldn't have overreacted so much," I admitted. "Pushing you was really uncalled for. But there's still so much shit in my head that I can't help but sometimes . . . Freak out."

Lucas nodded. "I understand," he said. Then he backtracked. "Well actually, if I'm honest, I really don't understand, but . . . I'll try. If nothing else, I'll respect how you feel. I know you've got a lot of," he paused. "I don't want to ever invalidate your feelings, and I'm sorry that I did."

I couldn't help but smile, because once again Lucas Morgan had managed to say all of the right things. Just like that, we were okay again. Right then, at the peaceful closing of an argument, it seemed wrong not to kiss him, so that's exactly what I did.

Lucas took my hands as I pulled away, intertwining our fingers together. "This isn't going to be easy," he said gravely. "You and me. It won't even be close. But I really want it to work out, and I'm willing to fight for it."

I nodded. "Effort," I said. "It'll take effort."

He smiled. "I'm down for effort."

He hugged me then, and I returned it in earnest. We stood like that for a while, embracing and thinking to ourselves, and that was all we needed.

Lucas was right. This wasn't going to be easy, not one bit. He was out to the public, I was heavily closeted. He was fully okay with his sexuality, I was still a little fucked in the head. He was so brash and outspoken, I kept my true opinions to myself. He was so open, yet, at the same time so closed off. And as people, we were just so different. We had little in common.

To any outside perspective, we were doomed to fail. Maybe we were. But it would be a goddamn pity if we didn't at least take a shot.

The following Friday, Lucas kept his distance in the locker room. And during the drive home. We drove the same way we had when we were only friends—we talked, and nothing else. But the moment we'd shut his front door, he wrapped his arms around his neck and kissed me hard.

Which, of course, I was not opposed to.

But I was hungry.

"Mh, hold on," I murmured, backing away. "Food first."

Lucas snorted. "And they say romance is dead."

I was already halfway to his kitchen. "Shut up, I'm hungry."

The Morgans always had a shit ton of food at their place—maybe that was why I liked Lucas so much. I shuffled through the fridge and the pantries, pulling out anything that looked even slightly appetizing.

"Jesus," Lucas whistled, his eyes roaming over the pile of food forming on the counter. There were chips, fruits, cookies, salad, and every possible sandwich ingredient I could find. "You look like you're about to host a picnic."

I turned slowly toward Lucas, wide-eyed at his unintended genius. "Great idea!"

"Oh, no." He wagged his finger in instant refusal. "Oh no no no."

"C'mon!" I insisted with a childish pout. "It'll be like a date."

Lucas' expression was as dry and unimpressed as ever. "Outside," he dead-panned. "In the cold."

"It'll be cute," I insisted. Lucas sighed.

"I don't like the cold."

"Yes, but you like me, so it's worth it."

Lucas leaned against the wall with a huff—his way of silently giving in. With a sense of victory, I said, "Awesome. Now where can I find a cute little checkered blanket?"

"I think we have one in—"

"And a picnic basket," I added.

Lucas directed me reluctantly, and when I finally had a cliché, aesthetically pleasing setup together, I dragged him outside. "It's cold," was the first thing he said.

Indeed, it was. A thick layer of snow coated the ground, and a new light snowfall had just begun, slowly adding to it. His backyard was framed on three sides by tall hedges to which snow clung delicately; they made the space feel closed off and private. As cold as it was, it was a lovely sight, and when I added the quaint picnic setup, it only magnified the scene. Even Lucas had a small, hidden smile on his face. "Okay," he conceded as we sat down. "This is cute."

I grinned and wrapped an arm around his shoulder, pulling him into me and offering whatever bodily heat I had to share. We dug into the simple yet delicious assortment of food I'd prepared and chatted about whatever came to our minds. School, TV shows, people we couldn't stand, people we secretly didn't mind so much. States were approaching just this coming weekend, and his Heathers performance the next; there was a lot to be excited for. We talked about how shitty our grades were, how annoying our teachers were, how horny our friends were, how happy we were. Long after the food was gone, we continued talking.

Shawn somehow found his way into the conversation. It was almost sad how quickly Lucas' expression darkened. It was risky, because I knew how he could shut off in an instant, but I couldn't restrain myself. I asked him about it.

And for the first time, he answered.

"We were best friends, you know?" He said quietly, his head resting tenderly on my shoulder. I knew the subject was hard for him, so I offered silent support in every way I could. I held him a bit closer, I intertwined our fingers, I leaned my forehead on the top of his head.

"We were attached at the hip. You couldn't separate us with a crane. For a good year of my life—the time when I was really struggling with my sexuality and . . . other stuff—I liked him a whole lot better than I liked myself. He didn't know what was bothering me, but he never pushed me to tell him. He just supported me however he could. He was my rock. He . . . he stopped me from doing a lot of really dumb things," Lucas' voice broke. I didn't like what he was implying. I didn't ask, though; that was a topic for another time.

"Sometimes I wonder," His voice was bitter now. "What would've happened if I'd told him way back then, before he'd gone and made up his mind; if things would be different. If he'd be on my side. If I'd still have a brother." He shut his eyes tight, and I almost told him to stop. That he didn't need to tell me. But I stayed quiet, resolving instead to rub my hand up and down his arm consolingly. "But obviously I didn't, and I don't. The change was so quick, Nate. And really unexpected. I'd told my parents long before, and they'd supported me. I sort of figured Shawn would do the same. And now . . ."

I realized after several seconds of silence that he wasn't planning on saying more. I wasn't sure how to approach comforting him—I'd never been great with words. I'd never needed to be; I'd never really had to support someone before. The only other close person in my life was my sister, and I was the last person she'd come to for advice.

I realized that I would have to work on that. Relationships needed support. For now, though, I settled for saying, "Let's build a snowman."

Lucas smiled sadly and nodded, pushing himself to his feet and offering me a gloved hand. "Let's."

Here's my confession: despite having lived in Nebraska my entire life, I'd never actually built a snow man. Lucas seemed to realize this pretty quickly, and found my incompetence hilarious.

"You're trying to make a ball, Nate. A ball."

"This is a ball!" I protested, holding up the sad lump of snow I'd made—it was no bigger than the palm of my hand, and it fell apart as soon as I lifted it, sending snow sloshing to the floor. Lucas looked down at the small pile that now decorated the ground, then back up at my now-almost-empty hand, his eyes sparkling with amusement. He was half-laughing, half-smirking.

"Mhm," he nodded sarcastically. "Looking good, champ."

I huffed and threw what remained of my snowman at him. He gasped as it his his face and slid off, leaving snow in his eyelashes and eyebrows, and on his nose.

He narrowed his eyes. "Oh, that's how we're gonna play, is it?" He reached down, grabbing a huge handful of snow that he formed, with alarming speed, into a deadly snowball. I ducked, barely avoiding being smashed in the face, but I leaned too far rightward and screwed up my balance. On the slippery landscape, my feet quickly lost their hold, and I found myself falling ass-first into the snow.

I sat up just in time to see Lucas racing towards me. "You can't hit me while I'm down!" I protested, right as he tackled me, forcing me back into the ground. Then we were tussling, pushing each other around in the snow and getting absolutely filthy in the process. We were laughing, too, like absolute maniacs. For the first time in a long time, I felt again like a child, with no worries about sexuality or college or where I would be in fifty years, who's biggest concern was winning at horseplay.

I eventually gained the upper hand and pinned Lucas down; he gave in, his body relaxing underneath me. We were both panting, our breath forming small clouds in the frosty air, and giggling like the young boys we once knew each other as.

His eyes were bright and excited—so different from the way they'd been minutes ago, when he was talking about his brother. Then he leaned up; I met him in the middle, and we shared the most cliché, most sweet, most awesome snow-kiss of all time.

As you could probably guess, the snowman had to wait a while.

***

Our States competition went well, with our team coming out on top. But then again, we almost always came out on top.

I talked to several scouts after the game, and the more they spoke, the more my heart swelled with the realization that I would make it out of Nowhere, Nebraska. My escape was coming, and it was coming soon.

The best part of States, though? It meant the end of the school soccer season, and therefore the end of my hectic schedule.

The Heathers showcase came the following week, on Thursday, Friday, and Saturday. I found fun in watching Catholic teachers and parents having heart attacks throughout more or less the whole thing as they realized it wasn't exactly a "pure" show. It was impressively good for a high school production, and I was so in love with watching Lucas perform, I went all three nights. His voice was so stunning, it almost made up for the fact that his character was a freaky psychopathic murderer.

After that weekend, Lucas' schedule cleared up, too. He did go to the Theater Company more frequently now that time allowed; instead of just most Saturdays and Sundays, he added Monday and Wednesday to the list. Which just so happened to be the days that I had club practice—we'll pretend that was an entirely unintentional coincidence—so our schedules matched up flawlessly.

In other words, we had a lot more time to spend together.

Mostly, we hung after school at my house, because Lucas' was only really empty on Fridays, whereas I was home alone ninety percent of the time. Shawn was just as much a dick about taking the car and leaving Lucas to walk home post-season as he was during, so he needed the rides one way or another.

We spent our time in different ways. Sometimes, we did homework together—or, more realistically, we procrastinated on doing homework together. Other times, we watched movies, or binged Rick and Morty, or played video games. Sometimes we just talked for hours, sometimes we just did nothing for hours. And sometimes we did . . . other things.

Finally, we had enough time to allow a real relationship. Sure, we were pretty much constricted to our houses, because the idea of going anywhere else legitimately freaked me out. And sure, we sometimes had to compete with unknowing others for time—Lucas had his theater friends, and I got dragged places by the soccer boys, both of which had no knowledge of the relationship they so often interrupted. But we made the best of what we had. For weeks, we followed the same routine, and we were fine with it. Hell, I loved it.

Let's have a chat.

This chapter is kind of important for a couple of reasons. If nothing else, take away this: these characters are not perfect.

I wanna talk about their individual reactions, because I feel like some readers might not quite understand them. Let's start with Lucas, some we don't get his POV at all.

Lucas gets a lot of shit from people. That much you all know. And if you remember, in the first chapter it was mentioned that no one ever hit him, but he did get shoved around quite a bit. People show him their distaste by spitting slurs and pushing and such. So yeah, he doesn't like getting pushed. At all. Especially not by his boyfriend. So he got pissed.

And when it comes to him not really understanding Nate's panic, anybody who deals with mental health issues or has a close friend who does can probably agree that it's not always easy to be understanding. Sometimes you get angry and forget to be considerate. That doesn't mean it's okay, but it happens.

As far as Nate goes, I feel like before I can talk about his reaction I've got to tackle the topic of mental illness. I'm sure some of you wonder about his mental state, but I don't really plan on confirming it in the story, at least not soon. Why? Because the story is in Nate's point of view, and he doesn't even know himself (hence the line "I wasn't sure exactly what was wrong with me", so it wouldn't really make sense. Also, I think a lot of people identify with his character, and for them it might be more beneficial to headcannon his state themselves in order to relate more. I definitely believe he struggles with mental health issues, but whether you think he has anxiety, depression, both, neither, or something else, is more or less up to you.

That said, to anybody confused as to why he freaked this chapter, it's literally a matter that he can't control. He knew he couldn't be caught, but his brain and his body reacted naturally with fear, and that's not something he had any semblance of control over. And that's not gonna go away just because he got an awesome boyfriend. It doesn't work like that.

Still, Nate shouldn't have pushed him. And even though pushing is a pet peeve of Lucas', Lucas should have been more considerate about Nate's feelings. They both screwed up. That's what normal, human people who make normal, human mistakes do.

Alright I'm done lol

13: Nathaniel Jean's New Dream

I came up with the title for this after watching Tangled lmao

Lucas tucked his hand into mine as we entered his house, sighing in relief at the rush of warm air that greeted us.

I'd told him in the car that school had pretty much sucked for me today. The guys were acting all weird around me for some reason, I'd failed a calculus test, and I'd earned myself detention on Saturday for falling asleep in class for the third day in a row. Club practice had drilled me into the ground on Monday and Wednesday, and with my parents home to add unneeded stress to my life, I hadn't been getting enough sleep. In short, I was exhausted. Of course, Lucas said it wasn't my fault, but my teacher thought otherwise.

He'd said he was going to make my day a whole lot better. I didn't know exactly what he meant by that, but I figured he was implying that he always made my day better—which, in fairness, he did.

"I've got something for you," he mused, trying and failing miserably to conceal a smile. I eyed him suspiciously as I hung up my coat—he was up to something.

"Yeah?" I asked, curiosity painted in watercolor across my expression.

"Yeah," he affirmed, re-grabbing my hand. "You wanna see?"

What kind of dumbass question . . .

"Well of course I wanna see!"

He led me upstairs to his room and sat me down on the bed. Then he disappeared into the closet, and I had nothing but the sounds of shuffling to use to guess what he was doing.

Then his form reappeared, holding so much stuff that he looked like he was about to fall over, and I choked on air.

A bouquet of roses. A pink teddy bear. A heart-shaped box of chocolates. Another box of red-sprinkled cookies. And, balanced meticulously on the box of chocolates, a long black box.

I thought back to my seventh period and asked myself what date I'd put on my paper. It couldn't be . . . There was no way . . . I would've remembered.

I recalled my messy handwriting absentmindedly scrawling out 02/14. Today was Valentine's Day.

I looked up at Lucas, who was staring down at me expectantly with his classic smile. "Oh my god," I breathed. "I forgot."

Lucas snorted. "Well I didn't. So?"

His prompting tone hit me like a slap in the face, and I finally realized that he'd bought all of this lovey-dovey shit for me. Me. Flowers, chocolates, a teddy bear . . . For me.

"Fuck," I cursed as I felt myself starting to get emotional. But I couldn't help it—I was a guy that had gone all of his life without getting gifts for events like Christmas or my birthday; unless money counted. No one had ever thought of me that way—as someone to put time and effort and thought into picking things out for. It had become normal for me by now. I didn't expect gifts from anyone; why set expectations for something that you know will just let you down in the end?

And yet here was Lucas, standing before me with a fucking boatload of gifts meant for me, and god I felt like a fucking girl because I was pretty sure I would either scream or burst into tears.

Instead, my voice seemed to lose itself in the twisted maze of everything I was feeling. My brain was a useless pile of hormonal mush. Only my body seemed to work, and I beckoned Lucas forward. He shuffled toward me obediently, still struggling with the mass of objects he was carrying

Then he, ceremoniously as ever, dumped the pile onto me and hopped onto the bed beside me.

In any other situation, I would've laughed. Now, though, I only stared down at what was around me. The first item I encountered was the teddy bear, which had landed quite perfectly on my lap.

It was as tall as my torso, and when I held it, it was soft. I'd only had a teddy bear once in my life, when I was little. Named it Fozzie after my favorite Muppets character. It had been my prized possession, until Jenna was born and my parents decided they would give her mine instead of buying her one of her own. Rich people, it seemed, were always the cheapest when it came to matters of affection.

Jenna had lost Fozzie at a park soon after. I'd cried for two nights straight.

The teddy in my lap brought back fond memories I'd all-but forgotten. My happiest times, when life was pure and simple. I silently named it Fozzie.

Then I looked at the flowers. Red roses. Typical of Valentine's day. I'd always thought flowers were a girl thing, but when I lifted them to my nose, I understood the obsession. There was something so romantic about being given something so fresh and lovely. Sort of symbolic.

"Thank you," I whispered as I took another deep inhale. I could feel Lucas' eyes on me, and wondered to myself if I was weirding him out. After all, he'd only meant to share with me a nice gift, as boyfriends do. And here I was, hardly talking, cuddling a teddy bear and sniffing flowers like a freak.

Then I felt his hand. It started at my lower back and moved upward slowly, then back down, and I knew he knew. That this wasn't just any gift to me, that it meant something. Even if he didn't know exactly what or why, he knew he'd done something more than raid the Valentine's Day section at the supermarket.

I probably could have spent all day cuddling that teddy bear and sniffing those flowers, but I forced myself to put them aside and turn to Lucas. Somehow, thank you wasn't enough. I wanted to communicate to him how much he'd changed my life—not just now, but so many months ago when he'd agreed to be my link. I was so much better with Lucas Morgan, it was uncanny.

Before I could even attempt to speak, however, he held up the long rectangular box. I'd forgotten all about it.

I took it in my hands; it was velvet, soft under my fingers. When I opened it, it revealed a silver band, hung over a thin chain. Words were inscribed across its circumference.

"Before you freak out," Lucas said beside me, "It's not a promise ring or anything. Obviously it's not an engagement ring. And I know you can't wear it around for the world to see—that's what the chain is for. And . . . Yeah."

I could tell by his voice that he was nervous. Maybe he thought I wouldn't like it, or would think it too much. I would've said something to reassure him, but I was once again caught in sweet speechlessness as I stared at the object in front of me. I loved it. Of course I loved it.

It was so pretty. So simple, but so pretty. I slipped the ring portion over my finger, just to see how it would fit when I could wear it out and about. Like a glove. Then I slipped the chain around my neck. It was so light, I feared I would break it. It felt like nothing.

I lifted the ring so that it no longer dangled in midair, turning it over appreciatively in my fingers. The words were in a neat, clear font.

At first, I didn't understand. I looked over the words again and again. I'll be your friend -L.M.

It was a nice saying, but what did it have to do with us? Did my boyfriend just friend-zone me?

And then I gasped softly as a memory I didn't think I had shoved itself to the front of my mind after five years of silence.

I was alone, on the back porch of this very house. I wasn't in the best mood, having been ditched by all the other boys. At the same time, I couldn't blame them. If I were them, I wouldn't want to hang around me either. God, I must have looked like such a loser.

Then approached a tall, skinny boy whom I'd always known but never really known. Lucas Morgan, a kid with skin was so pale he looked anemic. His nearly-black hair was messy and kind of long for a boy's. His eyes were almost too green; I thought they were fake. Colored contacts, maybe.

"You look lonely," he said, which to me seemed like a strange conversation starter. Nevertheless, I laughed, because I could tell just by looking at him that he meant no malice.

"What gave it away? My complete solitude?"

The other boy scrunched his nose playfully. "Nah, just a hunch."

I only hummed in response, and Lucas frowned. "Hey, c'mon, you're at a party! Lighten up a bit, have some fun."

"Oh, they don't want me in there." I blew a strand of my hair—which had been much longer and much blonder back then—out of my face. "I'm no fun."

"I don't believe that," Lucas said. I raised an eyebrow at him.

"Yeah? How would you know? You don't know me."

A determined look crossed the boy's face. "Well then I'll find out."

I snorted. "And how are you gonna do that?"

"I'll be your friend, of course."

"I don't think it's that easy."

Then again, I wouldn't know. I didn't have many friends.

"Oh yeah?" He held out his hand for me to shake. "Well I'm making it that easy. Let's be friends, Nathaniel Jean."

"I'm guessing you remember?" Lucas said in response to my drawn out silence. I turned to look at him, nodding slightly, and he grinned. "Good. It would've been really awkward if you didn't."

"How'd I get so lucky?" I breathed, half to myself, as I looked at the bear and the cookies and the flowers and the chocolates and the ring. Lucas smiled warmly and pressed a kiss to my cheek.

"Happy Valentine's Day."

"Happy Valentine's Day," I said, an unstoppable smile pulling at my lips. "I'm sorry I forgot."

"You know I don't care about that," Lucas said as he wrapped his fingers around the back of my neck, pulling my face toward his. Then, right before our lips touched, in a lower voice, he added, "I do care how you thank me, though."

Safe to say, he was more than satisfied with the way I showed my gratitude.

It was much later that night, after we'd somehow managed to go through all of the chocolates and cookies, that I found myself thinking about the future.

I was hovering over Lucas, who lay with one arm crossed behind his head and the other folded comfortably over his chest. I was kissing him, and he was half-responding, half-relaxing underneath me. I'd realized early on in our relationship that he loved it this way, though he never verbally admitted it. To just lay there and be kissed. To simply receive the affection that was often lacking in his day-to-day.

Things were actually serious between the two of us, I realized. This wasn't something either of us had dealt with before. We knew flings, not relation-ships. We could really go somewhere. Lucas had said that the ring didn't mean anything today, but who knew what could happen? Maybe in a few years there would be a ring that did mean something.

The thought gave me shivers. I'd never even considered commitment be-fore Lucas, and now I was thinking of marriage?

It wasn't unpleasant, though; nor was it scary. It was actually really, really exciting.

I felt Lucas smiling against my lips. Curious, I pulled away, and watched his too-green eyes flutter open. "What?" I asked. "Why are you smiling?"

Lucas shrugged. "Because you make me happy."

It was 6:40 PM the following Wednesday when my phone started buzzing on my bed. I'd been halfway through getting ready for soccer practice when it rang, and I may or may not have fallen onto my ass while attempting to answer the call and pull on my sock at the same time.

"Hello?" I greeted to whoever it was that had decided to call me. I never checked caller IDs—for no good reason besides my own laziness—and this was no different. That said, you can probably understand my surprise when I was met with loud-ass sobbing from the other line. "Uh . . . Hello?"

I figured now would probably be a good time to check who was crying incessantly in my ear. It was when I looked at my phone screen and saw the name Lucas M displayed that I grew alarmed.

"Lucas? What's wrong?"

But he just kept crying. I heard my name in between the sobs at one point, but that was all.

Worry flared up in my gut. "Are you okay? What happened?"

Had someone hurt him? Was it Shawn? Did something happen to a family member? What if it was something urgent?

Whatever the case, I was already on my feet. "I'll be right over," I promised. I managed to make out a few subtle, tear-muffled protests from Lucas, but I was already pulling a hoodie over my soccer uniform. Then my phone, at the worst time possible, died.

I moved as if I was on a quickly waning time limit. Ignoring the fact that I had one sock on and one only pulled half-up, revealing my shin guard underneath, I slipped on a pair of slides and hurried out of the house, taking the steps three at a time. The cold bit at me as soon as I was outside, reminding me that this hoodie was certainly not substantial for Nebraska's winter weather, but I hardly noticed.

Speeding was not something I did often—Sheriff Patberry was always more than happy to ticket us "rambunctious teens"—but I found myself surpassing the limit by fifteen, maybe twenty, as I hurried to Lucas' house. Maybe I was overreacting. Maybe there was nothing too serious going on. But all I knew in that moment was that my boy sounded upset, and that didn't sit well with me at all.

Lucas' garage was open, and within it I saw a sleek black Cadillac and a BMW SUV. Lucas' parents' cars. Shawn's was, thankfully, nowhere in sight—he must have already left for practice.

I hesitated for a moment. The Morgans were home. If I rushed in there worrying over Lucas, it would raise a question.

Then again, the Morgans were among the few people in this town who'd supported Lucas since the moment he told them he was gay. I was nowhere near ready to come out, but if anybody were to know, I supposed they weren't the worst option.

Then again again, I was friends with the boys who gave Lucas hell. His parents probably maybe wouldn't want me dating their son.

Maybe they'd be okay with it . . . ?

With this half-comforting thought, I stepped out of the car.

I hesitated again as I stood in front of the door. This was suddenly a lot scarier. I definitely wasn't ready, even if they were good people. They weren't the problem; it was the stress and anxiety that came with the idea of anyone knowing, having the power to do with the information as they desire.

But Lucas had sounded really upset. I knocked on the door.

It took a minute, but soon the dark wood swung ajar to reveal the face of Elena Morgan.

She was the mirror—though obviously more feminine—image of Lucas. The same thick, nearly black hair; the same pale skin, though hers had a more olive undertone; the same dimpled smile; and the same height. Yup—Elena Morgan stood at about six foot one.

She didn't hide her surprise to see me. "Nathaniel?" She smiled politely, but I could already see her less-than-positive opinion of me displayed in her eyes. I'd never noticed the slight accent in her voice until recently, now that I knew she was Romanian. "Shawn's not here, honey. He just left."

"Oh I'm not here for Shawn," I told her. "Is Lucas around?"

The change in her demeanor was instant. Her eyes narrowed, ever so slightly, and her entire form seemed to tense protectively. "Yes," she answered honestly. "But he doesn't need any trouble right now, alright? Come back some other time. Or don't."

She began to push the door shut, but I held out a hand to stop it. "Ma'am, you've got me all wrong," I said. "I'm not here for trouble. Your son, he called me. He was crying. I'm just here to see if he's okay."

Elena eyed me suspiciously. "My son called you," she said disbelievingly.

I nodded. "Yes, ma'am. We're . . . Friends."

She stared at me for a moment, and I realized she even shared Lucas' unnerving, analyzing, soul-reading gaze. Then her eyes rounded, just a tad, and her mouth formed an 'o' shape. "You're his friend," she repeated.

"Yes," I nodded quickly. "Close friend. Can I . . ."

"Of course," she stepped aside to allow me in. As I passed her, I noticed her slight smile; the left end of her lips lifted just beyond her right. Just like Lucas'. "Lucas! Nathaniel Jean is here to see you!" Then she turned to me. "Come on, hun. We'll meet him halfway."

She led me into the living room where I'd spent so many days alone with her son, unbeknownst by her. "By the way, he's fine."

Fine? Then why was he . . .

Lucas appeared at the entrance of the room, disrupting my thoughts entirely. He had definitely been crying. He still was. His eyes and cheeks were red and wet with tears. But he was smiling like a madman. A piece of paper was clutched in his hand.

"Lucas, what's wrong?" I asked, worried all over again. Instead of answering, he all-but ran forward, wordlessly shoving the paper into my chest and watching me expectantly as I read it.

I think I might have screamed.

Okay, I definitely screamed.

I must have squeezed the life out of poor Lucas, but he hugged me back just as fiercely. I swung him around in a circle, unable to contain my ecstasy for him, because my boyfriend had just been accepted into Juilliard.

I wasn't sure how long we stood like that, hugging and screaming and giggling like little kids, but I probably could have gone on for days. Words couldn't describe the immense pride I felt for Lucas in that moment, unrivaled by any I'd felt before.

"Oh my god," I breathed as we settled down; our grips had eased and the jumping and spinning had come to an end, though we still rocked from foot to foot in each other's arms. "I fucking knew it," I said. "I knew you would. I never had a doubt."

I'd never seen Lucas' face so bright. He was absolutely beaming, probably the happiest he'd been in his life. This was what he'd been training for, this was the start of his dream.

He sighed into my shoulder. I could feel my shirt growing wet, but now I knew that he was crying tears of joy, not despair.

"Nate, I don't wanna alarm you." His voice was a whisper that only I could hear. "But my parents are right there."

I glanced over Lucas' shoulder. Bruce Morgan, his father, must have been there the entire time, sat comfortably on the couch. Elena had joined him, and they were both blatantly staring at us.

Nervous energy seared my skin. "I know."

I wasn't sure why I did it. Maybe I was too high on happiness and nerves to think properly. Maybe it was some sort of unspoken message, aiming to show Lucas that I wanted to be with him and wasn't ashamed of it. Maybe I just really wanted to kiss him.

Whatever the case, I took that blissful moment to lift Lucas' chin, though admittedly with shaking hands, and bring his lips to mine, right in front of his parents.

It was quick, of course—I wasn't about to leave an indecent impression on the Morgans. When I pulled away, Lucas' expression was a lovely blend of awed surprise and Do you know what the hell you just did?

"Nate," he whispered. "What did you do?"

I let out a shaky, uneven breath. "Something very unlike me," I muttered, focusing on Lucas' face because I was pretty sure I would shatter like glass if I looked at his parents.

This wasn't about me, though. This was Lucas' moment. The focus should be on his accomplishments, not my . . . whatever the hell you'd call this.

"You're gonna be off to New York pretty soon, huh?" Was my not-so-subtle subject switch. Lucas smiled, apparently deciding to go with the change.

"Yup," he said, popping the 'p'. He wrapped his arms loosely around my neck. "And you'll be right up there with me, right?"

I returned his grin in earnest. "Wouldn't miss it—even if I fail to get into every NYC school in existence."

"Which you won't."

I realized then that my lifetime aspiration, which I'd held onto for so many years now, was quickly shifting. The destination was the same: New York City. But the picture was different, and momentously so, because now I didn't imagine myself fleeing to The Big Apple on my own. I didn't have to make my escape alone. My new dream included Lucas, and it was crazy to me how big a difference the seemingly small change made.

"Okay, hold on for a second."

The voice wasn't mine, nor was it Lucas'. It was much deeper, and held a very confused tone. "Am I missing something?"

I turned, half-terrified, to face Bruce Morgan.

"Sir, I . . ."

"Fucking finally," Elena muttered, effectively cutting me off. "I thought he'd never get a boyfriend."

"Mom!" Lucas whined. Elena grinned at him, blowing a cheeky kiss.

Bruce still looked wary. "You sure you're good news, Jean?"

I swallowed nervously. Bruce Morgan was a huge man, tall and bulky with muscle. He may not have been trying to intimidate me, but he sure as hell was. I finally understood the stigma around 'meeting the parents'. This was horrifying.

"I try to be," I told him, hoping he couldn't tell how much I was inwardly quivering under his gaze. I regretted the words as soon as they'd left my mouth. I should have said something more reassuring—a simple 'yes' would have sufficed. I'm such an idiot. Fuck, I'm gonna die.

Bruce crossed his arms sternly. "I know your type. I don't trust you."

"Dad," Lucas groaned.

I thought I might piss myself right there, but then Elena smacked Bruce's arm lightly and rolled her eyes. "Oh, stop it Bruce. The poor boy looks like he's seen a ghost."

Lucas snickered behind me. I couldn't understand what on Earth was even mildly amusing, until Bruce's lips twitched and I noticed for the first time that he was holding back a smile.

I had no idea what the hell was happening. So I, ever so intelligently, said, "Huh?"

Bruce gave up on suppressing his grin and chuckled, standing up from his seat on the couch. Despite his much friendlier expression, I had to command my feet not to step backward as he approached.

When he held out his hand to me, it took me a moment too long to realize that I was supposed to shake it. He laughed again; the sound was deep and hearty and genuine. "Lighten up, son. I'm just messing around."

I blinked, then glanced back at Lucas, who was still snickering behind me. Bruce's grip was firm but not tight. "Yes, Sir. I mean . . . Okay."

Bruce's eyes twinkled with amusement. "You're not gonna hurt my boy, right? He's dealt with enough shit as it is."

"O-of course not."

He smiled. "Great then. I'll spare you the rest of the dad talk—at least for now. As of this moment, I welcome you into the family."

And that was that. The Morgans invited me to stay for dinner—I figured this was worth dealing with the repercussions of missing practice—and any tension dissolved quickly. My nerves dissipated, because they were just too damn nice and funny and genuine to be nervous around.

They, despite who I was and who they'd known me to be, accepted me into their home just like that. Maybe they didn't quite trust me now, but they were willing to keep that to themselves and try.

They were the polar opposite of my family. And holy shit, I loved it.

I got to spend the next two hours laughing with my boyfriend and his parents, celebrating his success, feeling like I was finally becoming a part of something wholesome. I forgot about the fact that I'd just faced one of my biggest fears and come out to near strangers. I forgot about my fucked up family, and my shitty grades, and the fact that my 'friends' had been acting really, really weird around me lately.

None of that mattered right now, because my mind was occupied with better, prettier, more important things.

14: Nathaniel Jean's Friends

The guys were acting weird.

Like, really weird.

They weren't being mean, exactly. "Distant" was a better word. Every time I was around them, I got the feeling that they knew something I didn't. Something that involved me. And as the days passed, their behavior grew stranger and stranger, until I felt like an alien among my own "friends".

It wasn't that I was particularly sad about their newfound exclusion. It didn't bother me that they kept hanging out without me, or turning their backs to me at lunch. I'd much rather spend my time with Lucas and his family anyways. What bothered me was the underlying threat that came with these actions.

Their opinions of me weren't exactly on the top of my "important things" list, but I feared I would soon be friendless if things continued as they were. Without those guys, I was nothing, and I couldn't afford to be so defenseless. If they were upset at me over something—if they tossed me aside, told everyone whatever it was I'd done—I'd be an outcast before I could even try to salvage my reputation. I wasn't sure I could handle that.

But what was I supposed to do about it? They weren't exactly the type of guys to have a nice heart-to-heart.

Thankfully, I didn't have to do anything at all. After two weeks, when I was nearly positive I'd be at the bottom of the school's social ladder within another, they came to me.

I was walking with Lucas to my car when Damien and Cameron called me from behind. I knew before I turned what was coming. This was more or less the first real attempt they'd made to talk to me in a fortnight, so the chances of them wanting a casual conversation were less than likely. It was time for confrontation.

I told Lucas I'd meet him in the car and joined them wordlessly. They didn't bother to hide their glares as they led me all the way behind the school to the football field. There, Shawn was already waiting with Trevor and Tyler.

"What kind of cult shit is this?" I muttered as I approached the boys, who all stood with their arms crossed.

"Shut it, Jean," Tyler snapped. I had to hold back a snort at this little mini-man trying to puff out his chest and intimidate me.

"Shutting it," I said; I failed to suppress my snicker, and Tyler took a step forward.

"Something funny?"

"Not at all," I said with a smirk. "But seriously, was it necessary to drag me out here and stand around me in a circle like we're about the perform some kind of satanic ritual?"

"I said shut it," Tyler growled, reminding me of an overexcited chihuahua.

I put my hands up in mock surrender. "This is just really extra is all I'm saying."

He looked about ready to fight me, which I found both funny and somewhat disappointing. Funny because I'd squash him like a moth. Disappointing because he had, not long ago, called himself my friend, and now he was trying to square up with me. Things had changed so drastically, and I still had no idea why.

I rolled my eyes in annoyance at the whole situation. "This is dumb as fuck, guys. Just tell me what the hell's had your dicks up your asses for the last couple weeks."

"You really wanna say shit about dicks up asses?" Cameron said with a snort, his eyes narrowed accusingly.

The tone of his voice, the snickers from the other boys—they said everything. I quickly caught his drift, and what he was implying had me paling. A nervous stone settled at the bottom of my stomach, and I prayed that this wasn't about what I had a feeling—a horrible feeling—it was about. "The hell are you talking about?" I asked, trying hard to hide the hesitation in my voice.

"You know damn well what we're talking about," The worse of the Morgans snapped. I did. I knew exactly what they were talking about. Deep down, I think I'd figured this would come eventually, all the while telling myself that it wouldn't. That didn't prepare me at all for the monsoon of nausea that accompanied it now that it was happening, though. I felt like throwing up before Shawn even continued.

"You think we weren't gonna notice the fact that you're butt-buddies with my brother?" As my heart sank and fear rose in its place, I opened my mouth to protest, but he cut me off quickly. "You take him home every day. You're always looking at him in the hallways. And did you seriously believe I wouldn't realize one way or another that you spend half your time at my house—when I'm not there?"

My heart began racing from the pit of my stomach. This was really it. This was what I'd spent so many years trying to avoid. "I'm not a fag, Shawn," I rebutted instinctively. "Is that really what this shit's about?"

"How are we supposed to believe that?" Damien snarled. "You're at his house, Jean!"

"We have a project," I lied swiftly. "Am I supposed to just fail History because he's gay? You guys are so quick to assume absolute bullshit!" I was talking without thinking now. Anything to dig myself out of this hole.

Shawn shook his head disbelievingly. "You're gonna have to try harder than that," he said. "We sure as hell aren't gonna be walking around with a fairy in our ranks. You want us to believe you're not a faggot, you've gotta prove i t."

"I don't have to prove anything to you," I snapped. My voice was confident, but I'd long since hidden shaking hands in my pockets. My brain was hot-wired and short-circuiting. Despite the lingering late winter chill, the air around me felt too hot.

Shawn smirked maliciously. "You're right," he shrugged. "You don't. But remember this: whatever we know about you, everyone knows about you."

With those words, my lungs just about closed up. Shawn didn't know it, but he'd just threatened my entire future.

"I'm not gay," I said slowly, trying to even my breathing. "And you're all assholes for thinking I am. But if you need me to prove shit to appease your petty little heads, I'll prove shit."

A satisfied smile spread throughout the group. "Good," Shawn said. "See you later, then."

"Hm," I forced a smile. "Fuck you," I said, my voice sickly sweet, as I turned around and left them there, still grinning like the bunch of tools they were.

Once I was out of their field of vision, I practically collapsed against the school's brick walls. My hand instinctively went to my shirt, under which I could feel the outline of the ring Lucas had given me. My fingers gripped it tightly through the material, hoping to draw some sort of comfort from the familiar item.

Terror—genuine terror—flooded through my veins. If I couldn't convince them that I was something I wasn't, they would start rumors. And at that point, I'd be helpless to their attack. Their word would dominate mine. And it would spread, infecting first the students, then the faculty, and eventually, the whole town. It would find my parents. I had no doubt in my mind that they would cease to support me, if not disown me entirely. My savings wouldn't be enough to get me anywhere.

And so I'd end up stuck, an outcast in my town, for the rest of my life. The stress would lead me to be a horrible boyfriend to Lucas, and we'd quickly near our end. He would find his way to New York and make it big, alone. After some years, I'd see pictures of him and his groom—some handsome, clean-cut fellow with a theater degree, who was never afraid to show his affection—smiling in front of the Statue of Liberty.

That wasn't an option. I had to prove it to them somehow.

I couldn't breathe. My whole body was shaking, my forehead was beaded with sweat. My fingers clutched my ring too tightly through my shirt, my knuckles turning white. I sat there for a long time, leaning my head against the wall and imagining the worst, suspending myself further and further into panic.

When I finally recovered enough to stand, I was shaky on my feet. Nonetheless, I forced myself all the way back to the parking lot. My heart sank impossibly lower when I spotted Lucas still there, leaning against my car.

His eyes widened in alarm when he saw my distressed expression. "Is everything okay?"

I shook my head. "No," I said, my chest still rising and falling rapidly. "No, it's not okay." I glanced around. I saw no sign of Shawn or Damien or any of them. Nevertheless, my anxiety spoke much louder than my bravery, translating itself into the words, "Do you think you could, uh, walk today?"

He blinked in surprise. "Like, home?" I nodded. He pursed his lips, staring into my eyes and trying to figure out what was going on in my mind.

"Could you not analyze me like a cell under a microscope for once?"

I instantly felt bad for snapping. I wasn't mad at Lucas in the slightest. I was just so wound up and stressed, it seemed like the natural response.

I think he knew I hadn't meant any foul, because he nodded. "Sorry. Yeah, I can walk. Can I come over later?"

The answer would usually be a 'yes' without hesitation. Even now, I knew his company would probably ease me. But in that moment, the idea of spending my evening with him was strangely sickening, and I found myself shaking my head. "Not today, alright? We can . . . Tomorrow."

Lucas looked beyond concerned, but he didn't pry. Instead, he nodded again. "I've got theater tomorrow. And you have practice. Thursday?"

"Thursday," I agreed. The word left a bad taste in my mouth.

I had no appetite when I got home. My mouth was dry, but I felt sick every time I drank water. When I tried to focus on homework, desperate for a distraction, my mind refused to go anywhere other than where I didn't want it to go. I didn't read or write a single word. I had a headache. My stomach hurt. No matter how high I turned the AC, the house felt hot and clammy.

I didn't get a wink of sleep that night. I didn't even try. I stared for hours at my blank ceiling, telling myself over and over that everything would be okay, realizing over and over that it wouldn't. The mere thought of Shawn or Damien or Trevor or Tyler or Cameron or even Lucas made my stomach lurch to my throat.

I wanted to cry, but I didn't want to feel weak. I wanted to scream, but I didn't want to wake Jenna. I wanted to punch Shawn, or the wall, or myself.

In the end, I settled for sitting upright, hugging a pillow as tightly as I could to my chest and trying to cease my body's trembling. I counted my breaths, both for a distraction and to ensure that I still was breathing.

I couldn't even look at Lucas the next day at school.

I averted my gaze in the hallways. When Damien and Shawn stopped to p ick on him, I looked away and feigned a snicker. And when the day was ov er, I rushed home before he had even stepped into the parking lot.

I felt horrible for ditching him afterwards, but I knew I couldn't handle giv ing him a ride. Not after yesterday. There was so much pent up frustration in my head, I felt as though my brain would burst at the mere sight of him. When he texted me, I didn't open it. When he called, I let the phone ring.

It was unfair, I knew. My misfortune wasn't his fault. I didn't blame him, ye t I couldn't help but avoid him.

Thursday was just a repeat of Wednesday. The guys were talking to me now, at least, but it was obvious in their demeanor that they still had their suspicions. I didn't know what I could do to make them think otherwise wi thout being an even shittier boyfriend to Lucas.

When my doorbell rang that afternoon, I felt every inch of my body tense. I 'd been pacing the living room for the past thirty minutes, trying to prepare m yself for Lucas' arrival. Here he was now, just beyond the door, and I wa sn't ready.

Nevertheless, I forced myself to approach and open the door—he deserved t hat much after the way I'd been acting. When I did, his expression was no ne-too-pleasant.

"Nate what the fuck?" Were his first words. I stepped aside so he could e nter and searched my brain for the explanation I'd spent the last two days p lanning. Now that he was here, the words seemed to have simply vanished.

I silently followed him into the living room. When I sat on the couch, he re mained standing, staring down at me expectantly as I struggled to form a s uitable sentence.

He sighed. "I mean really, Nate. I don't want to be all clingy-boyfriend, bu t really. You won't answer—won't even look at me. What happened on Tu esday?"

Despite the aggravation clear in his voice, there was also obvious concern, which only worked to make me feel worse. I forced myself to meet his eyes a nd suppressed a shudder at the fact that he was, right now, linked to the p ossibility of my biggest fear becoming a harsh reality.

"I'm sorry," I muttered, running a hand through my hair. "They . . . they t hink they know, Lucas. They have an idea about us, and it's freaking me t he hell out."

Lucas's shoulders sank and he pinched the bridge of his nose. "That's why Shawn's been weird," he grumbled. "Weirder than normal, at least. God, Nate."

He sat down next to me, now seeming to sag under the same weight that was holding me down. It was silent for a moment. Then, his eyes trained on the blank TV in front of us, he said, "What does this mean?"

"For us?"

He nodded. "Yeah."

I sighed. "I don't know. I mean, we're not, like, breaking up or anything. So if you're thinking that, stop it." His lips quirked up ever-so-slightly, and he bowed his head in a breathy chuckle.

"You read my mind, Jean."

The fact that I'd been distant enough to lead him to believe that I wanted t o end things succeeded in making me feel a whole lot shittier. "I'm sorry f or being a prick. I'm just—god, I'm really freaking out. I don't know wh at to do. If I can't convince them—"

"You will," Lucas affirmed, sounding much more confident than I ever c ould at a time like this. He turned his head to face me. "I can walk home. An ytime we hang, we'll do it here, and I'll make sure Shawn doesn't see me le ave. I won't text you when I think they might see. I won't even look at you. It'll all work out. We'll be fine."

I groaned aloud. Everything he was saying was what I wanted, but I hated tha t I wanted it, and I hated that he was so willing to comply. "That's so fucke d up," I breathed. He was the living, breathing embodiment of "too good f or me".

Lucas shrugged. "I wanna help you be okay. If we have to up the hiding a l ittle more, so be it. I can handle that."

"I don't deserve you," I said, putting my head in my hands. I was recoiling far ther and farther into the closet, and I was pulling him with me. It was so w rong.

"Hey," Lucas said, his tone light. He wrapped an arm around my shoulders. "No one does, so don't feel bad."

I chuckled and leaned forward to connect our lips, hoping I could convey my gratitude with a kiss. Though he was joking, I was fairly certain that he was right. Not a single being on this Earth deserved him. "I'm sorry," I said, my v oice weak and hardly audible.

"It's okay."

It wasn't fun, but we made it work. We became even more of a secret—a notion that I hadn't thought possible. At least it succeeded in making the b oys back off—they seemed to believe me now.

Lucas was right; we were fine.

Until, after one week of normalcy, they started being weird again. This time, it was an entirely different kind of weird.

Suddenly, they had plans every single day. Tuesday, they wanted to go hang at Damien's. Thursday, it was Tyler's. Friday, Cameron drove us to the mall. Saturday, Trevor held an "end of the third quarter" party, which had to be the most bullshit reason to throw a party I'd ever heard. If it hadn't been obvious before, that event made it clear to me that they were doing this on purpose. They still didn't fully trust what I'd said. What they thought they'd get from taking up every bit of my spare time, I couldn't figure out.

Every time I had to text Lucas saying, no, I can't tonight, one of my nerves se emed to snap. It didn't help that I could practically feel Lucas' annoyance thr ough the phone, even if it wasn't directed at me.

The one time I tried to weasel my way out of their plans went a little like t his:

"Actually, guys, I've got a shit ton of missing work, and if I don't do it t onight my parents are gonna see my report card and castrate me."

"What does castrate mean?" Damien had asked.

Tyler had raised an eyebrow. "I call bullshit," he'd said as Cameron tried to e xplain castration to Damien. "You don't give a shit about grades."

I'd rolled my eyes. "Yeah, but I care about my balls, so . . ."

"Or," Shawn had prompted, shoving his hands into his pockets. "You care about running away with a certain someone, maybe?" The other boys had snickered. "You feeling deprived already?"

Arms crossed over my chest, I'd said, "Aren't we past this by now? Really, dude, I just wanna do my homework."

Shawn had shrugged infuriatingly then, a smirk present on his face. "Do what you want, and we'll think what we want. Deal?"

I'd glared daggers at him. "You guys are actual assholes, you know that?"

Again, Shawn shrugged. "See you tonight, Nate."

I didn't see Lucas until Sunday that week, and for a small window of time s ince he had to get to NNTC soon.

As we lounged on the couch, Lucas with his head against my chest, I'd apologized profusely. "I swear I tried, Lucas. They wouldn't give me a br eak. They're so fucking annoying. You know I'd rather spend that time wi th you, right? Any day. And I wish I could, they're just . . . I'm sorry. I'm being such a shit boyfriend, but I don't know what else to do."

Lucas had stopped my blabbering with a brief yet effective kiss. "I get it, N ate. It's not your fault. If this is what it takes, I can deal with it. We're here no w, and that what matters, right?"

I sighed, my fingers curling absentmindedly in his hair. "Yeah, but I hate th at you just have to sit here and take it. I'm sorry," I said again. Lucas kis sed my cheek.

"It's okay."

The next week—Spring Break—was twice as bad. Every damn day there was a different party to go to or house to hang at or drill to practice or place to eat at. I didn't see my boyfriend a single time over the course of the b reak, or over the following week. We might as well have been a long-distance r elationship, because we only ever talked over text and FaceTime. I was ab out ready to accidentally push Shawn, Cameron, Tyler, Trevor, and Da mien off of a bridge.

I would love to ignore them, if it wasn't for the fact—which they made p retty clear—that if I didn't obey their beckon fucking call, their rumor wo uld spread like a wildfire on a hot California day.

When Lucas was finally able to come over on Saturday night, he didn't look happy.

"I'm sorry I've been so busy," was the first thing I said when I saw his sour ex pression. However, he shook his head.

"That's not it," he said.

I blinked, confused. "Then what is?"

He didn't say another word until we were up in my room. When I joined h im on my bed, he held his phone out to me, revealing a picture on Trevor's s pam from one of the Spring Break parties, and I cringed.

The picture was of Trevor, shirtless and posing like a fuckboy. Next to him, however, was me, dancing a little too closely with Madeleine Montgomery.

"That was . . ." I trailed awkwardly. "Well, it was what it looks like, but not b ecause . . ."

Lucas raised an eyebrow.

"I was pretty pissy all night," I explained, figuring he could guess why. "T he guys tried to get me to lighten up, I guess. They told me to go dance wit h Madeleine—she likes me or something—and when I told them I didn' t feel like it . . . Well, you can probably guess what they said."

The story was all true. I hadn't wanted to be at the goddamn party in the first place, and they'd more or less blackmailed me into dancing with M adeleine.

Lucas nodded, but I could still see annoyance in his gaze. "I didn't enjoy it ," I added. "Obviously. First of all, she's a girl, and second of all, she's not you. But I had to."

Lucas shrugged. "You gotta do what you gotta do, right?"

I nodded solemnly. "Unfortunately. Can I make it up to you?"

Finally, he smiled. His arms went around my shoulders, pulling me closer, and I kissed him softly. "You sure can," he mumbled against my lips. I tried to ignore the guilt I felt at how forgiving he always seemed to be.

When his hands found the hem of my shirt, I pulled back just enough to s ay, "I really am sorry, you know."

"I know," he said. "It's okay." Something seemed off in his voice, but I told myself to ignore it. I was just being paranoid.

As I approached my car after club practice on Monday evening, I heard a scurry of footsteps approaching and turned to see Trevor hurrying to catch up with me.

"What's up?" I asked as he placed a hand on my shoulder. He grinned.

"You know you're my best pal, right?" He said. I internally rolled my eyes—sure I was, when he didn't want something from me.

"Right," I affirmed with a nod.

"And you know I believe you when you say you're not a fag, right?"

My teeth clenched. Just for saying that, I wanted to shove him face-first into the asphalt. "Right," I repeated, albeit more tersely.

"Awesome," he said. "Well, issue is, the other guys aren't so sure."

I huffed. Of course they weren't.

"And they want you to . . . Prove it."

"I've already proven it," I growled. Trevor held up his hands defensively.

"Hey, don't shoot the messenger. It's just that we—they—think it would be a lot more convincing if you weren't so scared of bitching at the fairy every now and then."

"We've gone over this," I said. "Many times. I'm what some people call mature, and I don't see the need to waste my time picking on people in the hallways."

I caught Trevor's eyes narrow the slightest bit. "Right," he said, his voice as chirpy as ever. "And I totally get what you mean. But Shawn says he won't re

ally believe you're not into Lucas until you directly show that you don't li
ke him anymore than the rest of us."

"And why couldn't Shawn tell me this himself?"

Trevor shrugged. "He thought I should do it since you and I are closer or
whatever."

We'd reached my car. "Cool," I said as I opened the door and climbed in, s
hutting it loudly in his face. Without another word, I backed out and left Tr
evor standing there.

I tried to ignore the sweat on my palms, the fact that my fists were gripping t
he steering wheel too tight. I wasn't worried. I was fine. Why wouldn't I b
e? Trevor was clearly bluffing. If Shawn cared, he would have told me hims
elf. I wasn't stressed. I was fine. I wasn't going to start picking on Lucas like
the rest of them—the idea was ridiculous. I wasn't anxious. I was fine.

I was fine. Absolutely fine.

I wasn't tired. That's why I didn't sleep that night. Not because I was up
set or scared or anything like that. Why would I be? I was fine.

Are you guys anxious yet???

15: Nathaniel Jean's Wishes

Tuesday, I continued my days as I had been for weeks. I kept my head down as Lucas passed, and when my friends decided to bother him, I turned a blind eye. Wednesday, too.

Thursday morning, I walked to class with Shawn as per usual, pretending to listen to him talk about his night out with Celia Looslie.

Of course, my mind was elsewhere. Specifically, I was thinking about the fact that, as of now, I was free this evening, which meant Lucas could come over.

"Where's your head right now, Jean?"

I blinked, shaking away my distraction, and hurried to find an adequate straight-guy response. "Madeleine Montgomery, that's where," I said, flashing Shawn a smirk. He grinned.

"No better place to be, man," he laughed. "But seriously, did you hear anything I just said?"

Now that I was out of danger, I figured honesty would do no harm and sh ook my head. "Nah, what'd you say?"

"I asked if Trevor talked to you."

Hoping that he wasn't referring to what I thought he was referring to, I sa id, "Dude, Trevor talks to me all the time."

Shawn rolled his eyes. "Yeah, but I mean on Monday. After practice. I as ked him to talk to you. Did he?"

Dammit. "Uh, yeah."

"And?"

"And I think it's pretty dumb that you want me to be a jackass just to prove t o you for the hundredth time that I'm straight—which, might I remind y ou, I shouldn't even have to prove in the first place."

Shawn shrugged. "If you don't like him, why is it an issue?"

"How about because I'm a good person?"

Shawn snorted. "Yeah, right, Jean. If you're a good person, I'm a good person. You gonna do it or what?"

The fact that my morality was just compared to Shawn's made me want to throw up. Not as much as the underlying threat in his voice did, though. "Dude, no," I said. "I'm not like that."

Shawn sighed. "I'm trying to be nice here, dude. Let's try this again. Stop being a pussy and prove that you're a fucking man, or I let everyone know y ou aren't. Kay?"

An anvil plummeted in my stomach. "Why are you still doing this?" I g roaned tiredly.

"Just to be sure," he said simply. Then he nodded his head. "Look who it is. Perfect timing."

Only a few steps ahead, putting some books in his locker, was Lucas. I clenched my jaw. "Cut it out, Shawn," I grumbled.

"Might wanna start taking me seriously right about now," he said offhandedly. He stopped walking as we reached the spot where Lucas stood. Said boy didn't even turn to look at us.

That is, until Shawn "accidentally" knocked the books out of his hands, sending them tumbling to the floor, like a classic bully.

Lucas huffed and turned to Shawn with an annoyed eye roll. "Really, Shawn? Could that have been any more typical?"

Shawn, however, wasn't looking at Lucas. He was looking at me, and I could tell from his gaze that he really was serious. I do this now, or I deal with the consequences.

"Pick them up, fag," I said, flinching at my own word choice. Of all words, I picked that one.

Lucas turned to look at me, his eyebrows raised like seriously? I could only hope that he could read the apology in my eyes as I continued. "What? Don't act like bending over isn't something you're used to. Pick them up."

Shawn laughed as I inwardly cringed. To both my surprise and his, Lucas actually listened. Without a word of retaliation, he bent over and gathered the books in his arms, smiling gingerly all the while. That was how I knew he was mad.

He shoved the books into his locker, flipped Shawn and I the bird, and walked around us to get to class.

Shawn clapped me on the back. "Nicely done, Jean. You might convince me yet."

I forced a grin and concentrated on telling my feet to continue forward i nstead of turning to run after Lucas. I wished Shawn would leave, so I cou ld at least just shut my eyes and hate myself for a good minute or two wit hout his interruption.

I could never forget the look in Lucas' eyes as he held up the books, a big f ake smile on his face. There was a line, and I'd just crossed it. I'd obliterated it .

I spent the rest of the day with a dry, awful taste in my mouth. More often t han not, I found myself clammy and nervous. As soon as school was over an d I was out in the parking lot, away from the boys who I could just abou t kill at this point, I called Lucas. Luckily, he answered.

"Lucas I am so sorry about earlier, I had t—"

"Can we not talk about this right now?" Came his voice. I could hear his a gitation in every word.

"Yeah, sure," I said, afraid of pushing him. My heart was beating u ncomfortably in my chest. "You still coming over later?"

"I'll be there."

"Lucas, you've gotta believe me when I say—"

"Later, Nate."

I swallowed the lump in my throat as he hung up.

"Hey," I breathed when he showed up at my door after six that night. He s miled, though it looked forced, and returned the greeting.

We walked in awkward silence to my room. My apology was on the tip of my tongue, but when we sat on my bed, Lucas spoke before I could.

"You were different," he said, not meeting my eyes. "That's why I liked you. A t the beginning of the year, I mean. Your friends would do their thing, an d you were always quiet. You didn't help, which kinda sucked, but you di dn't make things worse, either, and I took notice of that. It intrigued me, I guess. Set you apart from the rest of them."

I closed my eyes and took a deep breath, hoping I could at least clear my mi nd and not sound like an idiot. Without opening my eyes, I explained to him what Trevor had said to me on Monday, and what Shawn did today.

"I'm sorry," I said. "I'm sorry, I'm sorry, I'm sorry. I didn't mean a word of it , and god, I felt sick just saying it. But what else was I supposed to do? Plea se don't be mad at me."

When I finally opened my eyes, they were met right away with Lucas'. "I'm n ot mad at you," he said with a sigh. His eyes were tired. "Frustrated, sure, b ut not mad. I'm mad at the situation, because it really fucking sucks that t hey can just hold this over you and control you like a goddamn puppet. It s ucks that you're gonna have to do it again, and I'm gonna have stand there a nd listen to my boyfriend spit slurs at me."

I wanted to argue and tell him that it wouldn't happen again. The more I th ought about it, though, the more I realized it would. They'd expect me to say something tomorrow, too, and the day after. And I'd have to listen.

"I'm sorry," I apologized again.

"It's okay," Lucas said, but I could hear the clench in his teeth.

It all came crashing down when he left later that night. The moment the door shut behind him, I stopped and I let myself think. I knew what I was doing. I was destroying something that I needed about as much as I needed air. I was cutting off my own heartbeat. I was hurting the most important person in my life time after time, and I hated myself for it, but I didn't know how to recover.

I cried. God, I cried hard. But when the tears stopped coming and I was still alone in my living room, my back against the wall, I didn't feel any better. Just scared. Fear could make a man do stupid, stupid things.

The next day, as expected, Shawn nudged me suggestively as we passed Lucas in the hallway. And Monday, and the day after that, and the day after that.

Every day, I would call Lucas and apologize for whatever vile words I'd said. E very day, he'd say it's okay, each time sounding more strained than the last. E very day, I felt a rift between us growing larger, and every day, I found that I looked in the mirror and liked myself less and less. That sickness I used t o feel was coming back—the loss of sleep, the skipping on meals because I was so nauseous, anything I ate came right back out.

It was when I woke up the next Thursday that I noticed something heavy in side of me, something that wasn't entirely unfamiliar. I stood for several min utes with my hand over my stomach, wondering what the feeling was. The best way I could describe it was an overall discomfort—my heart beat slig htly faster, my stomach churned a little, the hairs on the back of my neck stood up the smallest bit, and something in my head told me that I didn' t want to leave the house.

I'd felt it before, that I was sure of. But when? And why now? Was I sick? Or just scared?

I pondered for a long time over what I was feeling and where I'd felt it be fore. My mind took me back to the seventh grade, when I'd first looked at a boy in the way I should've looked at a girl; then to freshman year, whe n I finally admitted to myself that I was far from straight; then to a few w eeks ago, when the boys had first brought up their suspicions; then to yeste rday morning, when I remembered that I'd have to spend another day as the main character in their cruel little game.

The more I thought about it, the more I realized that I felt like this every day . Every single morning, I got the same sinking feeling. Today, it was just stro nger than normal.

So many of my worst moments and fears were tied to a single place—my school. Those buildings, less than twenty minutes from my house, were the focal point of my anxieties. I hated that place so damn much, I dreaded dr agging myself there every morning.

That's what I was feeling now. Dread. Very strong, very overwhelming d read. Dread that I couldn't quite ignore, because it wasn't just in my he ad. It coursed throughout my entire body, making my heart race and my st omach churn and my hairs stand on edge.

I'd dreaded school for years. It was only now that my so-called pals had f ound some kind of sick enjoyment in extorting me, now that I genuinely co uldn't think of a single moment throughout the school day that didn't ma ke me want to throw up, that I realized it.

With that pleasant thought in my mind, I got ready for the day ahead.

"Give him a little shove this time."

The brilliant idea was Tyler Fiero's. My brilliant answer was "No."

"Come on," he insisted. "Don't be such a girl."

Cameron joined in. "Tyler's right, dude. Do it."

"I'm not gonna push him," I deadpanned. Shawn, stood on my right, raised a n eyebrow.

"I think you are, Nate," he said. He was giving me the same look again, the o
ne I'd grown to fear. The I won't take 'no' look. The do it or else look. Th
e don't forget, I could tear apart your whole life with two words right now
look.

"Dude," I said seriously, staring back with the same intensity. "No. You're
taking this whole thing way too far. I'm not gonna be a bully to give you
whatever sick satisfaction you crave. Quit getting off on this shit and find
something better to do with your time."

As Lucas' form, absentmindedly walking to class with headphones in his
ears, grew nearer, the boys' edging grew stronger. Do it, they said. It's not
a big deal, they said. Or else.

"No!" I said again, a little bit too loudly. My hand moved before I could
tell it to stop and pushed Shawn away from me, just hard enough to make
him stumble a little. The nagging stopped as his eyebrows quirked, and I
gulped in anticipation of what he might do next. I half hoped he'd hit me.
A fight with Shawn would be better than doing what he was asking me to do
.

Shawn smirked. "Okay," he said, and I felt my shoulders relax. He raised his
hands in surrender. "I'll drop it for today."

The words "for today" made me nervous, but at least the delay would give
me time to prepare, and time to warn Lucas.

Then, when Lucas' form was nearly in front of us, he cupped his hands
around his mouth and said, loud enough for everyone in the hallway and
its classrooms to hear, "Hey everybody, want some news? Nathaniel Jean's
a—"

His pressure ate at my brain, instantly corroding my resolve. In a desperate a
ttempt to protect myself from the knives he threw, I did it. I reached out an
d shoved Lucas by the shoulder.

I'd meant it to be a light push. Just enough to make him stumble a little, like Shawn had.

Maybe it was my panicked state of mind. Maybe I didn't know my own s trength. Whatever the case, a loud bang sounded throughout the hallway a s Lucas' hands smacked the lockers to catch himself.

The guys around me, along with more or less everyone in the hallway, laughed. The only people who weren't laughing were Lucas and I. I su ppressed a gag and forced a snicker in its place.

Lips parted and eyebrows raised slightly, Lucas turned to look at me. His expression was one of genuine disbelief.

Apologies and questions of concern rose in my throat. Sorry. Did I hurt you? Sorry. Are you okay? Sorry!

The word that I forced out was one I'd modeled after Shawn. After all, it was what he always said when he pulled stunts like this. A perfect blend of asswipe and douchebag. "Oops."

It happened too quickly for me to even react. Before I could register what w as about to go down, a thud sounded through my ears. I felt a dull stinging in my bottom lip. Lucas' fist was clenched, the ring on his pointer finger gl immering.

"Oops," he mocked, his eyes narrowed in a heated glare that was directed at nobody but me. I saw his eyes dart to my bottom lip, and the expression in them seemed to shift for a moment. Then he erected his walls and hardened his gaze once more. To be honest, the hit had been louder than it was hard—it didn't hurt at all, but he had managed to bust my lip with his ring.

What the fuck just happened?

Then Tyler Fiero was surging forward to take on someone seven inches taller than him. I grabbed his arm and yanked him back, hissing, "Chill," under my breath, all-the-while staring in shock at Lucas. My other hand moved to touch my lip. What the hell had just happened?

Everyone in the hall was watching now, laughing and shouting and making noise and throwing jeers. "Dude, you gonna take that?" Cameron snapped at me, giving me a slight shove toward Lucas, who had backed off now but was still glaring heatedly at me.

Without so much as glancing at him, I said the same thing I'd said to Tyler, who was still trying to get out of my grasp. "Chill."

Cameron didn't listen. He took a threatening step forward. Lucas looked away from me to meet Cameron's eye, and he didn't back down.

Then Cameron made to lunge. He didn't get very far, though, because—to everyone's utter surprise—Shawn held him back. "Get over yourself," he snapped. "Calm the hell down and get over yourself."

Lucas locked eyes with me again. His glare had only intensified, and with a contempt shrug, he turned and walked away.

Tyler whipped around to stare at me incredulously. "What the hell, man? You're gonna let him walk away like that?"

I didn't respond. I stared after Lucas as he stormed away, a sickening mixture of anger and confusion and regret playing tag in my mind.

An oblivious teacher decided to choose that moment to finally poke his out of his classroom and demand, "What's going on?"

"I'm going to assume you know why you're here?"

Principal Harlington stared down at me through her oval-rimmed glasses, the tip of her upturned nose pointing at me like an accusing finger.

I nodded. "I do."

In the chair beside mine, Lucas was silent. He stared blankly ahead, but I could feel tension radiating off of him.

"Good," Harlington said, folding her hands on top of the dark oak desk. She didn't so much as glance in Lucas' direction. "I like you, Nathaniel. You're a very nice young man. I expect better from you than getting into petty fights."

Her words were another unpleasant reminder that the adults of this town saw me as some sort of godsend. They stared at me and saw my angelic mask. They had such high expectations of me, and I was fairly certain that I didn't meet a single one of them.

"With all due respect, ma'am," I said, "I didn't get into a fight."

She raised a thin, arched eyebrow. "Witnesses say otherwise. From what I've heard, there was conflict with Mr. Morgan. Am I mistaken?"

She said Lucas' name as if it were a pungent odor. "I didn't get into a fight," I repeated.

Her eyebrow, if possible, rose higher. "Then please, do explain the cut lip. Was it a one sided act of aggression? Did Mr. Morgan assault you, Nathaniel? If so, that is a serious offense, and we will deal with him accordingly." She spoke about him as if he wasn't sitting right there—as if she couldn't turn her head forty-five degrees and address him as well.

Why she didn't haul her lazy ass to the monitors I was sure she had and check the camera footage herself, I didn't bother to wonder. If the confrontation had been with anyone else—Shawn, for example—maybe she would have. But when it came to Lucas, she didn't care enough about matters of guilt and innocence. Whatever I said, she'd trust.

I could feel Lucas' eyes on me now, burning into the side of my head. Silently waiting to see what I would say. Would I lie, or would I tell the truth?

A part of me—the part that was angry that I'd gotten punched in the fucking face—wanted to rat Lucas out. But then again, I was pretty sure I was mad at myself more than anything.

"No," I lied seamlessly. "He didn't hit me. We just had a minor verbal disagreement. I hurt myself in PE earlier today. That's all."

As soon as we left the principal's office, Lucas had reverted back to staring ahead and only ahead. I tried to catch his eye, but he stubbornly held his gaze forward.

"Not a word after I lied for you?" I said, irritated that he wouldn't even look at me. Then I realized how shitty that sounded, so I backtracked and said, "Please, talk to me?"

"I didn't ask you to," Lucas countered. I couldn't help it—I scoffed.

"Yeah? You want me to go back and tell her the truth?"

Finally, he turned to look at me. His green eyes were stormy. "Do you want to go back and tell the truth?"

I huffed, already feeling defeated. "No," I admitted. "I don't."

"Awesome," he said dryly.

"Lucas," I began with a sigh. "Please don't be like this. Can't you at least try to hear me—"

"You sure this isn't too public a place?" Lucas interrupted. "The cameras could catch us having a conversation, god forbid."

He clearly wasn't going to make talking easy, so I gave up on that approach. I grabbed his wrist and more or less pulled him toward the school's exit; he shrugged off my grip, but followed nonetheless.

The awkward tension between us was so thick, I felt as though I was trying to run at the bottom of the ocean. From the time we stepped onto the parking lot to the moment I pulled the car up in a very random, very secluded spot at the edge of the forested portion of the park, the air was sticky and uncomfortable.

"Okay," I said as I put the car into park, turning to look at Lucas. "One question. Why?"

Lucas kept his gaze on the windshield. "I thought we were putting on a show," was all he said.

I fought the urge to roll my eyes. "I really don't think I deserved it."

Lucas made a contempt 'hm' sound. "Then I didn't deserve to get pushed around."

"You know I didn't mean anything by it," I told him. "I didn't."

"Well then neither did I."

I shut my eyes tight and rubbed my temples for a brief moment, trying to ease my aggravation. If he would just look at me.

"Lucas . . ."

"If you get to be all asshole tough-guy around your friends, why can't I?"

"You know why I do it, though," I said, exasperated. "You know what they're doing . . . You know I can't take it."

And I really, really couldn't. I couldn't take it.

"And that gives you an excuse to shove me into a locker?" He snapped. "Again?"

Giving up, I sighed. "No."

He turned to face me. As frustrated as I was, I could see the distress clear in the downturn of his lip, the furrow of his brow, the sad glint of his eyes. It was more than a push to him. Fuck.

"Who's more important to you?" He asked. "Me, or them?"

"You!" I said without hesitation. "That's not even a question!"

"And when you're off to New York, who's going to be by your side?" He continued. "Me, or them?"

"You."

"That's the plan, right?"

I nodded. "Of course."

But he wasn't done. "And what if that plan goes up in flames because I can't keep pretending I don't mind you treating me like gum on the bottom of your shoe every time your friends open their mouths?"

I ran a hand through my hair and made a fist, my head leaning back against the car seat. "God, Lucas . . ."

Then I said the one thing I'd been thinking a lot lately. The one thing I really, really didn't want to say. "Maybe we should stop, then."

Lucas was silent. He didn't ask what I meant, but I knew he didn't have to. "That's what you want?"

God, it was the farthest possible thing from what I wanted. "I want to stop doing you more harm than good," was what I said. And I really did mean it. "I can handle hurting myself. Hell, I've been doing that for years. But not . . . not you. And that's all I've done these last few weeks."

Lucas rubbed his temples. "And if we stop now," he said, "Will we ever start again?"

I wasn't sure what I'd do if we didn't. The idea of ever moving to New York without him by my side was sickening.

Then, softly, he said, "What if I don't want to stop?" I was silent, so he continued. "Because I know what you're like, and I know that this situation is making you act like someone else. And I really can't stand that someone else, but I know you're still in there, too. And if we could just make everything else stop . . ."

I knew what he was asking for. A sacrifice. One that scared the shit out of me. But this was my future speaking.

When I still didn't respond—not because I had nothing to say, but because I had so much to say, Lucas started again. "Just," he breathed out through his nose. "Just tell me how you really feel, Nate. And we'll decide where to go from there."

The first thing that came to my mind was, "I feel like an idiot."

"Good start."

I glared at him. "You're not helping."

He was silent for a while. Then his expression softened, and he seemed to realize that it hadn't been a necessary comment. "Yeah, okay."

I thought over his question for a long moment. What did I want? I wanted a million things.

I wanted to be okay. I wanted to get out of here. I wanted to do better in areas where I was weak. I wanted to be smarter. I wanted to be nicer. I wanted to be free, for god's sake. I wanted to be a good boyfriend. I wanted to strangle half of the Listrougth High population. I wanted a closer relationship with my sister. I wanted any relationship with my parents. I wanted to be out of the closet. I wanted to stay in the closet.

I wanted Lucas to not be upset with me. I wanted us to have an easy, happy, seamless relationship. Now, though, my wants seemed like hopeless wishes.

"I feel like . . ." I began slowly, carefully picking my words. "I wanna make things up to you however you'll let me. I feel like I don't wanna lose what we have because of other people who don't mean shit. I feel like I wanna become better for you. I feel . . ." I paused, then said, "like I wanna fall in love with you."

God knows, I was already way beyond in love with Lucas. I was stuck on him, no doubt. He'd had me long before he knew he'd had me. Before he even knew he could get me. But this wasn't the time to say it.

His expression eased, and a bit of the tension seemed to leave his shoulders. With a sigh, he said, "Let me see," taking my chin in his hand. He examined my face, his thumb gliding over my lip. "I'm . . . I'm sorry. This was . . . I didn't do it out of anger, you know. I'm not like that. And the hit really was just for show—I didn't want it to hurt. I forgot I was wearing the ring."

I huffed, a small smile pulling at the corners of my lips. "Well in all fairness, it didn't really hurt. And I didn't mean to push you so hard. I wasn't going to go through with it, but Shawn . . . it doesn't matter; I did it. But yeah, I kn ow."

"I'm sorry," he said again.

"I'm sorry, too."

Lucas put his face in his hands, rubbing his temples, before looking back up at me. "You really have to mean that, Nate, because you've got no idea how much of a toll stuff like this takes on me. You made me feel like shit. You've been making me feel like shit. I know it's my fault since I keep telling you it's okay but I never wanna say anything because I know it's probably h arder for you and I know . . . I know it wasn't your choice; none of it was y our choice. And you can't do much about it. I'm not asking for things to g o back to the way they were, believe me. I can live with walking home and s eeing you less and any of that if that's what you need. But that push, and a ll of the jeers . . . that was too far."

"I know," I said; and I did. I'd been hearing it his voice for a while now—subtle, unintentional hints that it wasn't okay. Lucas, though he hardly ever agreed to share them, had his insecurities. He had a set of demons that he rarely unleashed, and there seemed to be a certain few things that set him off. I'd ignored the hints, though, because I hadn't known what else to do. I still didn't know what else to do, but I'd have to figure something out. "I know, and I'm sorry. I just . . . there's this voice in my head that keeps telling me there's nothing else I can do. It makes me sick, but I don't—I don't understand my own thoughts sometimes, you know? The only thing that makes any sense these days is how I feel, and I always feel so damn anxious, like I'm gonna puke at any second if I don't do what . . . and I act on that, and I pull some idiotic shit. But that doesn't make it okay, and . . . I promise I'm gonna stop, alright?"

"Promise is a strong word," Lucas said, searching my expression for hesitation.

"Yeah," I agreed. "And I mean it." I took his hand, letting my thumb run across his knuckles. "Okay? Also, I need you to promise me that you'll talk to me about these things. You're just as fucked up as I am, even if you refuse to admit it, and I know that. But, for all the time I've spent with you, you're still so hard to read. If you don't tell me when things are hurting you, my slow ass isn't gonna figure it out."

Lucas chuckled, but a shadow seemed to momentarily cross his face, and for a short second, he averted his gaze. Then he nodded and smiled slightly, intertwining his fingers with mine. "Okay. I—I promise," he said. "I wanna hug you now, but car hugs are really fucking awkward, so how about we go to my place? Shawn's going out after school, I think, and my parents haven't seen you in a while; they miss you. We can make sure you're gone before he gets back. You down?"

I grinned. I was supposed to be going out with Shawn after school, but if things were going to change, may as well start now. "Of course I'm down."

So, we weren't going to stop just yet. I'd call this a probation round; we weren't quite set in stone, either. But we were going somewhere, and if that somewhere turned out to be good, we'd keep on going. If not, we'd step on the brake.

I was nervous a lot. I'd grown so used to the feeling, it was more or less just how I lived now.

Today, though, I was more nervous than usual. It was Friday morning, and what I did today could very well be the worst decision of my eighteen years.

It wasn't as if I was going to do anything major. I wasn't going to stand on a table and scream I was gay. I wasn't going to tell my fuckboy friends to screw themselves and say whatever they wanted. I wasn't even going to do so much as to go up to Lucas and have a chat with him in the hallway.

But when the guys shared their plans for the evening with me, I told them I was busy and ignored their response. When they urged me to pick on Lucas as I passed him in the hall, I turned up the music coursing through my headphones. And at the end of the day, when I saw Lucas in the parking lot, I called him over and offered him a ride. Small changes—minuscule, even—but they didn't go unnoticed.

"The hell are you doing, Jean?" Shawn hissed in my ear. I snorted uncaringly; at the same time, though, I was hiding trembling hands behind my back.

"What's it look like, Morgan? I'm going home."

When Lucas joined me in the passenger seat, his surprise was clear in his expression. "Nate, what did you do?"

I took a shaky breath and buckled my seatbelt a little bit too violently. "I don't know," I muttered. "Committed social suicide, probably."

"Actually," Lucas said; when he turned to me, mischief was written all over his face. "Maybe not."

I turned my attention from the road to raise an eyebrow at him. "And how is that, exactly?"

He smirked. "You know Sister Marsy?"

Oh, I knew Sister Marsy. She had to be the strictest, meanest, most unbearable woman I'd ever met. She was one of the younger nuns—that is, she was in her fifties—but you'd never know by talking to her. She had the spirit of a ninety year old woman struggling with shingles whose house was infested with roaches and whose grandkids never visited.

"Unfortunately," I groaned. "Why?"

Lucas smirked. "Let's just say, I've got some newfound dirt on my brother dearest that may help you out of your situation."

I challenge you lovely readers to do this: analyze both sides of the argument. See it from both points of view. And if you want, leave your input here; I'd love to see it ;)

16: Nathaniel Jean's Creation

It was no secret the Shawn Morgan ran Listrough High. His peers, whether they liked him or hated him, never questioned his superiority. Adults, oblivious to his actions and the harshness of his personality, saw him as the polite, talented, better son of the Morgan family—the best boy in town.

His word was law, at least among his fellows. The school was wrapped around his accusing finger.

It was also no secret that Shawn Morgan was a ladies' man. He loved girls, and girls loved him. He was toxically charming when he wanted to be. He'd been playing the field since he was in diapers.

And when Shawn Morgan slept with a girl, everybody knew it. Even if the poor girl was interested in keeping her personal affairs to herself, the news would be out and about before school commenced the following morning.

He found some sort of pleasure in the numbers. Rallying up his "conquests" gave him a weird sense of validation. And if nobody knew about a conquest, had it ever really happened? In his eyes, the answer to that was no. As much as he loved sleeping with girls, he loved the attention he got from sleeping with girls more. He got satisfaction in knowing that the person to his left probably had some idea about who he'd been with—or better, in—the night before.

Until that day, I'd been sure that their wasn't a single girl Shawn had fooled around with that I hadn't heard about. He'd have to be ashamed of a hookup to refrain from sharing it. It would have to be with someone who he didn't want anyone, under any circumstances, to know about. An event he'd rather pretend never happened.

Which was probably why I'd never before known that Shawn Morgan had slept with the one and only Sister Marsy.

Lucas wouldn't tell me how he'd found out, and I didn't care to pry. I only cared that this could be my way out of the hole I'd fallen into.

Lucas also unfortunately said that I wasn't allowed to actually tell anybody Shawn's secret—I could only threaten him. It was sad how protective Lucas still was of his brother, even without realizing it, after all of the shit Shawn put him through. Nevertheless, I agreed.

If the secret got out, it would ruin him. His reputation would go straight to the bin. Everything Shawn did, it seemed, was catered around approval. He would have none of that if the world knew of his scandalous, rather disgusting affair. Adults would see him as nothing but trouble, sleeping with a woman who could be his mother and who was supposed to remain chaste. He wouldn't be able to walk a hallway without hearing jokes and jeers whispered and shouts. He would, in an instant, lose his reign.

I was hesitant, though. As bad as his secret was, mine was undeniably worse. His would bring him temporary disapproval—mine would bring me permanent exclusion. I could only hope that a threat would be enough to scare him into withdrawal.

If not, I would be dead meat. I could imagine a million ways it could go wrong. If I blackmailed Shawn, and it wasn't enough—if he realized that the rumor he was brewing would do me more damage than my secret would do him—I would be left worse off than before. He would be angry, no doubt. And in his anger, he'd disregard my threat, and I wouldn't have a chance to save my name. The other boys would all team up against me, and even if I tried to deny their rumor, or turn it back around against them, it would be too late.

It was really, really risky. But it seemed like the best shot I'd get at recovering. Hopefully, the fact that his threat was of a mere rumor he'd started, whereas mine was of a fact we both knew was true, would be enough. If it worked, Shawn would be quiet. And once Shawn was quiet, the others would be, too. And I could finally be a boyfriend again.

The risk was worth it. If not for me, then for Lucas.

And holy shit, it worked.

I'd never seen Shawn grow so pale.

According to him, he'd been walking to Beth Crampton's house, tripping on LSD and looking for a freaky hookup. Sister Marsy lived in the same neighborhood, and when Shawn knocked on her door, thinking she was Beth and too fucked up to see otherwise, the old nun hadn't told him otherwise.

Which was actually really fucked up. If I gave two shits about Shawn, I'd think Sister Marsy should be taken to court for screwing with a boy who was clearly out of it, or at least kicked out of the church because she clearly wasn't "holy". But I didn't give two shits about Shawn, so I kind of found the whole thing hilarious, and I couldn't find it in myself to be sorry for that. He was too concerned about his reputation to consider how horrible what she'd done had been, but that was none of my business. All that mattered was that he'd finally let up.

I wasn't sure what he said to convince the other boys, but they backed off, too. After weeks of dealing with their bullshit, being stressed every damn night, and being a horrible boyfriend, I was free from their grasp. I felt like Pinocchio—a puppet no longer dependent on his master. I could walk on my own two legs and swing my arms of my own accord, and they wouldn't say a word. No more threatening to start rumors. No more suspicion.

I wasn't going to suddenly get cocky and start acting like a moron. Some things wouldn't ever be able to go back to normal—there was no way I could spend every Friday at Lucas' anymore. But if I wanted to go to his house once in a while, I would, and I wouldn't be scared to do it.

My relationships with those boys would never be back to where they had once stood, I could tell. The awesome thing was, I didn't care. They were leaving me alone, and that was all that mattered; my relationships with them had never meant shit in the first place.

Part of me suspected that they were still suspicious. Another part of me suspected that they hadn't even really thought I was gay in the first place. They'd just been minions, mindlessly listening to their master, and now that their master had backed off, they did, too. The freedom was uplifting.

A rumor for a secret. That was the deal.

"Nate!"

I must have jumped a foot into the air when Lucas barged without warning through my front door, yelling my name as if he'd just had some life-changing experience.

"Jesus Christ," I breathed, pressing a hand to my chest and feeling my heart's erratic beating. "Lucas, what the hell?"

Without proposing any sort of explanation, he practically ran to join me on the living room couch. An envelope was in his hand, and he shoved it towards me.

"The mail man was here and he dropped this off and oh my god Nate look."

With my eyebrows raised in amusement, I gently pushed Lucas' hand down, choosing instead to focus on him. "Okay, you're excited," I said, which was pretty obvious. "Which is awesome, but also hello. How was your day?"

"Nate," Lucas whined. "We can do that later! This is important!"

"My day was great," I said, more to annoy him than anything. "Thanks for asking."

Lucas rolled his eyes and held the envelope up to my eye level so I had no choice but to look at it. Cheater. With a huff, I gave in and scanned its surface.

Then I saw who the sender was, and any sign of joking fell from my expression.

The letter was from New York University.

It wouldn't be the first college letter I'd gotten. I'd applied to several universities in and around New York—some had accepted me, some hadn't. None of them mattered as much as this one, though. None even got close. I wanted it. I really, really wanted it.

Now that I was finally taking him seriously, Lucas took my hand and placed the envelope in it. "I can't open it," I said, my voice only barely surpassing a whisper. My heart was still racing, but now for entirely different reasons. "If I don't . . ."

"You will," Lucas said reassuringly. He wrapped an arm around my shoulders and pressed a loud kiss to my temple. "You will."

"But if I don't?"

My life wouldn't end if I didn't get into NYU. There were other schools that I could go to.

But my dreams were tied to this particular school. They had been since I was a child. Ever since my cousin Kenny told me that he would go to NYU someday, it had been my destination.

"Nate," Lucas said softly, giving my shoulder a squeeze. "You've gotta open it. One way or another, you need to know."

I took a shaky breath and leaned my head into the crook of his neck. "I know," I said. "I know I have to. But I don't know if I can."

"Don't freak," Lucas said. "I know how you're feeling, alright? When I got my letter from Juilliard, it took me thirty minutes to finally open it. And those turned out to be thirty minutes completely wasted. Panicking won't help—you're just going to think more and more until you've thought to much. You'll think about the bad until you can't think about the good. You've gotta, you know, rip off the bandage."

I snorted. "Easier said than done."

"But not impossible."

"No," I agreed. "Not impossible. But really fucking hard."

Lucas gripped my chin, forcing me to raise my head, and nodded towards the envelope. Slowly, I opened it with shaking hands and pulled out the paper inside. Unfolding it proved to be a whole other struggle.

"Almost there," Lucas encouraged softly. "Don't stop now, Nate. You're almost there."

"Almost where?"

"NYU."

Shutting my eyes tight, I unfolded the paper.

"Nate," Lucas' voice seemed far away, but I could still here the urgency within it. "Nate, look."

I opened my eyes. The paper fell out of my hands.

I'd only really processed one word. Congratulations.

"Congratulations," I muttered aloud. "It said congratulations."

Lucas was beaming. "You made it, Jean."

"I made it."

When he wrapped his arms around me in a tight, congratulatory hug, I couldn't help but mumble the words to myself again. "I made it." And again, because saying it felt so damn good. "I made it. I made it."

"You didn't just make it," Lucas said, pride dripping from his voice as his hand rubbed up and down my back. "I told you you'd get the scholarship."

I froze. "What?"

Lucas pulled away just enough to look at me, his eyes wide with excitement. "Did you not see?" He he asked. "Oh my god, you didn't see!"

I hastily grabbed the slightly-crumpled paper and took the time to actually read it, scanning each line carefully. By the time I reached the end of the page, my eyes were watering, threatening to spill onto my cheeks.

A full scholarship.

They were going to give me a full scholarship. I'd been laughing when I applied for that ages ago, thinking no way will this ever actually happen. And there it was.

I couldn't contain my elation. I practically tackled Lucas, crying and cheering and melting into an absolute mess at the fact that I'd been offered a full scholarship to the university of my dreams.

"That's what you get for being a fucking prodigy!" Lucas said joyously, leaning his head back in happy laughter.

People had been impressed enough by my skill to offer to pay to have me come to their school and play for their team, regardless of my weakness in other areas. That was insane to me. Out of this world. I couldn't quite believe that it was true, but I also couldn't quite tell myself that it wasn't.

Lucas planted a congratulatory kiss on my lips. I held him there when he moved to pull away, basking in the joy of knowing that everything was finally starting to fall into place. He'd made it. I'd made it. Come fall, we'd be in Manhattan, far away from all of the bullshit that loomed over us every day. We'd made it. Our home was there, not here, and the life we began there would be ours and no one else's. We'd build from the ground up until we were above the skyscrapers, casting our shape upon the horizon, throwing a monumental shadow across the city. Our lives would be our creation. And that creation started now.

"I love you," I said against his lips, overcome with joy and wanting nothing more than to finally let him know how I'd been feeling for so long now. "God, I love you. I love you so much."

Lucas' arms wrapped tightly around my neck, pressing our bodies together. His lips left mine to kiss my cheek. "Say it again," he murmured.

"I love you, Lucas Morgan," I said. "I love you, I love you, I love you."

Lucas' lips abandoned me altogether. His grip loosened enough so that he could lean back; green eyes met blue, and the smile on his face was one I'd keep with me, always.

"And I love you, Nathaniel Jean," he said. He shut his eyes and leaned his forehead against mine, our noses just barely brushing. "I love you, I love you, I love you."

I tightened my arms around his torso, pulling him against me in an embrace that did just about everything it needed to do to communicate our feelings. As I held him and he held me, we knew. We both knew. We knew everything we needed to know. And it was beautiful.

Everybody was in a good mood on Friday. The school day had been shortened to leave room at the end for a stupid pep rally that was meant to "lift our spirits for the upcoming finals". The rally itself was bound to be a waste, but nobody cared—less school was less school, after all.

I, of course, was feeling good for different reasons. Two days after I'd received the NYU acceptance letter, I hadn't been able to wipe the smile off of my face.

What made the victory even sweeter was how well Lucas and I were working now. No more Shawn or Damien or anyone to put a strain on our relationship. We were still a tightly kept secret, of course, but now we were a secret that didn't hurt to keep. We were happy. I was happy.

For once in my life, I was one of the smiling faces in the crowd. As I walked toward the rally, there was a little bounce in my step. I couldn't help it. Everything was just so good.

Of course, I would have enjoyed the rally more if I wasn't surrounded on each side by the idiots that I called my friends. All they did was talk too loud, hoot like idiots, and make comments about which cheerleaders they would—or already did—sleep with. In my opinion, the cheerleaders, who were supposed to be keeping the spirit of the rally, looked absolutely dead inside.

Nonetheless, it was bearable. I'd dealt with worse.

Until one of the guys caught sight of Lucas, who was sitting in the bleachers a few rows below us with his friends.

"Dudes," Tyler said, smirking ridiculously. "Let's throw something at fairy boy."

I rolled my eyes as the other boys expressed their agreement. "How immature can y—"

"Don't be a buzzkill, Nate," Trevor groaned. "It's just a bit of fun."

"Yeah," Cameron agreed, punching me in the shoulder. "We'll throw something soft."

Damien's eyes lit up. "I have an idea!" He exclaimed, which ways like a snake saying I have legs!—it didn't happen often, so it was an event to be remembered when it did. "I've got a sandwich in my bag. No harm in a sandwich, right?"

"You're gonna make a mess," I groaned. "Really, can't you just not be a child for, like, ten minutes?" Damien waved a hand dismissively, using the other to search through his backpack.

"Oh, hush," he said as he pulled out a plastic bag, inside of which was, as expected, a sandwich.

Shawn's eyes widened as he looked at it. "Wait, hold on. Don't throw that."

Tyler rolled his eyes. "C'mon Shawn, we only need one mom-friend in the group."

Damien pulled the sandwich out of the bag, swatting Shawn's hand away as he tried to snatch it. "Damien, I'm serious! Don't throw that!"

I had no idea what Shawn's issue was, but I was happy for the backup. "Seriously, dude," I said. "It's not necessary."

Damien ignored us both and raised his arm. "Hey, Lucas!" He called. Lucas turned around at the sound of his name, his eyes searching for the caller.

"Damien, stop!" Shawn yelled, much louder this time. But it was too late. Damien chucked the sandwich at his victim. It hit Lucas's face, causing said boy to yelp and jump in surprise, then slid down until it fell to the bleachers, leaving a smear of peanut butter on his cheek.

Then chaos broke loose.

Beside me, Shawn jumped to his feet and grabbed Damien by the collar, pulling the other boy up with him. Everyone around us watched in surprise as a streak of yells and curses left his mouth and he shook Damien violently. People started shouting, cheering for a fight and making the gymnasium ten times louder, drowning out the sounds of crappy pop music blaring from the speakers.

I didn't understand why Shawn of all people had gotten so upset until I looked ahead and saw what was happening around Lucas.

Saeyoung Park and Lucas' other theater friends were freaking out, screaming for help and yelling at curious watchers to step back and give him space.

And Lucas—oh God, Lucas. He was gasping for air, his hands grabbing at his neck as he struggled more and more to breathe. He was allergic to peanuts. How could I forget that?

In a second, I was down in that bleacher row with him. "Where's his epipen?" I yelled to Sae, who looked more than a little surprised that I'd come to help him.

"H-his backpack," she said nervously. "In the theater classroom."

"Well where's the fucking theater classroom?" I snapped.

We didn't have time for her to stumble over her words and be nervous. Whatever she thought of me, she needed to forget it for a minute and just talk.

She seemed to realize this herself, because her gaze steeled and she said, "Room 249. His backpack is—"

I didn't wait for her to finish. I ran.

I ran harder than I had at any soccer game. My legs moved faster than they could, not slowing in the slightest until I reached the theater room—room 249.

The teacher inside, Mr. Lourwy, looked up in surprise as I banged on the door. He must have sensed my urgency, because he rushed to open it and let me in. "Mr. Jean, what's—"

"I need his epipen!" Was all I said, which didn't do much to ease Mr. Lourwy. I ran to the desk that held Lucas' familiar backpack and frantically searched the pockets. Thankfully, I quickly found the pen.

Mr. Lourwy seemed to realize what was happening, and he followed me as I ran back to the gym, keeping up surprisingly well. He was saying something, asking questions, but I didn't hear him. I only heard Lucas, panting, asphyxiating.

I burst through the gym doors and was back at Lucas' side in an instant. His face was dangerously red, and his lips had begun to swell up. Since I'd been gone, a crowd of teachers had surrounded him, telling students to back off. One was on the phone with the ambulance.

Where I'd been sitting, two administrators were holding Damien and Shawn by their arms. Shawn had a bruised cheek, and Damien was sporting a black eye and a cut eyebrow. The gym was buzzing with the excitement and confusion of students who knew something interesting was happening but didn't actually know what interesting thing was happening.

It wasn't until the needle was submerged in Lucas' thigh that I started breathing, or even realized that I'd stopped breathing in the first place. I gripped his hand tightly, not caring who was around and absolutely despising the fact that that was all I could do. In this situation, I was powerless. I could only sit and wait and hope the injection would do its job.

Thankfully, it did. It was relatively soon that Lucas' gasping began to ease, and his breathing began to slow. Within another minute, the ambulance had arrived, and I'd been forced to release his hand as they pushed him away on a stretcher.

I drove after them to Nowhere, Nebraska's tiny little hospital, but once again found myself pretty useless as I was instructed to sit outside of his room and wait.

Sit and wait. Sit and wait. It was agonizingly painful to sit and wait.

Lucas' parents were soon there, too, panicking and asking everybody within a five meter radius what had happened over and over again. Saeyoung was there, along with a few other friends who I recognized but didn't really know. Shawn was probably still at the school, getting in trouble for fighting.

Time seemed to pass in slow motion, minute by minute. I did everything to keep myself distracted, but my mind kept falling back to the image of

Lucas' anaphylaxis. The picture of him, red faced and clawing for breath, burned a permanent scar into my memory.

It was my fault. I should have remembered. He'd mentioned the allergy to me once, months back, but it hadn't really come up again since. If I'd remembered, there was no way that sandwich would have left Damien's hand. Lucas would have never gone through that.

"Hey."

I startled at the soft voice coming from my right, turning in surprise to see that Sae had sat down next to me. "You okay?" She asked. She had a very smooth, very lovely voice.

I rubbed my eyes. "If Lucas is."

Sae smiled slightly. "He will be. I've known him for a while; this isn't his first time. He'll be fine. But it is scary."

I nodded in agreement. "Very scary."

She seemed to hesitate, as if contemplating whether or not she should say something. "Can I ask you a question?"

Here it comes. "Yeah."

"No offense, but why do you care?"

I turned my gaze forward and found myself locking eyes with Mrs. Morgan. She offered me a smile, and I truly did finally understand why people spoke of the importance of parental figures. In the few months I'd known her, she'd become like a mother to me. Her smile gave me encouragement, but also a choice. What I said to answer Sae's question was nobody's decision but mine.

I made the choice that was so unlike me, I could hardly believe I was doing it. The choice that would've made Nate at the beginning of the school year—Nate a few weeks ago, even—shit his pants. I said, "Don't people usually care when someone they love gets hurt?"

My voice was quiet, lowered so that only Sae could hear. The words still had the same effect, however; her face went slack and her lips parted in genuine shock.

"You?" She whispered almost incredulously. In a different situation, her surprise would have been funny. "Wait, are you talking friend love, or love love?"

My stomach wasn't entirely happy with me for boldly sharing my sexuality with no preparation or warning, but I swallowed my nerves and said, "Love, love."

I lifted the chain around my neck, which I'd long since pulled from under my shirt to fidget with while I waited, and showed her the ring.

I could tell that Sae was trying hard not to gape and make a scene. "How did I not know about this?"

I shrugged. "We didn't tell anyone." Then I raised my eyebrows purposefully. "We still don't."

"Oh," she said, nodding. Then her eyes rounded. "Oh. You think—oh god no—I would never. Your secret's safe with me. That's a promise."

I smiled. "Thank you," I said, right as the doctor—Madeleine Montgomery's mother—exited Lucas' room.

"He can take visitors now," she told us. Her lips were tight, and I could tell from her expression that she wasn't happy to treat Lucas. That was a personal issue, though—a doctor is a doctor, and a doctor does as a doctor does. "Only a few at a time, though."

Lucas' parents went in to visit him first. When they emerged a few minutes later, Lucas' friends took their place. Finally, after everyone else had seen him, I went in alone.

He smiled as I approached, holding out his hand. "Hey, hero."

I chuckled. "I'm far from a hero," I said. I wanted badly to lean over and kiss him, to savor the feeling of him, alive and well. I'd shut the door on my way in. Still, there was a dark part of me that hadn't quite died yet, and it was scared. Scared of what would happen if somebody saw. Scared of what would happen if my parents found out.

Then a thought occurred to me. What would happen if my parents found out? What could they do to me now that would hurt me? Yell at me? Yeah, because their opinions meant so much to me after they'd been absent for more-or-less my entire life. Take away my college plan? I didn't need that money anymore—I was going to college for free. I had some money in my wallet, and a few cards to pull from, I could hold my own without them, at least for a while. I could get a job, or two, or three, or however many it took to be completely independent of them. I didn't need them to hand me my life on a silver platter. I could make it on my own.

I didn't need them.

And if I didn't need them—if I could make my way out of this hell-hole with or without their help—then what was the point of even hiding any-more? I didn't want to spend the rest of my time here as a social outcast, but would it really be so bad? School was over in less than two months. We'd be gone soon enough.

And in those two months, maybe I could finally ease some of Lucas' bur-den by sharing it with him. If there was someone else walking around with a target on his back, maybe Lucas wouldn't have been in a life threatening situation today at all.

"What are you thinking?" Lucas asked, disrupting my thought. I didn't answer. I just kissed him.

He made a noise of surprise, but he didn't pull away. On the contrary, one of his hands found the back of my neck, pulling me closer.

"I need to come out," I said, breaking the kiss to look at him.

For a moment, it was as if he hadn't heard me. Then his eyes widened. "What?" He said incredulously. "Are you out of your mind?"

Okay. Not quite the reaction I was expecting.

"I thought . . . I thought you'd want me to," I said. Lucas made a face.

"Why on earth would I want that?"

"Because then you wouldn't have to take all of the heat," I explained. "We could share it."

Lucas' gaze softened and he smiled warmly. "Nate, that is the sweetest, most thoughtful, dumbest thing I have ever heard."

I blinked in surprise. All this time, I'd thought our secretiveness was a product of my fear alone. "You seriously want us to be a secret?"

He pursed his lips. "If we were somewhere else, in a different situation, no," he said. "But here, in this town, it's not worth it. I don't think the backlash would be good for you. And if it's not good for you, it's not good for me. I'll take all of the hits for you, okay?"

"That's not fair to you," I argued. It wasn't okay that he could nearly die of an allergy attack and I would just sit there, letting him take all of the hits.

"I can handle it," Lucas insisted. "I have until now, haven't I? Let me be the punching bag."

"That's so fucked up," I groaned, but I didn't argue further. His mind was pretty clearly made up, and he knew more than I did. I trusted his thoughts more than my own.

We both turned our heads at the sound of a knock on the door. A nurse entered, holding a clipboard and a pen. She smiled kindly as she approached.

"I'm just gonna do a few quick tests, okay?" She said. She was young—mid-twenties, maybe—and I had never seen her before. Her skin was dark and rich, and her densely curled ebony hair was tied up on top of her head in a large bun. Her name tag read Natalie. "You should be free to go in another hour or two."

She told me I could stay if I wanted, so I sat down in the stool-like chair next to Lucas' bed and watched as she did her work. She made small-talk while she ran her tests, and I could quickly tell that she was one of those genuinely nice people that you so rarely found in this town.

"Alright," she said finally, her eyes quickly scanning her clipboard once more. She looked back up at Lucas, giving him an affirmative nod. "Everything looks normal to me. I'm going to hand the information over to your doctor, so expect her here shortly, okay?"

Lucas groaned, and I watched as Natalie tried and failed to hide a laugh.

"Oh, she's not so bad," Natalie said, though her eyes said otherwise. She turned to leave, but right before she opened the door, she turned back. "I, er, I hope I'm not sticking my nose where it doesn't belong," she said, her gaze trained on her feet. "But I heard what you two were talking about earlier."

I choked on air and she quickly lifted her head, her eyes meeting mine as she frantically backtracked. "Don't get me wrong! I wasn't eavesdropping or anything, but I was waiting outside the door and I didn't want to intrude and I kind of just . . ." She cleared her throat awkwardly. "Heard. Anyways, I'm new to this place if you couldn't tell. I moved here because my boyfriend lives here—you might know him, his name is Renaldo Suarez."

I did know Renaldo Suarez. Or at least I knew of him. His parents owned a cute little restaurant a mile from my house, and he helped them out sometimes. They were some of the nicer people in town, and their younger son was one of Lucas' close friends from theater. They were among the few that didn't mind him the way he was.

"My point is," Natalie continued, "he's told me enough about this town for me to know that it's not always the . . . kindest place. And I know it's probably not easy for the two of you. Renaldo and I just bought a little house off of South Street and I guess what I'm trying to say is that I know I don't know you but I'm always willing to help you. I don't mean to be weird or anything but . . . my sister and her wife went through a lot when they were your age, and it was hard to see her deal with everything our asshole parents put her through, and . . . You guys seem nice. Nice people don't deserve bad things.

"So I, a complete and total stranger, am offering you help if you need it. Now or ever."

She took a pen from the pocket of her scrubs and a sticky note from who-knows-where and quickly scribbled something down. She handed the paper to me and I found myself staring at a phone number.

I looked up at her, stunned. She smiled. "I pray you'll never have to use it," she said. "But just in case."

Lucas beat me to talking. "Gosh, Natalie," he said, looking sort of awestruck. "Thank you so much. We don't . . . There aren't many people like you around here."

I kept glancing between the sticky note, Lucas, and Natalie. Her gesture seemed unreal to me. People were never this nice. It just didn't happen in a place like this. "Is this serious?"

I'd half meant to keep that to myself, but I wasn't embarrassed to have said it aloud. Natalie nodded. "One hundred percent. I don't know what your situation is, but if you find yourself in a rough spot, shoot me a call."

She left after that, offering a final smile before disappearing to fetch Lucas' grinch of a doctor.

402-052-5600

That night as I tried to sleep, I couldn't quite forget what Lucas had said to me earlier.

He was so right.

I'd been talking like a fool in the aftereffects of my adrenaline rush. The stress f Lucas' allergy attack compounded with the relief of his well-being had left me with dangerously high levels of confidence. The kind of confidence that could have made me do something stupid.

Sure, I didn't need my parents. I genuinely didn't care what they thought about me—they'd never been more than figureheads trying and failing to have a family. But I wasn't sure I could survive walking around like an alien among my own people. To be shunned by everyone who, just a day before, had admired me. To be picked on in the hallways, or disliked by teachers, or glared at on the street. Just picturing a mother pulling her child away from me made my throat itch uncomfortably.

I realized then that my fears extended far beyond getting out of this shit town. Being stuck here was a nightmare, but being hated here was no prettier. Living amongst others who wanted me gone; surrounded, with few exceptions, by hate and hate and more hate.

Thinking about it alone made my heart race. I didn't like the image of being an outsider. I wanted it out of my head. But I'd brought myself here, and now I couldn't un-think it. The idea was stuck firmly at the front of my mind. The possibility of being cast aside, no longer a part of anything. It didn't matter that the school year was soon over, and come summer I'd be gone. I wouldn't be able to handle the heat for a week, let alone the next two months.

Now I really, really wanted to stop thinking about it. But the images only got worse and worse. I saw my sister Jenna, disgust written in bold on her face. I had no idea how she would react, but if it was bad . . . No more Sunday movie marathons or races in the backyard. That was what got me.

I didn't sleep that night. As horrible, truthful pictures flooded my brain, each worse than the last, I could feel myself losing the fight between calm and panic. Heart racing, palms sweating, breath shaking, I let myself descend into the dark as my room shrunk around me, suffocating me.

I had to be careful.

Epilogue

I couldn't pull my eyes away.

From the people, hundreds of them, bustling in the streets below me. Every shape, size, and color imaginable. From the buildings I looked down on, and the ones I had to lift my chin to see the tops of. From the lights—so many of them that not a single star could be seen in the night sky. From the cars, the sidewalks, the everything.

My hands were pressed against the glass; my nose, too, because no matter how close I got, I felt as though I wasn't close enough to see it all. I wanted to see it all.

I nearly jumped at the sensation of arms sliding around my sides from behind, a chin resting on my shoulder blade.

"Pretty crazy, huh?" Lucas chuckled, pressing a kiss to my shoulder. "It's all there."

"I feel like it's not real," I said, my voice coming out distant. "Eighteen years of dreaming, right there."

"Is it as good as you imagined?"

I felt myself smile—one of those smiles that you absolutely can't control, but it's okay because you would never want to. "Of course it is," I whispered. "It's just like the pictures—the physical ones and the ones in my head. But the feeling is totally different."

"Yeah?" Lucas mused, and I could feel him smiling, too, against my back. "What's the feeling?"

I turned around to face him and put my arms around his neck, took a good moment to just stand there and look at him and relish in the fact that he was mine, and that uncontrollable smile got bigger. "It feels like victory," I said. "Like . . . Like I'm not just surviving anymore. I'm actually winning. It feels weird."

"Are you . . . crying?" Lucas asked, trying and failing to suppress a chuckle. "Since when are you the emotional type, Jean?"

"Fuck off," I laughed, looking up at the ceiling and blinking tears out of my eyes as my cheeks turned pink. "I can't help it, I'm happy."

Lucas leaned forward to rest his head on my chest and hugged me close. "I know," he said. "I'm happy, too."

Happy. We were really, really happy. War was over, and the struggle of battle made the triumph so much sweeter.

We were unlimited. Not in concrete concepts, of course—money and time were not infinite, and we would learn that time and time again in the years to come. But more abstract ideas—the mushy ones, like love and joy and freedom—were ours for the taking. The American big city was a complete contrast from the American small town. The American big city didn't care who I was or what I did.

A rush of excitement came over me, just as uncontrollable as my smile, because we were free at last, and despite having just spent hours driving, I was full of a sudden, incredible energy. I grabbed Lucas around the waist and, with a triumphant whoop, spun around with him in my arms, pulling his entire body with me. His yelp turned into a giggle, and pretty soon we were both in hysterics, laughing and crying even though there wasn't anything real to laugh about; after all we'd gone through, we deserved some laughter.

Ecstatic. That's what we were.

He leaned up to kiss me—our first kiss in New York City—still chuckling against my lips, and I felt every butterfly, every chill, every spark imaginable.

I think I really could have stood there all day, kissing him in our new, wonderful home, but my eyes itched for another look.

The apartment was small and partially furnished—Lucas insisted on spending the extra money for furnishings because he "refused to spend our first day in New York sleeping on the floor like peasants"—and littered all over with boxes and bags of our things. One bedroom, one bathroom, a living room, a kitchen, and a dining area—all that we needed. I absolutely loved it, because it was ours, and it was here.

And from the huge window on the far wall of the living room, what seemed like all of Manhattan stretched out below us.

I pulled Lucas closer to it—the poor boy practically stumbled into the glass—and said, "Look."

So he looked, and the awe in his expression grew to meet mine as he stared, not for the first time and certainly not for the last, at the life we were entering.

"I don't care what kind of shit the world throws at us now," he said, slipping his hand into mine and lacing our fingers together, his eyes trained on the unending commotion outside. "We can handle it. You know that, right?"

"We'll do better than handle it," I said with a confidence I didn't know I had, but also couldn't let go of. "New York's not gonna know what hit it."

He nodded, and I could see his elation in every detail of his face. His wide eyes and big dimpled smile made him look like a child at Disneyland, and seeing him so animated only worked to increase my own eagerness. "Kings at last," he said dreamily. He lifted our hands, pressing his lips to the edge of my palm, and the small gesture made me feel like a twelve year old with a crush all over again—heart pounding in my chest, butterflies going mad in my stomach, nervous energy in my veins. Those lips curved into a playful smile, and I wondered if I'd ever be able to stop looking at them, or thinking about them, or kissing them. "Bet you I look great in a crown," he said, biting his bottom lip in that Lucas-way he always did as his smile spread.

Never.

Chuckling, I said, "I don't doubt that for a second." Lucas looked good in everything. "But forget crowns—I bet you'll look great on Broadway."

Lucas turned to look at me, and I saw the sparkle of a dreamer in his eyes. "Bet you'll melt hearts in a U.S. soccer uniform at the World Cup."

"I don't want to melt hearts," I said with a cheesy grin. "Just yours."

Lucas scoffed. "You're such an idiot," he said, pushing his hand into my hair and pulling my face down to meet his.

"'Course I am," I muttered into the kiss. "That's our thing, isn't it?"

I felt Lucas smile—it seemed that neither of us could stop smiling, and that was the best feeling ever. He pulled back to look at me, and I fell in love all over again with his face, absolutely glowing. He was so damn cute. "I can't wait to see you in the history books," he said, and I caught a break in his voice as he choked up a little.

"Now who's the emotional one?" I teased.

"Still you," he said, which, to be fair, was also true.

"Shut up," I said. He opened his mouth defiantly to say something else, and this time, I made him shut up.

Then, because fate had apparently decided to kill the moment, there was a knock on the door.

"Visitors already?" I whistled, wiping under my eyes in a sorry attempt to pull myself together before I faced anyone new. "We must have friendly neighbors."

When I opened the door, however, I wasn't met with friendly neighbors. My breath caught in my throat.

"So, are we supposed to do the straight-guy-handshake-half-hug thing, or will it not completely destroy your fragile masculinity if we hug for real?"

I tossed my head back in another excited, giddy laugh and practically threw my arms around my cousin, Kenneth Jean.

"You little fucker!" I exclaimed. "You didn't tell me you were coming!"

Kenny laughed, hugging me back just as tight. "I wanted to surprise you," he said. I thought back to all of the times I'd greeted Kenny this way when we were younger, because he'd been my favorite part of the year, and I'd been unable to contain my excitement whenever I saw him. Right now,

I was feeling eight years worth of that excitement all at once. He still felt familiar. "I kind of couldn't wait."

Kenny. My cousin Kenny, who I'd idolized so much as a child. Kenny who, when my parents found out was gay, had been ripped suddenly and painfully from my life. Who they'd made me hate, who they'd tried so hard to destroy.

But certain things—certain people—could never be destroyed, no matter how hard you tried. I'd learned that lesson with Lucas before, and now I was learning it again with Kenny. Eight years later, seeing him in person still felt like a gift. A treat I would only get twice a year, so it was something I treasured. I treasured my cousin.

He leaned back to look at me, and I could see that his eyes were glazing over with unshed tears. What a sap. Then again, I'd been crying for the last five minutes, so maybe I couldn't say anything about being a sap.

"Damn," he breathed. "If someone had told fifteen year old me that I'd see my little cousin again someday, I wouldn't have spent so much time crying like a baby during Dancing with the Stars."

"Dancing with the Stars," I snorted. "That's pretty gay."

"That's my brand," he joked, "But more importantly, how the hell are you taller than me?"

I scoffed. To be fair, the difference was only a few inches, but it was funny nonetheless. "How the hell are you shorter than me? You seemed massive when you were fifteen."

"Yeah," he said grudgingly. "I was. And I haven't grown since."

I looked at him—really looked at him—for what felt like the first time. The shitty-quality FaceTime camera had completely obscured the freckles all over his face, and my memory hadn't done them justice. His eyes were a lighter brown than they'd seemed. His hair, too. I laughed and pulled him back in for another tight hug, before letting him go so that he could greet Lucas.

"Where the hell is Nick?" I asked when they pulled apart, anxious to see Kenny's fiancé. I'd spoken to him over the phone several times, and he was an absolute gem. Just as Lucas had become Kenny's friend, Nicholas had become mine.

"He's out in the hall," Kenny said, and I raised my eyebrows incredulously.

"Why is the poor boy waiting in the hall?" Lucas asked before I had the chance, looking both amused and bewildered.

"Because," Kenny said smugly, "We have a little housewarming gift for you."

He made a show of reopening the door and retreating through it. When he came back in, he was holding one end of a box too large for him to bring in on his own, while Nicholas carried the other half.

Lucas and I watched, wide-eyed, as they stepped through the door sideways and set the box, which claimed to contain a sixty inch TV, on the floor.

"I'm sorry, do you know what a housewarming gift is?" I said in disbelief, unable to look away from his "little" gift. "Because that sure as hell isn't one."

Nicholas smirked. "We thought a coffee machine would be too basic."

Nicholas Abadi was a twenty-five year old giant, standing at a solid six foot four. He was Egyptian on his dad's side and Greek on his mom's, and it showed in his olive skin and dark features, typical of a Mediterranean. He was the human embodiment of the phrase tall, dark, and handsome. He laughed at my shocked expression and stepped forward to give me a hug. "Welcome to New York," he cooed.

I shook my head as he stepped back, still staring at the TV. "We can't take that," I said.

"Hey, speak for yourself, headass," Lucas scoffed. Then he beckoned to Nicholas and said, "Get over here, Nicky, I want a hug," because we all knew he absolutely despised that nickname. While I stared between Kenny, Nicholas, and the TV like an idiot, Lucas was the normal functioning human out of the two of us, thanking them profusely.

"How much did this cost?" I asked.

Nicholas put a finger to his lips. "St. Nick never tell his secrets."

"Don't worry, hun," Kenny chuckled. "I'm a trust fund baby and I own a company. My boy is a sales manager. We can afford it."

When he put it so bluntly, it seemed impossible to argue. So I laughed instead, shaking my head in lingering disbelief, and gave them both grateful hugs.

"You better keep him around," Lucas said to me, grinning slyly. "Picture the birthday gifts."

"My god," Kenny breathed, tossing his arms around Lucas dramatically. "I think I might be in love with you. Nate, can I steal your boyfriend?"

"Sure thing," I laughed, wrapping an arm around Nicholas' shoulders. "Long as I can get yours."

"It's a deal," Kenny said, giving Lucas' cheek a noisy kiss. "Real talk though, I'm one hundred percent down to be a sugar daddy for the two of you. Always been a dream of mine," he joked, shimmying his shoulders suggestively, and I rolled my eyes.

"You're such a dork," I teased. "Anyways, since you guys are here, how about you give us a tour?" I couldn't keep the eagerness from my voice. The opportunity to explore was screaming my name, and I wouldn't try to ignore it.

"Right now?"

"When else?"

Kenny laughed. "Aren't you tired? The drive from Nebraska to New York is what, a day long?"

"I don't care," I insisted. Besides, we'd stopped mid-way to stay in a hotel for the night, so it wasn't that bad. "I don't think I've ever felt more awake. The city is right there. I wanna see it all!" I was practically bouncing now, hyper with anticipation.

Nicholas rested his elbow on my shoulder, his eyes amused behind his glasses. "I'm not sure we can get it all done tonight," he said. "But we sure as hell can start."

So we left the apartment, went down what felt like two hundred flights in the elevator, and emerged onto the city streets. It took all of my self-control not to break into a run.

The scene was so unfamiliar to me, I felt as though I were in a new world, not a new state. I was Alice, and Manhattan was my Wonderland. People walking instead of driving. So many of them out and about, even though the sky had long been dark. The lights never seemed to dim, and neither did the noise. It was breathtaking.

"We walking or driving?" Kenny asked.

"Walking," Lucas and I said at the same time. We shared a glance, and when he smiled, I couldn't help but think that even he looked different.

Maybe it was the illumination of his face in the street lights, or the fact that now I was looking at him when he was surrounded by everything I'd been anticipating for my entire life. Maybe it was just the liberty that I could see in his gaze, framed by happiness and wonder and every good thing imaginable. Maybe it was all of those, maybe none. It didn't matter—the sight of him now, whatever had changed, was just as stunning as the city in which I stood.

When I looked ahead, I saw that Kenny and Nicholas had already begun strolling down the sidewalk, the latter with his arm around my cousin's waist, their heads bent close together as they spoke to one another. Kenny kissed Nicholas' cheek.

"C'mon," Lucas said, and he, too, started walking, though I didn't miss how his eyes had darted to my hand for a moment so brief, anyone else—anyone who didn't know him like I did—would've never caught it. I hurried to keep up with him, noticing that he kept a decent distance between us. He didn't want to scare me.

The sad thing was, I did feel scared. I wanted to put an arm around him, or kiss his cheek, or hold his hand. But I couldn't help but think of the place we'd just come from, where such a gesture would have torn me down before I could even begin to put my defenses together. I could easily picture spending the rest of my life here receiving glares from every passerby and being shunned wherever I went. I wouldn't be able to run away as soon as the damage was done, like I had in Nowhere, Nebraska.

I reminded myself that this was New York, not Nebraska. That the people I was passing on the sidewalk now, I would probably never see again. That those people didn't care either way. But the nerves were still there, beyond my control. Even after I'd left that place behind, anxiety followed me here.

Anxiety had controlled me for so much of my life. If only Paranoia were a physical being, so I could stand up to him until he backed down and agreed to leave me alone. But no—it seemed that he could torture me for as long as he liked, and I would have to sit and take it.

Except I wouldn't. Paranoia was bullshit, and it was about time he released his grip on me. If I couldn't get rid of him, I would at least get used to him, because I wasn't about to let him keep dominating my life. Not here. Not in New York.

So I inched closer to Lucas and took his hand firmly in mine. He turned to me in surprise, and when I grinned at him, albeit a bit sheepishly, he smiled whole-heartedly back.

"You okay?" He asked. His voice was soft, but it didn't need to be. Privacy lent itself here in the form of car horns and passing conversations.

My smile only grew, and grew and grew until I was beaming. "I can say," I told him, "With absolute certainly, that I have never in my life felt better than I do right now."

And it was true. Paranoia was still there, but I tried my best to ignore him. Just as, I realized, the people we passed ignored me. Not a single one of them took any interest in me or my boyfriend—or Kenny and his—and if they did, they didn't show it.

We caught up to the other two, and from then on we spent the night exploring the city, or as much of it as we could fit into a few hours. They pointed out to us every random shop they adored, told us which restaurants were the best and which were the worst, made plans to take us to see the Empire State Building soon. Just the four of us, walking and talking and laughing; it was perfect. The best possible way I could've spent my first night in New York.

Kenny and Nicholas became a permanent part of our lives after that. I saw them often, whether we were going for a walk or to see Aunt Lacy and Uncle Brock—who quickly became my New York parents—or to shop or to hang out or to go on cheesy little double dates. Kenny showed me around the NYU campus, and anytime someone asked if the two of us were brothers, we said yes, because we might as well have been. It felt like we were.

Kenny was great. But he wasn't the best thing about coming to New York. I had a boyfriend for that.

Being with Lucas—uninhibited—was what made the experience so indescribable. We could finally do the Boyfriend Thing. The dates and exchanged looks, touching and flirting. It took some time for me to adjust to the prospect of being fully open, and I still struggled with it sometimes, but we quickly learned to be who we were and not care too much about the consequences because there weren't any consequences.

I got to wake up to him every morning, and go to bed next to him every night. Every time I sat down to eat dinner, he was there with me. We could waste hours cuddling on the couch watching shows and movies, or playing games, or doing nothing at all. I got to see him whenever he walked out of the bathroom after taking a shower—I got to be with him in the shower. He helped me shave in the mornings sometimes, because he was better at it than I was and my body was finally figuring out how to produce facial hair. He didn't seem to know what it meant to wake up before ten, so I liked to make him breakfast, because he couldn't cook for shit and I loved the expression he got whenever I did cute little things like that.

So yeah, the Boyfriend Thing was pretty fucking great.

I got a job at a local gym, and he worked as a barista at a cute little café nearby. Sometimes I'd visit him during his shift and he'd sneak me a free drink, then walk around with me during his lunch break. Training for the soccer team started early on in the summer; it was long, extensive, and absolutely exhausting. Whenever I came home from a particularly rough practice, he would take me out on a mini-date and spoil me for a bit.

I wasn't super comfortable with PDA, and he respected that, so we found other ways to express our feelings when we weren't behind closed doors—after months of hiding, we weren't gonna settle for being buddy-buddy. He liked to play with my hands a lot when we were out, maybe because he knew it made me blush every time. Whenever we were sat next to each other, we'd find some way to be touching—a hand on a knee, a shoulder brushing a shoulder, a thigh against a thigh.

Simple things, and I loved them. I loved him. More than anyone, and I wasn't afraid to admit that—in my head or out loud, at home or in public. As corny as it was to say, he was the best thing that ever happened to me. Hands down.

I was so glad—more than I could ever put into words—that I'd met him in the seventh grade. That I'd gone to see the school's production of Wicked. That he'd asked me for that ride home, then another, then another.

It was weird, and kind of scary, to think that we probably wouldn't be together now if Shawn hadn't challenged him, compelling him to try out for the soccer team.

Shawn. He was a whole other topic.

As promised, he'd come with his parents to New York a few days after Lucas and I left. He lived in an apartment not far from ours, but he was spending his summer in a rehab facility.

Lucas went to go see him several times a week. Sometimes I went, too, and watching them interact was really, really weird. At first, Shawn was just like he'd been before—moody and mean—minus all of the homophobic slurs. I really did wonder if he'd ever actually been homophobic, or if that had been a costume he'd put on to fit in in nowhere, Nebraska, and now that he was here, he took it off. If he was homophobic, it wasn't to the extent he'd made himself out to be.

Still, he wasn't nice to his brother. I saw right through him, though. He must have wanted Lucas there, because he'd given the staff permission to let him in. I could tell Lucas knew, too, because despite Shawn's attitude, he left with a smile on his face each time, and he was never disheartened when his brother snapped at him.

Shawn's demeanor shifted gradually. Eventually, he stopped being mean and was just . . . quiet. He didn't say much, but listened as Lucas spoke. Then he became somewhat responsive. Then one day, while Lucas was talking about some random thing or another, Shawn went on a tangent that neither of us had been expecting. I felt almost like an intruder—the moment was between Shawn and Lucas, not meant for me. But then again, whenever Shawn was saying something he wanted to keep private, he usually said it in Romanian, so maybe he had wanted me to hear.

"I wanna do good in school, you know," was how he began, completely out of the blue. "Actually study for once. And quit doing dumb shit, like drugs, but I'll need time for that. And get a job. A girlfriend would be nice, too—okay, maybe not yet. Playing the field is kinda fun." He smirked, looking a lot like the Shawn Morgan I was used to. "But when I'm over that, in a few years, I'll settle down. Eventually, I think I even wanna get married. Get a dog. And two kids—a boy and a girl. I wanna play pro league, where all the big shots are, and make some serious money. And when I'm old, I wanna get a house upstate and one of those rocking chairs I can put on my porch so I can yell at kids as they walk past, like the morphine lady from To Kill a Mockingbird."

"You wanna do all that?" Lucas asked, chuckling.

He nodded. "Yeah. And I guess . . . I guess I realized I've gotta be alive to do it. So I wanna do that, too. I want to live."

Lucas had nearly cried then. Hell, so had I. Improvement was a beautiful, beautiful thing to witness, and we saw it every week with Shawn.

He would be leaving the hospital when school started in the fall—he agreed to finding a regular scheduled therapist after that. The fact that he so clearly wanted to feel better was probably the best part of it all. He got nicer, too—not friendly yet, but maybe on the way there.

Shawn wasn't the only one seeking improvement. I started seeing a therapist, and I learned some things about myself that I hadn't known before. That I was clinically depressed and suffered from anxiety. A lot of things made sense after I found that out.

I'd grown so used to the way I always felt, I'd thought it to be normal. But as it turned out, normal worked a bit differently than I did. And being with Lucas had helped me go from terrible to bad, but one boy couldn't cure a mental illness just by loving me. Nothing could, really. But therapy helped. Medication helped. And I liked how I was feeling now a lot more than how I'd felt before. Everything seemed to get better as I grew to understand myself more and as my mental health improved bit-by-bit—my self-esteem, my performance in school, my relationship.

So Shawn Morgan and I had more in common than I'd previously thought. It was crazy how understanding yourself more could help you understand someone else more, too.

I wondered if, in weeks or months or years, he would become a friend, someone who came over to hang out. Or even an acquaintance. If he and Lucas would ever be close again, or if they'd just hover in the realm of mutual respect, acknowledgment, and appreciation. If we'd ever play soccer as a team again, or maybe against each other. If, in some years, he'd be Lucas' best man at—okay, that was a stretch. But it wasn't impossible. Nothing, I finally realized, was impossible.

Except for a fish sprouting hooved legs that it whirled like airplane propellers and used to fly out of the sea. Shit like that was definitely impossible.

"What're you thinking about?" Lucas asked, having caught me spacing out. We were on the couch in our living room, which was finally beginning to look like our own—we'd put some things up on the walls, and even bought a few houseplants and such. Lucas' favorite was a little succulent in a rainbow-colored vase that sat at the center of our coffee table—he'd been responsible for buying it, of course, because only he would want to make our apartment as gay as possible.

His head was rested on my lap, his eyes amused as he looked up at me instead of at the Friends reruns that were playing on the TV that Kenny and St. Nick had given us. My hands rested against his bare torso, my fingers absentmindedly tracing the tattoo on his side. Grinning, I said, "Flying propeller fish with legs."

He blinked once. Twice. Then, laughing and shaking his head, he pulled me down by the collar of my shirt to kiss me and said, "God, I love you."

fin